DARING DARLEEN, QUEEN OF THE SCREEN

DARING
DARLEEN,
QUEEN OF THE
SCREEN
ANNE NESBET
CANDLEWICK PRESS

This is a work of fiction. Names, characters,
places, and incidents are either products of the
author's imagination or, if real, are used fictitiously.

First edition 2020

Library of Congress Catalog Card Number pending
ISBN 978-1-5362-0619-7

20 21 22 23 24 25 LBM 10 9 8 7 6 5 4 3 2 1

Printed in Melrose Park, IL, U.S.A.

This book was typeset in Hightower.

Candlewick Press
99 Dover Street
Somerville, Massachusetts 02144

visit us at www.candlewick.com

A JUNIOR LIBRARY GUILD SELECTION

For my friends who love their silent films
with a side of gelato

Chapter 1

Safe as Houses

Sometimes the real danger is not what you thought it would be at all. Real danger likes to curl itself up small and hide away just out of sight so that it can catch you by surprise.

Darleen had not yet had this insight at the time our story begins. She was busy dangling off the edge of a cliff, hundreds of feet above a wild river. What's more, her nose was prickling unpleasantly in the cold, and a masked villain was brandishing a knife and threatening to send her plummeting down into the churning waves below.

Under ordinary circumstances, that would be enough danger for anyone. But Darleen's circumstances were not in the least bit ordinary.

For instance: it was Darleen's own uncles who had just tied her up in those large and showy ropes and lowered her (feet first, thank goodness) right over the lip of the rocky cliffs, and while they did so, they had said incongruous things like "There you go, dear! Safe as houses!"

Safe as houses!

Perhaps not, thought Darleen.

She was twisting slightly as the rope shifted in the wind (not a pleasant feeling), so she kept catching glimpses of birds sailing above the shining river so very far below her dangling self, and then other glimpses, when the rope turned, of the crinkly rocks of the cliff only inches from her cold nose, and occasionally even third or fourth glimpses of redheaded Uncle Charlie with his megaphone, shouting directions from the out-jutting boulder where her Uncle Dan (whose hair was the color of his voice: a quiet brown) was cranking the little handle on the side of the great box on legs that was the moving-picture camera.

A camera makes everything it looks at un-ordinary! And yet Darleen had been doing something quite ordinary and everyday (for her) as she dangled from her rope: she had been worrying about her Papa.

Her Papa had made her a tasty bowl of oatmeal and jam that morning. "Strength for my chickee," he liked to say before long filming days. And he had tied a ribbon in her hair with his clever, callused, loving hands. They had eaten their breakfast as they always did, seated at the scarred old table in the kitchen of their tiny house in Fort Lee, under the old photo of Papa and Mama and baby Darleen, all huddled together like birds in the happiest of nests, and her father had said what he always said before they went off to the Matchless studios, across the street (where once there had been cornfields, in Papa's farming years): "Feet on the ground, my darling Dar! Don't fly away!"

"Yes, Papa," she had promised, as she did every day. "Feet on the ground" was their family motto: Papa's heart had lost too much of itself already when Mama had flown away due to inflammation of the lungs.

Sometimes when Darleen was younger and shorter, she would pull a chair over to the kitchen wall and climb up to stare at that photograph of the Darlings taken so many years ago, in 1906 or 1907. The three of them were posed in front of scenery with palm trees painted on it, her Papa in a borrowed jacket and hat, her Mama in a stiff sort of dress, softened by bunches of lace around her throat, and a very happy, very small Darleen perched on a stool in front of them, holding on to her parents' hands. Darleen never spent much time staring at her younger self, who looked like a mound of ruffles topped off with an extra portion of light brown curls. It was the other two faces that called to her so: the one belonging to her

Papa, so young and so glad and so obviously trying *not to laugh* (because it would have blurred the photograph), and the face of her Mama, whose eyes were brimming with love and yet always seemed a little sad, too, as if she already knew that she would fly away one day and leave two hearts aching from the lack of her.

You would never think that the woman with the sad and loving eyes had once been a dancer on tightropes in the circus! But she had! She had been Loveliest Luna Lightfoot (that's what the old posters said, rolled up in the corner of the broom closet), and she had come down from those high places to marry Papa and become Darleen's dear Mama and try to grow roses around their little farmhouse in Fort Lee. She had done that out of love: kept her feet on the ground.

And now only Darleen was left to stay true to that promise, and to keep the wounded pieces of her father's heart bound carefully together.

But it occurred to her now that this current business of dangling from a cliff did not seem much at all like keeping her feet on the ground. She didn't mind on her own behalf — to be honest, Darleen was tired of everything in her life being always "safe as houses" — but suddenly she found herself thinking, What would Papa say when he saw the pictures emerging from the chemical vats in his laboratory that evening or tomorrow? This was Episode

Six of *The Dangers of Darleen,* and her father, truth be told, hadn't much cared for any part of Episodes One through Five. He didn't even like her walking on the tops of trains or jumping from car to car. And that had really, truly been safe as houses compared with dangling above the Hudson River.

"Not quite the quiet cottage life we dream of, Darleeny," he liked to say. "But we'll get there when the money's a little better. We'll retire you from danger and smell the roses all day. That's the thought I cling to, that all this awful jumping about you're doing is merely *temporary.*"

What would he think about cliffs and rivers?

"Uncle Charlie," she called out, but of course her voice was swallowed up right away by the breeze.

"Darleen, dear! *Darleen!*" Uncle Charlie had the megaphone to help his voice be as loud as it could possibly be. "Less chitchat and a little more struggle, please! And a hint of a sawing action from you, Mr. Lukes."

Darleen made an obedient show of wriggling in her ropes. "But Uncle Charlie, what about my Papa?" she started again.

"Oh, can we just dump her in the river and be done with it?" said the masked villain from above Darleen's head. That Jasper Lukes! He could be trusted to come up with something awful to say whether or not he was playing the part of a villain. At the moment, Jasper Lukes was peering over the edge of the cliff and waving his dagger about for the camera. "Crying for her Papa! You know, this morning I woke up with a fine question in my head. Want to know what it was?"

"No, I do not," said Darleen, gritting her teeth.

Darleen's uncles had been looking after Jasper Lukes for years, ever since his no-good parents had tiptoed away. The Lukeses and the Darlings had been theater people together long ago, but then came the catastrophes, one after the other in quick succession, short scenes that belonged in a tragic melodrama with (joked Uncle Charlie—but poor Papa couldn't even joke about it) a one-word title:

CURTAINS!

ACT ONE: The curtains catch fire one night! The Darlings' theater, the Golden Bird, burns to the ground!

ACT TWO: But wait! The theater was insured! There is hope! The Golden Bird, phoenix-like, will be rebuilt and rise again!

ACT THREE: And then one morning, Mr. Lukes (father of Jasper) and the cashbox turn out to be missing. The insurance money—all the hope—as gone as gone!

Epilogue: Oh, there was much weeping and lamenting, especially by the actress who had wandered into town to take on the role of Mrs. Lukes a few years before and who was left behind with a golden-haired baby (Jasper) in her arms. She wept and lamented for a while — at least when she had an audience — and the Darlings tried to console her, and then one day she received a mysterious letter, addressed in handwriting oddly like that of old Lukes, and off she went, leaving young Jasper behind to be raised by the Darlings as best they could.

Perhaps it was understandable that a boy abandoned by two parents in a row might have a chip on his shoulder, but Jasper Lukes seemed to go out of his way to be mean. You wouldn't think so to look at him: with his golden hair and uniquely pointy little ears, Jasper Lukes, even now at seventeen, was "a faerie prince pulled right from a storybook picture." That was Aunt Shirley's opinion but definitely not Darleen's. Aunt Shirley hadn't spent her whole childhood being teased, tripped, and tormented. Five years older than Dar, and he had never yet grown out of his basic meanness. Darleen's secret theory was that Jasper Lukes's heart must be as small and pointy as his ears.

At some point in childhood, golden-haired Jasper Lukes had scrambled right onto the stage and then, once the age of the moving pictures arrived, into the photoplays. And still it seemed like he never missed a chance to poke a sharp word into Darleen's side.

"Well, I'll tell you, then," said Jasper Lukes now with a sneer. "The question was 'Why am I still playing second fiddle to this stupid little girl who can't even act?' Ooh, and look at this!" he added. "This fake blade has an actual edge on it after all!"

And he began to saw away at the rope for real.

He was trying to scare her now, of course, but all she felt was fury.

"Stop that, you!" she said to him, and her angry hands accidentally started working themselves out of the rope coils.

"LOOKS GOOD THERE, JASPER," bellowed the oblivious Uncle Charlie through his megaphone. "We'll add a close-in shot of the knife and rope later. But Darleen, could you give us MORE DRAMA, please? No need to dangle there like a grumpy sugar sack on a rope! Dangle like the Crown Princess Dahlia Louise of St. Benoix. Dangle like a princess posing as Daring Darleen!"

Because *that* was the story in the motion pictures they were making. A princess in disguise was brought to America by her exiled Royal Father, but trouble followed them — oh, yes, it did! And the poor princess's tragic circumstances had turned her (by Episode Two or Three) into the bravest of heroines, known across America as Daring Darleen.

That was one thing the real-life Darleen Darling and the fictional Crown Princess Dahlia Louise had in common: they both had to pretend to be Daring Darleen. The princess (being fictional) perhaps had a slightly easier time of it, thought Darleen as she dangled from her rope and listened to the venomous nonsense coming from Jasper Lukes above.

"Saint *Benoyks*!" Jasper was saying now. Darleen didn't like it when he made fun of the way Uncle Charlie spoke. Jasper's mother had had a fancified way of speaking, apparently, and Jasper had spent all these years waiting for his superior parents to come rescue him from the inferior Darlings.

Ben-wa or *Ben-oyks* — who cared? It wasn't like the camera could hear what any of them might be saying. But that also meant Jasper Lukes could say whatever nasty things he wanted, because the camera could only see, not hear, and the uncles, who did have ears, were too far away to hear exactly what he was saying.

Uncle Dan cranked steadily, and sixteen times every second a little rectangle of film paused just long enough in front of the lens to have one frame's worth of reflected light hit it. It was "the picture leaving its fingerprint," said Uncle Charlie, who had his poetical side, "leaving its fingerprint, over and over and over again."

Jasper kept sawing away like the villain he was.

"Jasper, you'd better be careful with that knife!" Darleen said.

"Oh, is our Darleen scared?" said Jasper, and he paused from his sawing to give the knife a jaunty twirl. "Well, then, maybe you should thank me, don't you think? Since maybe this will improve your performance. Your uncle's right, you know: you're just a tiresome sack of sugar on a rope, and that's all you've ever been. I'm sure we've all had just about enough of Darling Darleen. I know I have."

"I'm not *darling,*" said Darleen through her teeth, "not anymore," but still she flinched a little. Did he think it had been easy, being dumped into a flour barrel at the age of six? Or spreading strawberry jam all over her face? Or tucking four squirmy kittens into a cradle? And having to do all those things under the constant instructions of a director, a cameraman, grown-up actors, and all the rest of an exceedingly theatrical (and bossy) family? But it wasn't anything to be ashamed of, she knew. Those *Darling Darleen* pictures had saved the studio. They had! Money came rolling in; the cashbox was happy again. The Matchless studios grew and expanded. That was worth a lot of silliness with strawberry jam.

Anyway, she hadn't been Darling Darleen for ages now. Expanding the new studio had put them back into debt, and Darleen was too big now to be properly darling. What to do, then, to bring in some money again? Chases, plunges, trains, and villains—that's what the public wanted these days. The year 1914 would surely go down in history (said all the uncles) as the age of the adventure serial: a new episode every week, and tension galore! So Darleen had lost her *l*—she'd gone right from *Darling* to *Daring*—and everyone at Matchless was hoping that the people who came to watch the photoplays week after week would be happy with the change, even if her Papa was going gray from worry.

"Say whatever you want, *Darling Darleen*; we all know the truth," said the unpleasant Jasper Lukes, still working away with his knife. Darleen could see some of the little strands springing up like little stalks of hay where the blade had already sliced them in half. "You'll never amount to anything, really. You're not an *actress*—not really—you're just *pretending* to act. And what's more . . ."

Pretending to act! thought Darleen. What did that even mean? Of course she was pretending to act. Wasn't that what acting was all about? That was her job!

But meanwhile, Jasper Lukes was actually sawing away at the actual rope.

"Jasper, stop! Uncle Charlie! THE ROPE!" Darleen shouted, wishing she had the megaphone in one of her now-almost-freed-up hands. Uncle Charlie waved encouragingly.

"And what's more," said Jasper Lukes again. "What's more, I tell you, I'm better than all of this. When my parents come back—"

And then they were interrupted by a noise that seemed out of place: the engine of a motorcar that was driving (or so it sounded) almost right up to the edge of the cliff. Darleen's eyes were naturally fixed on that wounded stretch of rope above her. She had her hands completely loose now, and she began to kick her feet free of the coils.

The door of the motorcar slammed shut. Darleen could hear what sounded like steps—heavy, quick, excited steps—punctuated by shouts. Aunt Shirley, business manager of Matchless studios, was saying something about . . . the newspaper?

"Now, Shirley," said Uncle Charlie, but the rope had twisted again, so he was out of Darleen's limited vision. "Can't you see this is a delicate moment? Keep cranking, Dan!"

Aunt Shirley's laugh fell on Darleen's ears like a jagged waterfall, pouring right over the edge of that cliff. Aunt Shirley had never had any respect for delicate moments. She was always exploding onto photoplay sets, bearing news of one kind or another or asking how much that last shipment of film stock had cost.

"It's lunchtime. Aren't you people done yet? We're in the newspaper! Oh, look at you hanging there, Darleen! My goodness, that's almost too exciting! But is it quite safe, with just that rickety platform underneath you? And, oh, Jasper Lukes, watch what you're doing with that knife!"

That was when everything happened, more or less all at once.

Jasper Lukes stood up in disgust and said, "You know what? I've had enough of you all. I should up and quit! See how you'd like *that*!" And just to add drama to the point he was making, he tossed his knife (the pretend knife with the very real edge) over the cliff, where it swooshed by Darleen's almost-frozen nose and banged onto the safety platform below.

Jasper Lukes was always threatening to quit and then breaking things. That was irritating, but usually mendable.

The problem this time was that the entire safety platform, hit by that one little knife flung from not all that far above, shuddered, groaned, and began to sag. Not so much "safe as houses" after all!

Darleen had already kicked her feet free. She was not exactly thinking now. She was swinging herself right up to the cliff and reaching out with her hands and her feet.

There were friendly cracks in the rock, thank goodness. And her arms were strong. She clung to that cliff like a barnacle — a nimble, exultant barnacle!

She felt something tumble down her back now. That was the rope actually breaking and springing away from the cliff. Darleen, exultant barnacle, had no attention to spare for that rope. Let it fall!

Far away, the uncles were shouting. Farther away than that, a bird cried out in the wind, and then that very wind came ruffling through Darleen's hair and awoke something wild in her spirit that she had not known was there. She had found a new crack for the toes of her left foot and a good rock up a bit higher for her right hand, and she did not stop moving even then, because climbing up a cliff with the wind cheering you on and your heart unfurling inside you is something that must be done in a glorious rush, all at once. She was not acting: she just *was*, and her muscles pulled her up and up again, and the river glittered far below her and her spirit rejoiced, and a moment later she was hauling herself over the top of the cliff, where Aunt Shirley, pale as a sheet, babbled with horror as she hauled her away from the cliff's edge: "Oh, Darleen, oh, Darleen, what an accident! Goodness! But you're safe now. Don't be afraid, don't be afraid, don't be afraid." And meanwhile the uncles were scrambling over from their camera ledge.

And that was when Darleen realized the terrible truth: *she had not been afraid.* She had been *alive.* And she was still more or less *alive* now as she lay panting there on the top of the cliff, though the feeling was already fading.

There was a force in her that must have been coiled up very tight, just waiting for a moment like this to spring free and unfold. A terrible, powerful, untamable force that did not want to keep its feet on the ground. What danger could be more dangerous than that?

A force like that might make a person suddenly start clambering up perilous rocks or balancing on tightropes; it might make a person break all the promises she had ever made to the person she loved most: That she would be careful. That she would stay safe.

Oh, Papa! thought Darleen, and terror on his behalf filled her so suddenly that every one of her limbs started shaking.

Cliffs and trains and bridges are dangers that stay politely outside us, after all. But when danger wells up *inside,* there is no place safe to hide, is there?

And the danger facing Darleen was worse than any broken rope or runaway train. The danger was this: she might be like her Mama after all.

Chapter 2
Sizzle and Salt

Ham and eggs, apple pie, and hot, bitter coffee. That was the meal they always had after filming on the Palisades. And they always had it at the same place too. Alongside the road in Coytesville was an inn called Rambo's, an unpretentious sort of establishment with a porch in front and a single gable raising its eyebrow at the goings-on in the dirt road outside. All the photoplay people went to Rambo's. Sometimes they even made movies there when they needed a set for a Wild West shoot-out or something.

In warm weather the guests sat at tables outside under the big tree, but they were now only a couple of weeks on the sunny side of a month of blizzards, and Darleen couldn't stop trembling, so Aunt Shirley shepherded them all indoors, even Jasper, whose face, far from remorseful, was one big sulk.

"What got into you there, Jasper?" said Uncle Charlie as they took off their coats and settled into their chairs. "You went and ruined one of my ropes."

Jasper scowled.

And Darleen indulged in a fiery thought for a moment: *He almost ruined a whole lot more than a rope!*

"There, there, now, Charlie," said Aunt Shirley. "Accidents do get people upset. Don't be riling the poor boy. He had the wrong knife! That would upset anyone, wouldn't it?"

Jasper scowled some more.

As for Darleen, her teeth went for another round of chattering. Wasn't that just like Aunt Shirley to be fretting on behalf of the boy who had almost sent Dar plummeting to a watery grave?

Anyway, it smelled of sizzle and salt inside Rambo's, and that was a comfort.

"Busy day today out there, was it?" said the waitress as she slapped down their plates, and then she took a second look at Darleen and shook her head. "You look chilled right to the bone, honey. Isn't your family treating you right?"

Everybody here knew the Darlings of Fort Lee; the Matchless studios were basically a Darling extended-family operation. The Darlings had been show people and theater people, way back in the past century. And then in the nineties, Darleen's Papa, who was a genius with machines and chemicals, had gotten a job helping Mr. Dickson (Thomas Edison's assistant) down at Edison's laboratory when they were making the first moving pictures out in the backyard in a funny tanklike studio called the Black Maria.

One of those first pictures had been of Darleen's Mama, fluttering her silky robes against the black velvet—she had come down from her tightropes and high places to let the camera capture the miracle of her—and that had changed the world, if by *the world* you meant not only the history of moving photography but also the lives of Loveliest Luna and the young handyman Bill Darling, falling in love as the Black Maria swiveled around to capture the sun.

They moved to the little farmhouse in Fort Lee to live a different kind of story, a story in which engineers and tightrope dancers turn into people who live quietly in cottages, have a sweet little baby girl, and *keep their feet on the ground. . . .*

But then the Golden Bird Theatre burned down over in the big city of New York, and the rest of the family—all those theatrical but homeless Darlings—decided to join their brother in Fort Lee and move right on into the moving pictures, and Papa's quiet dreams were swallowed up again by chemicals and clever bits of machinery, and the little farm became instead a great barn of glass in which photoplays grew instead of corn or beans.

"Temporarily!" he said sometimes, with mournfulness around the edges of his words. "We'll get back to our roses one day, Darleeny, see if we don't. When the money's a little better . . ."

But that's one thing farms and photoplay studios have in common, seems like: the money is never much better. There is always new machinery to buy and pressure to expand and grow. But building huge glass "barns" so that you can shoot your photoplays in any weather is even more expensive than building the ordinary wooden kind. Matchless was always desperately short of money.

And the Darlings' dreams were always one plot twist away from coming to nothing again.

Darleen thought about cliff-hangers and shivered again.

"You all right there, young lady?" asked the waitress.

Jasper made a scoffing noise down where he was sitting, but Darleen took care not to look his way.

"I'm fine, thank you," said Darleen. That was acting. She wasn't actually fine at all.

She kept remembering what it had felt like, having that wild force of a feeling spread its wings in her.

I will be so careful, she promised herself (and her Papa). *I will be careful forevermore. I won't go near cliffs. Or steep places.*

She would push that feeling into a squished little ball and push that ball into the corner of her soul and never trust herself again. That's all.

"Eat up, now," said Aunt Shirley briskly. She lifted her fork to demonstrate how it was done. "Nothing like ham and eggs after you've had a bit of a shock."

"Mmm," agreed Uncle Charlie. He smacked his lips. "Say, what was that newspaper business you were so excited about, Shirley?"

"Oh, my, yes," said Aunt Shirley. "I've got it right here. Darleen, I know you think you don't like it, but drink some of this good coffee. Coffee is medicinal. It will warm you right up."

Aunt Shirley unfolded the newspaper. Darleen caught glimpses of headlines about troubles in Europe, troubles in Mexico, flooding in Russia, "The Richest Twelve-Year-Old Girl in the World?" (not about Darleen Darling, clearly!), and a dog show where dogs worth fifteen thousand dollars would be competing for ribbons.

"No, no, no — oh, here it is!" said Aunt Shirley, pointing to a column on the lower-right-hand side.

"NEW STRAND THEATRE TO OPEN APRIL 11," shouted the top headline, and then right underneath: "Full Programme Planned in Modern Wonder Theatre."

Aunt Shirley read the list aloud: "'Programme will boast a full orchestra with twenty-seven musicians, short subjects, opera stars, the latest episode of the new serial sensation *The Dangers of Darleen*—' There we are! There we are! Let's see now—no, that's all. Next bit is all about the featured drama they'll show after intermission. Never mind that now."

Down at the grumpy end of the table, Jasper stabbed a piece of ham. Darleen kept her eyes on her aunt.

"What's the film, Aunt Shirley?" she said by way of ignoring Jasper more thoroughly.

"The new Kathlyn Williams photoplay, *The Spoilers,* set in the wilds of Alaska, apparently. But who cares about that? The main thing is our picture will be there too—*before* intermission! Darleen, darling, what a thrill this is! And I've had the most brilliant idea for making the most of it! Want to hear, all of you?"

"Spill it, Shirl," said Uncle Charlie.

"Yes?" said Darleen with some suspicion. Darleen knew to be cautious when Aunt Shirley had her plotting face on.

Jasper made some sort of scoffing and complaining sound—*mmmmph*—but Aunt Shirley had already set down her fork.

"Well! Guess what? It's because of all the things you see in the paper that I had this idea. People follow things in the paper, don't they? Like the horrible snows we just had, or murder trials, or that old Mrs. Berryman dying and her fortune going to the poor-little-rich-girl orphan granddaughter and suchlike. So that gave me this idea, see—"

They were all beginning to stare at Aunt Shirley. Even Jasper had stopped chewing for a moment.

Uncle Charlie banged his spoon against his cup.

"All right, now, Shirley! Better get to the point. What's this 'idea' you're talking around?"

Aunt Shirley added a couple lumps of sugar to her coffee and stirred it happily with her spoon.

"What I'm saying is, *let's get our girl kidnapped!* It would raise *such* a lovely fuss!"

"WHAT?" said Uncle Dan, in what Darleen could tell was spoken in capital letters.

Jasper, down at his end of the table, laughed out loud for a moment and then stabbed another piece of ham. "Kidnapped!" he said, as if the thought made him happy.

"What I'm saying is, people simply *love* a good story, don't they? That's how people are. That's why they like *The Dangers of Darleen.* And that's why they like the newspapers so well. Good stories! And so we should give them one they can really feast on. Daring Darleen goes to the opening of the Strand—and gets herself *kidnapped*!"

Uncle Charlie set down his fork so that the tines were resting against his slab of ham. It was rare for

Uncle Charlie to set down his fork midmeal, especially at Rambo's.

"Kidnapped? Our Darleen?" he said. "You mean, in the photoplay or for real?"

"What's the difference, really?" said Aunt Shirley. "Isn't it just the most beautiful plan? In the previous episode, she can receive a mysterious invitation to the opening of the Strand. And then our real-life Darleen will show up at the real-life Strand and get herself *kidnapped* while Dan cranks his camera, yes. And the news will go into the *papers,* won't it? Maybe even right into the Pictorial Section of the *Times,* next to all the visiting princesses and blizzard pictures? See how lovely? So in real life, they'll all be reading the newspapers and worrying about Darleen, and meanwhile, the whole story of it — the kidnapping, the escape — that gets worked into Episode — Wait, what'll we be up to by then?"

She counted on her fingers.

"Nine! Episode Nine: *Daring Darleen, Kidnapped by the Wicked Whatsits!*"

"Salamanders," said Uncle Dan, who remembered the details of things even though he didn't do much chattering about them. In the story their moving pictures were telling, the Salamanders were the mysterious masked villains chasing after the Crown Princess Dahlia Louise and the exiled King.

"Exactly," said Aunt Shirley. "Kidnapped! All week long in the newspapers — little bits, you know, that we feed the readers now and again — and then, guess who will come to see the picture the next week, to see how our Darleen manages to escape?"

She tapped her spoon against her saucer: "EV-RY-BO-DY, that's who. It's gold. It's a simply golden idea, you have to admit. And we really need the money, if you don't mind me reminding us all of that fact."

There was a silent moment then while they all digested Aunt Shirley's golden idea. Uncle Charlie actually went back to chewing on his slice of ham, because he believed thinking worked better on a happy stomach.

He took two bites, and then he said, "Very clever, Shirl! A sort of real kidnapping at the Strand! I like it!" And then he took two more.

"But Shirley," said Uncle Dan. "The police. Won't they maybe get confused?"

That was a pretty long sentence for Uncle Dan. Aunt Shirley gave him a warm and confident smile.

"We will *inform* the police, don't you worry," said Aunt Shirley. "They'll know to stay away from the Strand that evening — or at least not to worry about kidnappings going on under the bright lights! Jasper, please pass the toast down this way, won't you, dear?"

"Oh, please, *please*, have her kidnapped for real," said

Jasper, and he made a face that Darleen saw only out of the corner of her eye.

Darleen's stomach was doing puzzled little flips and twirls.

"Aunt Shirley—" she said, but then she was interrupted by the arrival of wedges of the famous Rambo's apple pie.

"What, dear? You feeling better now?" said Aunt Shirley.

No. But how could she even begin to explain? She had been dangling from a cliff on a rope—that had been fine. And then the awful Jasper had accidentally (right? accidentally?—anything else was surely too terrible, even for Jasper Lukes) cut her rope, and a new feeling had spread its wings inside her and sent her scrambling in joy up that bit of cliff, when any normal person would have been weeping from fright. And now they wanted to have her kidnapped, at least sort of. And that would make anyone's insides feel a little peculiar, wouldn't it?

Everything today seemed to be leading somewhere she was sure she shouldn't be going: into danger.

Her adventure on the cliff had changed something. Had woken something up in her. Even with the tangy sweetness of apple pie on her tongue, Darleen was no longer entirely sure that she was *real*. She thought maybe she was more like the shell of an egg that might be shattered into pieces by that strange something new trying to spread its wings inside her.

So that was already about a thousand tangled worries. Darleen settled for the one everyone at that table would surely understand:

"But what will my Papa say?" she whispered.

Well, he said no, of course. At first, anyway. Uncle Charlie and Aunt Shirley spent a few hours talking him around in the kitchen of the little house where Darleen and her father lived, and Darleen's part of the conspiracy was not to let slip any part of the truth about what had happened that morning on the Palisades cliff.

"No need to trouble your Papa about what's past and done, now, is there?" Aunt Shirley had said on their way back to the studio in Fort Lee. "Accidents are accidents. The important thing is, nothing bad actually happened."

Maybe nothing happened, thought Darleen with some discomfort. But even unspoken, that felt to her like a lie.

"I don't understand what you're saying," said her Papa to his siblings. "Let Darleen be *kidnapped*? But that's *illegal*. That's a *crime*!" They were all stubborn people, each in his or her own particular way, so he had already made that point a couple of times, and they had already repeated what they thought was a clear and rational explanation of the kidnapping plan.

But Papa didn't like Darleen being put in any kind of danger. And being an honest and cautious type of person, he really, really, really didn't like things that seemed like they might be breaking the law.

"Not *really* kidnapped! Just for publicity, Bill," they said patiently. "You know how important publicity is these days. This isn't the nineteenth century anymore. This is nineteen fourteen!"

Darleen's Papa was sitting under the old photograph on the wall, and the contrast between his wrinkled, worried head and the smaller, happier version of himself in the picture made Darleen feel sad and guilty both, so she tried watching her fingers make patterns on the red-checked tablecloth instead.

"What I don't understand is, you say it's for the photoplay story, but then you say they'll be kidnapping Darleen herself at the new theater. Is it just a play you're talking about, or is it real?"

That was a question Darleen kept finding herself wrestling with, too, so she looked up to see what her uncle or aunt might have to say about it.

"But now, that's the new way of things, Bill," said Uncle Charlie. "Blurring the boundary lines, don't you know, between the story and what's real. Seems that people like it when the characters they see in the photoplays come out into the world and show how they're real people too. Makes the photoplays realer for them. Makes the people come back and back again. *Half real* is real good for business, seems like."

Darleen's Papa was shaking his head.

"What's a half-real kidnapping? Sounds risky to me, doing that right out there in the world, where people will be confused. We don't want Darleen in half-real danger. I don't even like having her in pretend danger! And messing with the law is worse than jumping off trains, seems like to me."

Darleen thought about the cliff that morning, and the broken rope, and how far from make-believe the dangers in photoplays sometimes turned out to be, and she bent her head over the tablecloth again, organizing her right hand so that all the fingers were resting on white squares, and her thumb was on a red square. Then she moved her fingers over to the neighboring squares, walking them from white to red. And then back again. It calmed the guilty thump of her heart a little.

Aunt Shirley didn't seem to feel guilty at all, though. She just laughed.

"Oh, Bill! It's just going to be acting. All pretend. And the police will be in on the joke, don't you worry. Nothing dangerous about it at all."

And that was how they talked him into saying something like yes.

When they had left, Darleen went over and perched on his knee for a while, like in the old days, when she was littler, with her arm around his worried neck.

"Are you really all right with this, Darleeny?" said her father. "Seems like they keep asking more and more of you. I guess I liked it better when you were still in those frilly dresses and throwing flour around in front of the camera."

"I couldn't keep being little Darling Darleen forever, Papa. You know that. Maybe people will really start coming to see *The Dangers of Darleen* in droves — by the millions — if we get the publicity they're talking about. Maybe we'll have money to mend the porch stairs and fix the roof and get you cozy slippers that aren't falling apart."

(Her father's slippers looked like they had been chewed on by kittens and then left in the sun to fade, but Papa didn't mind it. He was opposed to spending money on "nonsense," which meant anything for himself.)

"If you're safe, I don't care one single whit about porches or roofs or slippers," said her Papa. "And I'm sure that's all your Mama ever wanted too: for you to be safe. *Feet on the ground,* Darleen. Remember that, if they start trying to kidnap you every second Tuesday."

Feet on the ground. Feet on the ground.

Oh, dear.

It had been such a long day, with too much surprise and guilt in it.

When Darleen lay down on her comfortably lumpy little bed tucked under the eaves upstairs, her eyes couldn't help wandering to the window, where a bright wedge of moon glittered, rising above the glass roof of the Matchless studios, right there across the road. Maybe it was the moon's fault, then, that Darleen found herself trapped in the dream that had haunted her for as long as she could remember:

She was always looking out a window in this dream. She was always very small. And she was looking out the window because something — an angel or a bird or a butterfly — was dancing on the roof ridge that stretched outside her window, moonlight rippling across its supple, magical, fragile wings. Oh, how her whole heart filled with longing for the magical, fragile dancing creature, and for the creature's beautiful dance! And then the feeling in the dream would shift, every time, and her longing became fear. She would reach out her arms, but her mouth could make no sound, and the dancer spread its lovely wings and flew away.

Chapter 3

The Only Sprig at the Strand

Anyone might have expected there would be a great clan of young Darlings by the year 1914, considering that Darleen had not just a Papa (Bill Darling) but two uncles (Charlie Darling, who directed the pictures for the Matchless studios, and Dan Darling, who ran the camera) and one aunt (Shirley Darling, who managed the business side for Matchless). But that's not how it had all worked out. As Uncle Charlie liked to say, Darleen was the only sprig on the family tree.

She tried to live up to the responsibilities of being the Only Sprig, but sometimes — like for instance now, as she bumpity-bumped down Ninth Avenue on the El, her uncles on one side of her and Aunt Shirley on the other, all talking business as if they didn't even notice the wonder of being on a train that flew (noisily) past the upper windows of what must be eleventy thousand tall buildings in a row — sometimes, Darleen keenly felt the lack of fellow sprigs (whether cousins, brothers, or sisters) who would understand how extremely thrilled she felt right now, who might clasp her hands in their own and grin with her and maybe even squeak right out loud with delight on the curves. *An elevated train!* That was basically as wonderful as riding the Big Scenic roller coaster at Palisades Amusement Park, but nobody in this car on this Saturday afternoon seemed to notice. The other passengers looked bored or annoyed. Aunt Shirley was nattering on and on about how much newspaper coverage the opening of the Strand was likely to get, and her uncles (balancing camera and suchlike between their knees) were talking about lighting. Darleen tried not to be resentful, but she felt very alone in her appreciation of the rattle-bang magic of New York City.

"I hope the searchlight will do," said Uncle Dan.

"You'll make it do, Dan," said Uncle Charlie. "And what an achievement it will be — a night scene *actually filmed at night!*"

Darleen had already heard every syllable of this discussion many times: the Strand Theatre had lights at its entrance, of course, but that wasn't the sort of bright light you needed to capture an image on a filmstrip. Over at the Matchless studios, they pretty much never filmed anything at night. They filmed during the day and tinted the nighttime scenes blue so the audience would understand that the burglars were creeping around at midnight, not at noon.

But Uncle Dan liked a challenge. And that was why he was lugging along a big black box with a light in it. He would use what the Strand had to offer by way of lighting and add a spotlight of his own into the mix.

"It'll depend on you, then, Darleen," said Uncle Charlie, and Darleen jumped a little on her bench because, up to this point, they had seemed perfectly happy to talk about technical details forever, without needing to bring any reference to her into the discussion. "You'll have to be sure to go right into the spot where the light is brightest."

"When the evil kidnappers appear," said Darleen.

"Goodness, child," said Aunt Shirley. "No need to sound so gloomy about it. It's going to be a great scene for Episode Nine, even if Jasper's not part of it, poor fellow."

Jasper was in another one of his moods; he was off somewhere today on "personal business," whatever that might mean. Darleen tried not to let Aunt Shirley see how happy she was that Jasper would *not* be part of anything today.

"Well, anyway," said Aunt Shirley. "At least we can all be relieved that your poor father decided to stay at home tonight. He seems to be worrying himself into a state about this whole thing. I'm sure he thinks the police will be carting us all off in their wagons, even though I've told him a thousand times that we've got all that covered. The police will stay well away! I declare, if Dan and Charlie hadn't calmed him down with descriptions of the wonders of the new Strand Theatre and its ceiling with special holes poked all through it and its suffering lighting, I'm sure none of us would be here now—"

"Self-suffusing," said Uncle Dan. "Not 'suffering.' *Semi-direct, self-suffusing lighting.*"

Aunt Shirley made a shrugging motion that conveyed how little concerned she was with the actual details of the Strand's lighting system.

"Anyway, dear Darleen, you'll be safely kidnapped and home again in Fort Lee before the rest of us even get there, so Bill will have no reason to worry a single extra moment, and you can tell him all about the lights and the ceiling and whatever all else he wants to hear about. Which we know won't be the movies themselves, bless his dear, machine-oriented heart."

(*Bump!-bump!-bumpity!-squeak!*: those were the comments of the Elevated Line.)

Darleen certainly didn't mean to complain, but a small sigh did escape her then.

"I just wish I could see a *little* bit of Alaska," she said, as the train threw her against her aunt and then back against Uncle Dan.

That was her bitterest regret: they were having her kidnapped during the first half of the program (they wanted to get some shots of the crowd entering the theater, but they didn't want that crowd blocking the shot of the kidnapping), and that meant she would miss the Kathlyn Williams picture. It seemed a tragic waste to Darleen to be coming all the way across the Hudson to New York City only to miss seeing Kathlyn Williams in Alaska.

"Not a single snowflake," said Aunt Shirley, who could sometimes be awfully heartless. "And don't look sad. Think about your poor Uncle Dan, who won't even get to peek inside! He'll be out with his camera the whole time, waiting for you. He won't even get to see the *self-suffering* lights or anything."

"*Hmm,*" said Uncle Dan pointedly about the lights, but he didn't bother to say more than that.

And then they were at their station, and it was time to get off the train.

Time passed strangely — very slowly and very fast both at once — and before Darleen knew it, Aunt Shirley and Uncle Charlie were shepherding her through the lobby, which was filled to bursting with what Aunt Shirley called "the very cream of New York society." If people were milk, thought Darleen, then this was a milky flood. So many mothers and daughters in nice dresses and fancy coats, and more spilling in every second through the front doors. It did look like everyone who was anyone would be coming to the Strand tonight.

No one recognized Darleen, at least not at first. She wasn't in her Daring Darleen get-up of simple white blouse and rugged skirt, perfect for jumping off trains; under her spring coat, she was dressed like all the other twelve-year-old girls in the theater. No one would suspect a girl in a "stylish dress of batiste and Swiss embroidery, trimmed with washable lace in tasty design" (to quote Sears, Roebuck and Company) — a girl dressed in something ordered from a catalogue for the bargain price of $1.55 — of being either a princess or a photoplay star famous for her feats of derring-do. But then again, an exiled and fictional princess with Daring Darleen as her secret identity would not have worn her crime-fighting clothes to the theater! At the end of Episode Eight, Crown Princess Dahlia Louise had received a mysterious invitation to the opening of the Strand, with hints that she might learn something about the whereabouts of her missing Royal Father. It was only now that Darleen realized she would have to do stunts in this slightly flouncy dress all week unless the episode had a change of clothing worked into its story. Botheration!

And then she saw that a young boy had stopped right in front of her and was staring at her hard. Darleen shook the worried thoughts out of her head and tried to smile like a completely ordinary person of twelve.

"Why, hello, there," she said when the staring didn't stop.

"You know, you look a lot like—" said the child.

"Come along now, Edward!" called a woman who seemed likely to be young Edward's mother.

"Aren't you—" said the child.

"Shh," said Darleen, putting a finger to her lips. "What if there are wicked Salamanders hidden in these crowds?"

"Oh!" said the boy, and he ran off to follow his mother.

Shirley was already taking Darleen's hand to guide her inside.

"Well, here we are. Time for us to enter the palace," said Aunt Shirley. "And it had better be a palace! A million dollars it cost them to fit out this place, that's what the newspapers said. I surely hope they know what they're about."

(Aunt Shirley, apart from her inability to see the true nature of Jasper Lukes, was a very practical sort of person.)

The Darlings joined the crowds and pushed through the lobby doors into the center of that palace.

It was really like stepping into a castle in fairyland. The seats swept all the way across the great space of the theater, and the whole place glowed gently, like the inside of the largest, pearliest oyster shell the universe ever made.

"Oh!" said Darleen, won over immediately. "Oh, Aunt Shirley! It's *magic*!"

"Now, Darleen," said Uncle Charlie, but he was smiling. "What would your father say to that? What we've got here is a triumph of architecture and science. And on Bill's behalf, we mustn't forget to admire the ceiling!"

For a respectful moment, the three of them looked up at the ceiling, which Darleen's Papa had read all about and thought deserved some admiring.

Apparently it was dotted with secret little holes to help with the circulation of the air. Secret little holes are hard to see, of course, but the dome was as lovely as you could wish, and on the walls were many decorations in the sort of tasteful colors only the most sophisticated fairies prefer: old rose, French gray, and gold. And then there was the stage itself, which was magnificent and large.

A red velvet curtain hung from a gilded arch decorated with plaster characters, and above that arch, there was a symbolic sort of mural, of people in flowing robes waving their hands in the air gracefully. What that had to do with photoplays, Darleen had no idea. They looked dreamy and floaty, like people who had been mesmerized into thinking they were clouds on a spring day.

"And actual, real fountains!" said Aunt Shirley with a sigh of pleasure. "How beautiful it all is! I don't believe actual, real Italy could be a smidgen nicer!"

Indeed, three little fountains sparkled there, in front of the place where the conductor would probably stand. The fountains had special lights focused only on them (Uncle Charlie pointed out) to help with that sparkle.

The Darlings were seated to one side, near the front, so that Darleen could sneak away at the proper moment. Uncle Charlie saw Aunt Shirley and Darleen settled in their seats and then slipped back out through the crowds. His place, he always felt, was at the side of Uncle Dan so that Uncle Dan wouldn't lack Uncle Charlie's firm opinions and suggestions. Uncle Dan was photographing the people pushing their way into the theater now.

When the audience was settled in their seats, the lights all dimmed together, as if twilight had come to the fairy-tale land.

"Isn't that nice," whispered Aunt Shirley.

The little real fountains in the pretend garden still twinkled away in the gloom. There was an expectant hush in the crowd. And then the curtains parted, and the audience could see a stage set up within that larger stage. And the center of that stage was what must be the screen, behind yet another curtain, with the grandest columns on either side.

The newspapers had promised that the projection and the music would all be first-rate, and they certainly were. When the second set of curtains opened and the screen lit up with an enormous waving flag, the orchestra, tucked behind fake hedges, only a short distance from where Darleen was sitting, broke right into a rousing edition of "The Star-Spangled Banner," and Darleen's heart jumped around from the sheer thrill of it.

Darleen would be able to experience only about fifteen minutes' worth of the show, so she was determined to enjoy every bit of that time just as much as she could.

Twenty-seven musicians, the papers had said. Imagine the expense of that! But the sound was glorious. The crowd applauded with so much enthusiasm that the theater seemed just simply awash in sound.

"Ladies and gentlemen!" said a man who came out onto the stage in a fancy suit. "We are so pleased that you could join us tonight for this world-historical first-ever programme at our new Strand Theatre. Tonight we celebrate the opening of the most luxurious and well-appointed dedicated picture palace in New York City! And now, to help introduce a larger audience to America's newest junior crime-fighting princess, here's a special behind-the-scenes glimpse at the glamorous life of DARING DARLEEN!"

To be mentioned like that on such a grand occasion! Darleen wasn't a blushing sort of person, but she did feel the heat rising in her cheeks. She was actually a little relieved when Aunt Shirley squeezed her hand and said, "Almost time, dear."

Past the artificial bushes and the orchestra, some titles appeared:

"America's Baby
Grows Up
In Front Of The
Moving Picture Camera."

They showed a little bit of one of the *Darling Darleen* episodes now, the one where she made a whole complicated machine out of dolls and tin soldiers and blocks, just to get herself out of her crib so she could play with the kittens downstairs. Dar groaned, but at least it was funny, and the crowd was in the mood for it. (Though did they have to laugh *so loud*?)

"We Loved Her Then!"

said the screen. Then it offered a picture of Darling

Darleen in those awful frills and laces. Dar tried to cover her eyes, but her aunt had a firm hold of her hand.

"Weren't you sweet?" murmured Aunt Shirley into Darleen's ear. Dar groaned again.

"And Now That She Has Gone
From *Darling* To *Daring*
We Love Her Still!"

And there she was! Her own self, dangling from that awful cliff. She squinted critically at the screen and thought she had done a passable job of "dangling like a princess" while Uncle Dan cranked away. And then, after another shot, in which smiling Darleen, in her sensible crime-fighting costume (dark, practical skirt and white shirtwaist) was introduced, there was the title card for the series:

"Our Own *Daring Darleen,*
Serial Queen . . .
Daring Star Of . . .
The Dangers of Darleen!"

"Ahhh!" said Aunt Shirley.

She meant, *What a success!* Aunt Shirley had her mathematical look on at that moment: the look of someone who was adding up the nearly three thousand people seated in that audience and imagining them all flowing back, week after week, to see Daring Darleen triumph over set after set of celluloid obstacles.

"AND NOW, EPISODE EIGHT:
DARLEEN ON THE EDGE."

Aunt Shirley checked her watch and clucked her tongue.

"And that's that. Off you go, now, Darleen," she said. "Look for Danny, and you can't go wrong. Oh, and here's your prop, so make sure the camera sees you have it."

Her prop was a note with a fancy wax blob on it that was supposed to be the secret seal of the Order of the Black Salamander. When they filmed a close-up version, the note would surely say something like "COME TO THE THEATRE ENTRANCE IF YOU WOULD LEARN SOMETHING OF THE WHEREABOUTS OF YOUR ROYAL FATHER. SIGNED, *AN ANONYMOUS FRIEND*," but for now Aunt Shirley had simply scrawled on it, "Smooth as silk and nary a tangle!"—which was her all-purpose good-luck phrase.

It is tempting to blame Aunt Shirley's good wish for somehow having gotten itself mixed up and reversed on its way up to the clouds, because two things were soon to become very clear about this little kidnapping caper:

Unsuspecting Darleen was at this very moment walking into a most treacherous tangle, and nothing—nothing at all—would end up going "smooth as silk."

Chapter 4

Kidnapped!

The idea was that Darleen would emerge from the theater, spot Uncle Dan behind the camera, make a show of consulting the note in her hand, and then look around for a suspicious-looking fellow and his suspicious-looking automobile.

But in fact, as soon as she stepped through the theater's main doors, everything began to go awry.

First of all, Uncle Dan's camera was there, and the lights were blazing, but her uncles were nowhere to be seen. Darleen looked around in consternation. Had they gotten the timing wrong somehow? Should she just stand around until Uncle Dan appeared? A single episode of *The Dangers of Darleen* used two reels of film and lasted about thirty minutes. That meant there wasn't much time to waste. Soon enough, Episode Eight would end, and the crowd would swell through these doors at intermission, ruining all possible shots.

And just as she was thinking these grumpy thoughts, two things happened:

A man in an ill-fitting jacket came slithering out the theater doors (*slithering* was the word! Darleen had never seen a human being who moved so very like a snake!) and glanced around wildly. He looked like someone who had just lost something terribly important and was sure he would soon be in heaps of trouble. But before Darleen could finish imagining her list of things this man might have lost (a champion poodle? his wife's emerald brooch?), a hulking black motorcar squealed around the corner and stopped abruptly, right in front of the theater.

The worried man leaped forward as if he had been expecting this car and yanked its front door open.

"Couldn't find the girl!" he cried, and then there was a stream of angry shouting from the driver, who wanted the side-winding man to *shut up*, to *not be an idiot*, to *stop leaving everything for him, the driver, to do*, and to *hurry up and get in out of those lights*.

The side-winding man, still confused, tried to peer

into the back of the car. He was being very slow about opening that door.

Oh, bother, thought Darleen. *Does everyone in this world have to be so screamingly incompetent all the time?*

And then she glanced left, and there was Uncle Dan, racing back to his camera, followed by Uncle Charlie. "Something came up at the side entrance!" Uncle Charlie seemed to be saying. But then he saw what was happening here and changed his comments to "Go, go!"

Maybe the scene could still be saved, then. Darleen hurried up to that side-winding man as fast as she could manage while still pretending to be anxiously looking at her note. She practically had to bump into him to get his attention, however. What an amateur this actor was proving to be! She did that thing of pretending to pull away while he turned and gaped at her, his right hand on the open motorcar door, and his eyes darting from Darleen to the cameraman behind her. Incompetent beginner! Even the silliest extras knew better than to cast wild-eyed looks at the camera — or to freeze in front of it.

"Oh, for heaven's sake, be quick!" Darleen hissed at him, trying to maintain a terrified expression for Uncle Dan's camera. "You're supposed to get that door open and *push me in*! Or move out of the way, at least!"

Thank goodness moving-picture cameras could not record the words anyone said!

It had started badly, but the stunt turned out remarkably well. The side-winding man opened the back door, and Darleen managed to tumble into the car quite as if he had pushed her himself—just as another hulking black automobile squealed up behind them. What was that about? Darleen didn't remember a second car being part of the plan.

There was a lot of shouting. Uncle Charlie shouted, and the men jumping out of the second car shouted, and the driver of *this* car spat some very harsh words at the incompetent side-winding man, who was still just standing there, gaping at the door.

That was when the sidewinder *finally* woke up. He slammed the back door behind Darleen, jumped into the front seat, and slammed that door, too. The fancy motorcar lurched forward and away, as if it were the only thing in this whole sorry crew that had remembered all its lines.

The driver and the side-winding man kept shouting at each other in the front of the car. As well they might, considering how they had mangled this entire operation. Still, the driver seemed to be courting another kind of disaster, to be driving so fast while carrying on an argument with the sidewinder sitting next to him. Darleen was trying to think of some way to address the issue tactfully—because she knew that "Slow down" almost never actually worked, when addressed to an overheated driver — when something bumped into her feet.

Something moving! At her feet!

She took a closer look: there was a large lump wriggling on the dim floor of the motorcar — a roughly human-shaped lump with a large burlap sack over its head and with feet wearing a pair of shoes made from what looked like good leather.

Darleen gasped. What else had these amateurs gotten wrong? But before her mind could form another coherent thought, her hands were already pulling the burlap sack off the lump's head, and her arms were hauling the lump up from the floor to the seat of the motorcar.

"Oh, no!" said the lump and Darleen, both at the same time.

Because the lump was not merely a lump. It was a girl!

This girl, whoever she was, seemed to be about the same size as Darleen. In the gloom it was hard to tell what she looked like exactly, but her voice was pleasant, and her dress gave a general rustling impression of elegance. In the colorless flicker of light and shadow from the street-lights, she looked, to tell the truth, almost like a character in a photoplay.

This girl was looking at Darleen with as much distress as Darleen herself felt.

"My heavens, you poor thing," said the girl. "What have these wretched criminals done now?"

Considering that the mysterious girl had just emerged from confinement in a burlap sack, her worries about Darleen seemed very generous—indeed, almost out of place. And the full horror of this situation was beginning to dawn on Darleen.

"What they've done is—they've made a mistake!" she found herself saying. "Oh, how awful, I'm so sorry. We have to tell them—we have to stop this motorcar—to take you back. Hey, misters!"

And she was so horrified that she leaned right up to interrupt the arguing men in the front seat as the car lurched its way uptown, but before she could say another word, the girl put a warning hand on her arm.

"Oh, do be cautious! I'm afraid they're dangerous, desperate men. The driver has a firearm. I saw it! And then he put the sack over my head—"

"A firearm? That's got to be a prop," said Darleen, feeling oddly short of oxygen.

"A prop? You mean, a theatrical property? Only for the stage? No, I don't think so," said the other girl. "I'm afraid I recognize the make from sad experience in the West."

What? thought Darleen. And that *what* went very deep indeed, through layer after layer of Darleen's mind and soul.

"So we mustn't provoke them," said the girl. "But, oh, dear, why have they taken you? What a dreadful thing this is. We have to find some way to reason with them, to explain about you. I can't bear the thought of an innocent bystander being swept up into my troubles."

Darleen had to digest that speech for a moment. Weren't these *Darleen's* troubles they were both mixed up in at the moment?

Then she said, a degree more feebly than before, "Excuse me, but I'm pretty sure *you* are the innocent stander-by here, and I'm sorry. They were supposed to be looking out for me. They knew I would be waiting out in front. How *could* they have messed up so badly? And wherever did they find *you*? The uncles will be awfully embarrassed when these idiots show up with two girls instead of one. I'm so sorry. It's an awful mistake they've made. An awful, terrible mistake."

The two girls looked at each other in silence — two shadowy faces lit up by the little lightning flares of street-lamps — while the motorcar sped recklessly through the busy streets of New York, jostling its back-seat prisoners quite roughly as it went.

"How strange," said the other girl. "You seem to believe these awful men meant to abduct *you,* but why would you think such a thing? And — if I may — are we possibly acquainted? There is something about your face, although of course it's rather dim in this motorcar, that seems so very familiar. 'Better to confess a forgotten name right away than to writhe in internal agony all through dinner' — that's what my dear Grandmama used to say."

And she reached forth a delicate, kid-gloved hand.

"I am Victorine Berryman, and if I should know your name and have forgotten it, I do apologize sincerely."

Victorine Berryman!

For a moment Darleen could not manage to speak a coherent word beyond "Oh!" — though she did remember to take the offered hand.

Miss Victorine Berryman!

But that was the Poor Little Rich Girl herself, orphaned scion of the Berryman railroad empire! She had been in the papers quite a bit over the course of the past year. All those stories about how the matriarch of the Berryman clan had raised her granddaughter while traveling in luxury to all corners of the globe. And then the grandmother had very recently died, and there had been a search of some kind for relatives to take charge of the orphaned heiress. "And dine off her diamonds, no doubt," Aunt Shirley had said, tut-tutting and shaking her head. "The vultures will gather, poor lamb, mark my words!"

All of that was flooding through Darleen's memory, so she said only, "Oh!" another time, or maybe twice more, as ideas began to bump into other ideas in her head.

"And you?" said Miss Berryman. "Poor dear girl, I know this must all be such a terrible shock. I confess I'm quite shocked myself."

"Oh, but I'm Darleen!" said Darleen in a rush, remembering her etiquette. "Darleen Darling."

Miss Berryman's face lit up as if a spotlight had just been turned upon it.

"Daring Darleen!" she said, and suddenly she looked so much younger. Really, she had to be almost the exact age and size of Dar herself, despite her fancy way of speaking. "Oh, can it be? Miss Darling! But it's as if I've fallen right into a photoplay! *Daring Darleen* — yes, of course, if we weren't in this terrible gloom, I surely would have recognized your face right away! Oh, wonderful! I was just watching your picture when the notice came, calling me so urgently to the side entrance. But never mind that. So you are here to rescue me!"

"Rescue you?" said Darleen. "Oh, no, it's all pretend, Miss Berryman. I'm sure you must know that. It's for the advertising, you know. They are *pretending* to kidnap me, but really they'll just hurry me back to Fort Lee. It's all a stunt, that's all it is — something to draw the public in."

At that moment, they were flung quite hard against the partition between the front and back seats of that motorcar as it screeched to a sudden halt. The driver turned around to look through the gap in the partition. He had a glinting pistol in his hand, although there was no camera clickety-clacking away anywhere around to justify such overacting.

"WHICH OF YOU IS THE BERRYMAN GIRL?" he snarled at them.

Darleen's breath caught in her throat, and Miss Berryman, next to her, gasped too. They were surely both realizing at this very moment that the two of them, although not exactly what anyone would call identical in appearance, in fact both had more or less brown hair and were about the same size. What's more, both were wearing white dresses (though in a little more light anyone who knew anything about dresses should have been able to see that one of those dresses came for $1.55 out of the Sears, Roebuck and Company catalogue, and the other was made of pure silk and might well have cost a hundred whole dollars, for all Darleen knew). Could it be — was it possible? — that the kidnappers really *did not themselves know* who was who? Because if so —

The girls clasped hands. It was strengthening to feel another hand holding on to your own.

"Why do you ask, sir?" said Miss Berryman, with only the faintest wobble in her voice. "And I do beseech you to lower your weapon. It is most disconcerting, and unnecessary."

"AND WHAT WAS THAT MAN DOING WITH THAT WOODEN BOX WITH THE TELESCOPE STUCK ON IT?"

"Anyone should know that. He was taking pictures," said Darleen, and she could hear the terror in her own voice, but a light bulb had just gone on in her head: Uncle Dan! These ruffians had better know they had not committed this crime *in the dark,* as it were. They had left a trace of themselves behind. "He's a cameraman. He was making a photoplay. I'm sure there will be pictures of what you did."

And while the stocky, dangerously armed driver and the side-winding man started another round of shouting at each other, Miss Berryman leaned close to Darleen and said, with a gentle squeeze of the hand, "As my Grandmama used to say, we will now have to think on our feet. And at least we can be grateful for one thing: we know that *your* feet are especially clever!"

Truth to tell, no part of Darleen felt particularly clever at that moment — not her brain, not her ears, not her feet. Her limbs, in fact, were beginning to tremble. Something had gone seriously wrong with her fake kidnapping. That was all that she knew for sure.

The side-winding man had just jumped out of the car and was now glancing nervously up and down the street.

"But it's all some kind of terrible mistake," said Dar.

She felt flushed and odd, like she was coming down with a fever. "It simply has to be."

"Look out now, Miss Darling. He's going to open the door," said Miss Berryman, and indeed, the door of the motorcar was flung wide, and the man out there was whisper-shouting for them to *Get out, get out quick, and not cause any trouble!*

Darleen glanced up and down the dark street and saw absolutely no one about, nor even a street corner that seemed reachable before the driver could make use of his pistol. Not to mention the fact that running away is much harder when there are two of you, and the second one of you is still in the process of emerging from the motorcar. *What should they do? Shout? Run?* But even as these thoughts raced through Darleen's mind, it was already too late to act on them. The side-winding man had clamped a firm hand on her arm, and a moment later he and the driver were urging them up the stairs of this not-very-lovely building.

"Don't you fret, now, missies," the driver was saying. "You be nice girlies, and maybe no harm will come to a single hair of your pretty heads."

That made Darleen's own actual scalp tingle with alarm.

The men hurried them in through the front door and then up three flights of stairs, with occasional glares and hissed reminders to keep quiet, although the kidnappers' own clumsy feet were making almost all of the noise. A minute later, they were in a not-very-fancy apartment, lit by the newfangled glare of electric lights, and a thin woman with angular eyebrows was putting her hand to her mouth in surprise.

"*Two* of 'em?" she said. "What have you oafs gone and done?"

Chapter 5

A Naccident

That was a good question, thought Darleen, quite aglow with outrage.

"Well, now, we've had a bit of an accident, Sally," said the driver, and he bent his head a little in apology. To Dar's eyes he looked like a poor actor impersonating a schoolboy about to be scolded.

"A what?" said Sally, and then her voice became sharper: "A *what?*"

"A *naccident!*" said the side-winding man. "One girlie we got at the side entrance, and the other out in front! Didn't mean to take two of 'em!"

"Oh, now, what?" said the woman called Sally. She was so angry that she took breaks between words to clench her lips tight. "Which one's our little pigeon, then? And which one's the extra baggage?"

That was when the driver said, "It was *awfully* dark, Sally."

And then the side-winding man said, "Except when the lights were blinding. We couldn't see anything, what for the lights, and then the dark. They was taking pitchers. I bet one of these girlies is a nactress, but I dunno which is which."

Then there was a lot of shouting from Sally about the *pitchers* being taken and whether the side-winding man had let himself get pinned into some *pitcher,* like the fool that he was, and how two grown men could be so stupid as to nab two girls when they were meant to nab one — and then not even know which was the right one!

While Sally shouted at the other kidnappers, Darleen squeezed Miss Berryman's hand, and Miss Berryman nodded very slightly in return. They might have been acquainted for only a few rough minutes, but Darleen was quite sure they were in agreement. It was hard to know whether it was preferable to be the "pigeon" or the "extra baggage" in this particular case, but surely it was better if the kidnappers stayed confused.

There was another pause while Sally grew angrier and

angrier and the kidnappers grew twitchier and twitchier under her glare.

"You gals!" snapped Sally. "Who are you? Names! Tell us now, quick-like."

In a photoplay, Crown Princess Dahlia Louise might have stood tall and proud at this moment, might have flashed her eyes in defiance and announced (with the help of a written intertitle), "I AM THE CROWN PRINCESS DAHLIA LOUISE!" But of course, Crown Princess Dahlia Louise, being fictional, had a certain advantage, didn't she? The photoplay might have her imprisoned and imperiled, but it would also always give her some, usually unlikely, way out of trouble. In real life, standing in front of real villains without any rescue written into the script, it turns out to be much harder to know what one should say.

"Do pardon me," said Miss Berryman, "but I'm quite sure the first question here should be, Who are *you*? And why have you brought us here, and so ungently?"

That was very brave of Miss Berryman. Darleen could tell she was secretly frightened underneath, however. She was speaking with as much dignity as possible, but Darleen was holding her hand and could feel her fingers trembling.

"Ungently!" sneered Sally. "Ha-ha! That's rich! I'll show you what *ungently* looks like, believe you me, if you keep taking that tone, you snooty gal. Don't waste our time. What's your name? Don't be lying to me now."

"*Lying!*" said Miss Berryman, her voice suddenly much less brave. Indeed, she seemed almost thunderstruck. "Oh, dear, is that what it is? Is it lying not to answer your questions? Oh, dear. It's just that—"

"It's just that we insist that you release us from this miserable place, and right away!" said Darleen, shamelessly interrupting. Miss Berryman seemed to be getting herself distracted from the main point, which, as far as Darleen was concerned, was *getting safely out of there.* Darleen did try to make her interrupting voice sound as high-class as possible: "Release us and take us home! Immediately! Because this is . . ."

She paused for a moment, since the words that were coming to mind were not very heiress-like, but Miss Berryman pulled herself together and came to her rescue:

"This is intolerable," said Miss Berryman.

"Yes, exactly that," said Darleen, adjusting not just her vowels, but her shoulders, to be as much like Miss Berryman's as possible. "In-tolerable. And also wrong. And we aren't going to tell you a *thing* more. From now on, *silence.*"

(And she gave Miss Berryman's hand a strengthening squeeze while she said that, to keep Miss Berryman on the right course.)

Miss Berryman echoed only that one last word, *silence,* and really, she could have been a queen in a photoplay when she said it, so straight and determined was her back.

The dreadful Sally looked about ready to leap at them like a disheveled wildcat: "What is this nonsense? Are *you* the Berryman gal? Or are *you*?"

The girls managed to stand in silence together in that dim and nasty place while the screaming and shouting ran circles around them.

When the dreadful Sally ran out of breath enough for screaming, she shifted to a hoarse menace, which was almost worse than the shouting: "You better tell us who you are, you selfish gals! Imagine your poor, dear, weeping families, waiting fer a word."

Oh! Darleen did feel a pang at the thought of her father finding out she was in actual, real danger—just as he had so unreasonably feared! But somehow she stayed silent, despite the pang.

Eventually the frustrated Sally turned back to the kidnappers, to whom she also had a lot to say, all of it furious.

"Oh, come on now! You dragged them into your motorcar. You didn't see who was who?"

"We was working awful fast, Sally," said the side-winding man. "And there was all those lights."

"And don't be blaming me," said the driver. "I know

there wasn't supposed to be two gals. Not my fault we ended up with two!"

"Hey!" said the sidewinder.

Sally hissed at them again for getting off the subject.

"The boss will have our hides," she said. "Hear me? *Our hides.* Sort this out now, I'm tellin' you, or he'll sort us all out, and there won't be enough of any of us left to feed a cat."

"So what do we do now?" said the sidewinder.

"Dump 'em *both* in the river?" said the driver.

He actually said that!

"Let's don't get ahead of ourselves," said Sally with much disgust. "We haven't exactly collected our wages out of anyone yet, have we?"

She took a pen and wrote some lines on a piece of paper, then blotted it with a really filthy rag, scowled, and handed it over to the driver.

"This here's the note. Take it to the Berryman house, but don't you let anyone catch you while you're doing it. Instructions are, you pin it on the door, nice and visible, and scoot. And then we have until the boss sends his man over here to figure out what's what and who's who and who goes where. And no more messing up."

"No, Sally," said the driver, already backing out through the door. He looked relieved to be leaving, thought Darleen. And who wouldn't? "No more messing up," he repeated.

Sally was eyeing the girls now, and her eye was nothing you'd want on you if you had a choice.

"You two," she said, and Darleen could tell she was trying to make her voice sound less scary, which was in itself a terrifically dreadful thing, since she was no actor. "You go on in here and think it over. You want to go in the river, or you want to be good gals and tell us who's who so we can get you home? Make no trouble, and maybe we'll none of us come to no harm."

At a gesture from Sally, the side-winding man pushed the girls through a doorway they hadn't properly noticed over to the left. In they went, and the door slammed shut.

"Oh!" said the girls, both at once.

It was a way of flinching in unison. Because, to be honest, things did not look very good: They were imprisoned. In a gloomy room. Behind a locked door. By kidnapping bandits. Who seemed to have no consciences to speak of.

And still!

They were not yet in the river.

And that, under the circumstances, had to be counted the very next best thing to hope.

The girls looked at each other in the dim light of that

room (a streetlight outside sent a faint shimmer through the window), and they both thought the same thought: *What do we do now?*

"They are threatening to drown us!" said Miss Berryman. "What dreadful, dreadful people these are."

She was already running her hand up and down the wall, looking for the light switch, but Darleen stopped her.

"Not yet, not yet," she whispered, and she pulled Miss Berryman toward the window. Light is a powerful and sometimes treacherous thing, as Dar well knew from the photoplays. "We'll be terribly backlit, Miss Berryman, and that awful man will see us—"

"And suspect you are already planning our escape, which I'm sure you are!" added Miss Berryman, clapping her hands quietly in the gloom. "How clever you are, Miss Darling!"

Darleen wasn't sure she could ever live up to the trust and hope shining forth like a beacon from Miss Berryman's every word, so instead, she pointed down to the street, where a man—recognizable in the streetlight as the stocky, forward-moving driver—strode along, a letter demanding ransom presumably tucked away in some pocket. Sure enough, at the corner, he turned around and looked up at the window where they were standing in shadow. He looked up and thought whatever evil thoughts a kidnapper thinks while the girls held still in the dark. Then he turned and walked off again, heading north at the corner.

"You know," said Darleen once he was safely gone, "I don't think they want to drown *both* of us. Aren't kidnappings usually about ransom money? Surely if they know who you are, they'll be confident they'll get a lot of money for you, Miss Berryman."

"I'm afraid that's not a certainty at all," said Miss Berryman so quietly that Darleen had to move closer to figure out her words. "It's quite possible that my guardians, my Brownstone cousins, may not want to pay a nickel in ransom for me."

"How can you say that?" said Darleen, shocked. "They're your guardians! Your *family*! Why, they must be dreadfully worried about you already. Of course they'll do whatever they can to rescue you!"

"Oh, Miss Darling, if only you knew," said Miss Berryman, shaking her head. "I was so hopeful myself when the Brownstones first turned up! It was during that awfully dark time, you know, right after Grandmama . . . Grandmama . . ."

Miss Berryman faltered for a moment but then gathered her pluck together and carried on.

"When my poor Grandmama's attorney told me he had found some actual relatives willing to take me under their wings, you can imagine how glad I was! And surprised too! The Berrymans have been a sadly dwindling family for years. Why, my only uncle—poor Uncle Thomas—died before I was even born, and then I lost my dear parents too. Grandmama never mentioned any cousins to me, but Mr. Ridge, the attorney, seemed so certain about these Brownstones. Poor Mr. Ridge—there cannot have been a great assortment of possible relatives to choose from."

Darleen's sympathies were entirely on the side of Miss Berryman, who was turning out to be even more of an Only Sprig than Darleen herself.

"Haven't they been treating you properly, your Brownstone cousins?"

"I'm afraid not," said Miss Berryman. "They moved in right away, and since then, I have not had a single kind word from them. All they seem to care about is Grandmama's art collection! But I try to remember that the Brownstones are only *distant* cousins. Perhaps that makes a difference when it comes to family feeling."

"How awful!" said Darleen.

"Never mind it, Miss Darling," said Miss Berryman. "I bring up my sad story here only to suggest that these kidnappers might have more luck seeking ransom for *you*. If they figure out that you are a star in the moving pictures, that is."

Darleen felt a despairing sort of smile crawling across her face.

"Oh, dear," she said. "You know, if they had any idea about the current finances of Matchless studios, I guess I'd be in the river already. All Aunt Shirley ever talks about these days are the studio's debts. There's certainly no money to be had from kidnapping *me*."

They stood silent for a moment, and then Miss Berryman sucked in her breath in horror.

"Well, then, to think that I nearly told them who I was! Thank goodness you stopped me in time. Who knows what they might have done! It was the *lying* thing, you see."

She paused.

"What lying thing?" said Darleen.

"She said it was *lying*!" said Miss Berryman. "That not telling them who I was would be *lying*! Is not answering a question telling a lie? I'm not sure. But when I think how telling them who I am and who you are would, you know, probably lead to them doing awful things to at least one of us, goodness knows I'd really truly rather not. What a terrible situation it is: when saving an innocent life — yours, perhaps, Miss Darling! — demands a *lie*! What a dilemma!"

That didn't seem like much of a dilemma to Darleen.

"I guess a lie here and there can't much matter under

the circumstances," Darleen said, trying not to sound impatient.

"But lying always matters, Miss Darling," said Miss Berryman quite firmly. "I've been realizing that recently, you see. When my Grandmama became ill, I started thinking a lot about—well, about things like telling the truth. I was trying to reform my soul, you know, since I knew I would soon be losing her steadying hand. And I started noticing how often people say things that aren't true. Have you ever counted lies, Miss Darling?"

"Counted lies? No!" said Darleen. She had never considered such a thing.

"Well, I tried it. And I'm sorry to say I caught myself telling tiny fibs many times in a single day, Miss Darling! So I made a solemn promise to tell the plain truth all the time, with no exceptions at all. That's why I was so worried just now, to think that not telling these awful people who we are might be the same as lying."

"What!" said Darleen again. If anything, Miss Berryman's explanation was growing worse and worse. "But, Miss Berryman! It doesn't make a single lick of sense to tell the truth to people who are trying to throw at least one of us into the river. We *are* trying to get out of here alive, aren't we?"

"I confess that when I made my solemn promise, I didn't expect to face a situation quite like this one," said

Miss Berryman. "What a test this is! Oh, Miss Darling, I can feel it: my virtue is wobbling. And I'll have you know, it has been three months, two weeks, and four days since I last told a falsehood. What a pity it will be to ruin that record now! It seems almost too much to bear, truly it does."

And her voice cracked a little, as if she were swallowing a sob.

All of this took Darleen so aback that for a moment she was speechless.

It was clear that, although they might look a little alike (at least to inattentive kidnappers), Miss Victorine Berryman and Darleen, Only Sprig of the Darlings, were very different people in many important respects.

And then Miss Berryman pulled herself together all of a sudden.

"Goodness, what would my Grandmama say if she saw me like this!"

"She'd call the police, I guess," said Darleen, looking around at their bare and dismal surroundings. "And get us some help."

Miss Berryman shook her head as if Darleen had misunderstood her.

"Oh, perhaps so, certainly," she said. "But *first,* Miss Darling, my Grandmama would say, 'Chin up, young Berryman! Chin up, and look on the bright side!'"

Chapter 6

On the Bright Side

O*n the bright side?*

That seemed a bit of a stretch under current conditions.

"Well," said Darleen after a moment, "at least it seems like they can't tell us apart for some reason. How funny, too, when all they have to do is glance at your gloves! I've never seen such lovely gloves. I mean, honestly, how could they ever mix *me* up with a Miss Berryman?"

"And I suppose they must not be regular viewers of photoplays," said Miss Berryman, wiping her eyes with the swift swipe of someone determined to move past her moment of despair. "Because if they were, you'd think they would recognize you, quick as quick. At least my picture hasn't been in the newspapers. Grandmama was always rather fussy about that."

"We have to think up a plan," said Darleen. "That's what we have to do. And if you find yourself tempted to tell them anything they shouldn't know, please just clamp your lips together tight and *don't*. I'm pretty sure not saying anything isn't the least bit the same thing as lying. Anyway, who knows? Maybe I can do some of the fibbing for you. But the main thing is to get ourselves out of this fix."

Miss Berryman nodded in the gloom.

"You are right," she said. "And while we're being so open with each other, please, Miss Darling, if it isn't too bold of me to suggest it—since we are, I'm afraid, in some danger—"

That was true enough, alas. At that very moment, Darleen was peeking again out the window. She was visually measuring the distance to the nearest fire escape, which, most tantalizingly, ran down the side of the building about six feet to the left.

Miss Berryman hadn't stopped talking for a moment. "Here's my idea: since we're in such danger together, I propose we do what the Swiss mountaineers do when they are high in the Alps."

"What?" said Darleen. "What do the Alps have to do with anything? What I see is, the foolish fire escape is just barely out of reach. Though I suppose they wouldn't have locked us in a room that we could simply step right out of."

Miss Berryman's mind was fully focused on her Swiss mountaineers, however.

"While they are high in the mountains, you see, where the dangers are great, they set aside all the formalities," said Miss Berryman. "So let's not stand on ceremony a moment longer. Let me call you Darleen, Miss Darling, and you must call me Victorine. Now, then, that's settled."

Darleen must have made some small sound of surprise, because Miss Berryman hurried to add, "It's a funny name, isn't it? My Papa named me after his favorite knife."

"His *knife*?"

"Well, yes," said Miss Berryman (Victorine). "It's one of those little ones that fold up and have very useful bits and pieces to them. See?"

From somewhere under her skirt, she had indeed produced a small knife and now opened one of its blades, so it twinkled for a moment in the streetlamp's glow.

"It's one of my most prized possessions," said Victorine, looking at it fondly. "My dear father bought it before I was born and called it his Small Victory, and then I came along, and he decided I was his Small Victory, too, but since I would live in the brand-new twentieth century, he thought the name could use some modern improvements. Hence, *Victorine.* Never Vicky, by the way," she added. "Victorine has more dignity, don't you think?"

"Oh!" said Darleen, who was sometimes called Dar and didn't much mind it. "All right."

Miss Berryman was still showing off the secrets of her wonderful little knife, one blade at a time.

"It's my one inheritance from my dear Papa, you know — until I come of age, of course, and inherit everything. It has several good blades, and scissors, and a little corkscrew, and everything, and I am never without it. Perhaps it may come in useful in our current predicament!"

"Perhaps it may," said Darleen, feeling more grim determination than confidence.

"I give you permission to throw it at these villains whenever you think that would be a good idea!" said Victorine. "I know how deadly your aim is with a knife — Episode Three, with those gold miners! — but of course my knife is not specifically designed for throwing . . . How *did* you do it, Darleen, tossing those knives in that clever circle, right around the head of Mean-Eyed Jack?"

Darleen remembered that knife-throwing scene quite well. She had never laughed so hard on a photoplay set before. She kept flinging knives that kept landing any which where, and Uncle Charlie kept saying, from back where the camera was cranking away, "Never mind, never mind, we'll paste in shots of them landing where they're supposed to go."

They would never in a million years have been foolish enough to let her pitch an actual knife in the direction of the poor actor playing Mean-Eyed Jack!

"Well, now, *knife-throwing*!" Darleen said, and found that her conscience was rather torn about what exactly to say. "You do know that not everything they show in the photoplays is *exactly* true? They're tremendously clever, the people who put the pieces of film together to make the story work."

"Oh, yes, I'm sure they are," said Victorine. "But you needn't be modest, Darleen. I can see that you are tremendously clever, too, with all your tricks and talents. I'm such a quiet sort of person! I've never thrown a knife at a scoundrel ever in my entire life. But then, for the most part, my life has not been as dramatic as yours, I suppose. May I tell you my wildest dream when I was a little girl? I told my Grandmama once I thought I would like to grow up to be a World-Wandering Librarian! There, you're laughing! Shh!"

"I'm only laughing because you're laughing!" said Darleen. "And because I don't know what a World-Wandering Librarian even is!"

They were both still laughing (but as quietly as possible).

"Someone — who travels — with *books*!" said Victorine. "I should think that would be obvious. It was just a child's dream, of course. Books are heavy, and why would people on the other side of the world be wanting books from me? I mean, it's not as though I could teach anyone anything. I have so far to go in my own education. My Greek is lamentable! I haven't had the advantage you surely have had, Darleen, of attending a real school with real teachers."

"Oh, well, um," said Darleen, whose attendance in school over the years had been spotty at best. "We're so busy, you know —"

"Say not a word more," said Victorine. "I understand entirely. We have both had irregular educations, then: mine because of my travels (though Grandmama was a formidable tutor) and yours because of your devotion to the arts. But the important thing, Darleen, is that I'm so grateful to have you here, brave as you are. Just tell me what we do next. I proclaim you our captain and guide, up in these alpine heights."

And that made Dar want very much to be, in life, the Daring Darleen that Miss Berryman so mistakenly thought she actually was.

Victorine gave her little knife a final tap, folded it up,

and slipped it back into its hiding place, attached to her stocking.

Darleen wasn't sure they were any closer to making their escape, despite the knife inherited from Miss Berryman's father and despite all the wisdom of all the Swiss mountain climbers in all the Alps everywhere.

"Well, here's what I've thought of so far: ropes. Ever since you mentioned mountaineers earlier, you know. They have ropes, and we could definitely use a rope right now. Otherwise, we really do seem to be trapped."

"Oh, good point," said Victorine. "A very long rope would be an excellent thing to have, just at this moment."

They looked very carefully all around the room. No ropes. There was a bed in the corner—with bedsheets that looked neither very clean nor very sturdy. They shook their heads over those bedsheets: one small bed's worth of linens would never make a ladder long enough to get them safely to the ground from the fourth floor.

"Well!" said Victorine after a moment of silence. "I never thought it would come to this. It reminds me of when that horrible man closed you in the tower a few weeks ago, just because you wouldn't divulge the whereabouts of your dear Papa, the exiled King."

Dar blinked. *Her dear Papa!* That made her think of her own dear, real Papa, who must even now be waiting up for her back in Fort Lee, with no idea that his daughter was in a patch of pretty terrible trouble. Soon it would be very late at night, and she would not yet be home, and her father would begin to worry *dreadfully*. For a moment, Darleen was so struck by the awfulness of what her father would feel when he found out she was missing that she could not pay proper attention to what Miss Berryman (no, *Victorine*) was saying:

"Like Rapunzel, only without the long hair to help you! And then when he filled the tower room with water! That was much, much worse than this! To be imprisoned *and* to face drowning! That was dreadful. You were so clever then, the way you found the exit through the roof."

Darleen remembered it well, but of course she remembered it all much differently. She remembered everyone on the film crew shouting as they struggled with the huge crank that lowered the set into a pool of water, inch by inch, to make it look on-screen as if the water itself were rising, and how glad she had been for the hot cocoa Aunt Shirley served up to all of them at the end of the scene.

Alas, no exit through the roof was visible here.

And then, just as they were leaning over the bed to consider it properly—once her gloves were off, Dar's fingers couldn't help but notice the miserable quality of those sheets—the door flew open, startling them all over again, and that awful Sally woman and the side-winding man came clomping into the room.

"Ready to be sensible yet, gals?" said Sally. "You there!"

And she poked Victorine quite harshly in the shoulder.

"What's your name, gal?"

Victorine opened her mouth and closed it again. (Good for her!)

Darleen thought of the fictional Crown Princess Dahlia Louise and the old woman who came to the door of the shed where the bandits had locked her in. That had been a case where the only way out was to melt an icy heart.

"Oh, please," she said, putting her hands together most beseechingly and quoting shamelessly from a title card in Episode Four. "'Do think of your own dear children, good woman, and release us from this place of bondage!'"

"Har, har, har!" said the wicked Sally, and she shoved Darleen a little harder than she had shoved Victorine. "*That's* rich, that is! My 'own dear children'! That lot would hit me over the head with a log till I was dead as a squished frog if they had half a chance. You speak nice, girlie. You the rich one, then?"

"'My identity is my secret and my burden,'" said Darleen. That had been another title card, and she liked the way it sounded.

"That's enough nonsense out of you," said the woman, and the side-winding man handed them a glass of water to share and a dry hunk of bread.

"It's wasting food on the soon dead, far's I'm concerned," said the mean Sally person. "But fine. You go to sleep now, you gals, and don't bother pounding on the walls or shouting for help. I'll hear you right away if you try any of those sorts of shenanigans. Believe you me, you don't want us angry with you, I assure you of that!"

The sidewinder smiled at them so threateningly that Dar and Victorine grabbed each other's hands again and shuddered.

As the door closed, they heard the side-winding man say, "Ha! They've gone and lost their sweet minds, ain't they? From fright, most like."

For a moment they stood quite still, and then Victorine whispered, "Oh, well done, dear, daring Darleen, *well done*!"

But Darleen's brain had been busily going over the previous scene.

"Wait! Did that woman really call us 'the soon dead'?" she said. "That doesn't sound good at all, does it? Victorine, we have to figure something out!"

Half a moment later, they were back at the window, surveying that forbidding wall of brick and stone.

Impossible tasks sometimes look slightly less impossible when the other option is being thrown into a river by heartless villains.

"All right, here is part of an idea, anyway," said Darleen. "I know we can't make a ladder that would reach *all* the way down, but the bedsheets *might* be long enough to get us over there to the left, where the fire escape is. Not quite as grand as Rapunzel's braid, but what do you think? Would it be too terrible?"

Victorine took a look through the window, her brow tying itself into worried knots.

"It does look *quite* terrible," she said, "but I think you are right. I should warn you right away, however, that I may have to hum my way across. That's a trick I learned on the rope bridges of Assam."

"Hum?" said Darleen, but she was hardly paying attention. She was busy trying to calculate distances. It was strange: just looking outside made something flutter again in her chest. The wall was like a cliff made of bricks. How fierce and free and wicked a person sometimes felt on a cliff!

Victorine was standing next to her, looking out and down at the same wall.

"Humming, dear Darleen, helps keep fear at bay. Oh, but I will be careful to hum very quietly, of course."

"Well. Anyway, first we will have to tear the sheets

into wide strips," said Darleen. "They may hear *that* in the next room. Too bad we don't have any scissors. Oh, but your knife! I almost forgot!"

Victorine clapped her hands together (quietly) in the dark.

"How clever you are, Darleen!"

"It's decided, then," said Darleen. "We'll wait a while — pretend to be sleeping, you know — so that they let down their guard. And then we'll see what we can do with your scissors and these bedsheets."

"How bravely you say that!" said Victorine. "But then, of course, you dangle from cliffs practically every day of the week."

"Not quite *every* day," said Dar modestly.

They were clever to wait before beginning their escape, as it turned out, because while they lay on that miserable bed and pretended to be sleeping, the door to their room opened again and someone looked in, sniffed at the sight of them, and locked the door again. They heard the awful woman's voice in the next room:

"Sleeping like babies," she was saying. "Good."

"But babies don't actually sleep all that well, do they?" whispered Victorine, her fingers nervously fingering a necklace that had been tucked into her dress. The pendant was very odd — it looked like two keys. "I have traveled in enough trains to have learned that very well, alas. Is it time for me to try my scissors?"

"Yes, don't you think?" said Darleen. "Unless you want to wait until the awful man comes back from asking your family for money."

Victorine sat up straight and pulled the first sheet off their bed.

"We mustn't wait another moment," she said. "I put no faith in my greedy cousins, and I definitely don't want either one of us to end up drowned."

Victorine turned out to be very good with her scissors. She cut each of the two bedsheets into thirds, and then Darleen used the Double Fisherman's knot her uncle had taught her (Uncle Charlie had had a stint in the navy in his wayward youth) in order to tie the lengths cut from the top sheet and those from the bottom sheet safely and sturdily together.

"Your knots are very lovely," said Victorine, eyeing one of those double lengths. "But I'm not sure about the strength of these sheets. Do you think they'll really hold us?"

"Not as they are," said Dar. "That's why we're going to braid the strips together. Everything's stronger when braided."

"Clever girl!" murmured Victorine. "Of course!"

So they ended up with a thick braided rope of about

sixteen feet in length. And that, thought Darleen grimly, would just have to be enough.

Fortunately the little bed was flimsy. The two girls moved it up next to the window without making noise of any kind.

To attach their braided bedsheet rope to what she could only hope would prove to be the most solid part of the not-very-sturdy bed frame, Darleen used another of her Uncle Charlie's knots: the Round-Turn Bowline—good enough for the professional daredevils who *do* go up and down cliffs (and tall buildings) almost every day.

"And those climbing fellows are *much* bigger than we are and would plummet like lead if their knots should fail!" she pointed out to Victorine (and to herself).

From Victorine came only the gulp of someone determined not to say a single uncourageous word.

They took off their stockings and shoes and hats and gloves and gathered them into a little parcel that Victorine fitted cleverly onto her back. Darleen tied the other end of the bedsheet rope around her waist.

Then they had a scary moment getting that window open. It was stiff, and it threatened to creak—but they eased it open slowly, and it did not give them away.

All of these preparations had the advantage of keeping their minds busy so they would not be thinking too much about what it meant to be exiting a window four stories above the pavement, but finally, when they were about to have to face that thought square on, they saw a man coming around the corner at a trot, looking at the houses as he went.

The girls drew back to one side of the open window.

"But that's not the man who drove the car," said Victorine into Darleen's ear.

And the man looked up, a bit wild-eyed, as if he were worrying about something and rushing to a place he did not know well, and as he did so, a shard of light from a streetlamp caught his very distinctive face and his shock of golden hair. Darleen gasped.

It was *Jasper Lukes*! What in heaven's name was *he* doing here?

He vanished as he entered the door of the very building they were currently trapped in. Only four flights of stairs, and Jasper Lukes would be right outside their door. And that brought another urgent and dreadful thought.

"Oh, no! We have to go *now*!" said Darleen. "We have to go now — and fast. That man knows who I am — and that means they'll know which of us is *you*!"

And not wasting a single moment more, she hopped onto that windowsill and started feeling around for a crack in the bricks that would be friendly to her toes.

She had been so careful for so long, ever since that

cliff-side incident, about trying to keep her feet on the ground, but oh goodness, here she nevertheless was.

I'm just doing what needs to be done, Darleen told herself. *I can't help it, can I, if getting out of this mess means another cliff.*

But at the same time, a deeper, more inward voice was saying, *Oh, Papa, I'm sorry!*

Because she realized, to her horror, that as her toes reached out for the helpful crack in the bricks, that feeling must have woken itself back up in her chest — because she couldn't help it: she could feel herself *smiling.*

Chapter 7

Half-Spider on the Wall

What kind of monstrous person smiles on cliffs?

Oh, Papa! Darleen thought. *After this, I promise my feet will stay on the ground.*

"Hurry *carefully,*" said Victorine, looking out that window. "Oh, my. Do please be as careful as you possibly can."

They were in luck: there was a useful crack in the brickwork running along a few feet below the window, and for a while, of course, an actual sill to hang on to.

Facing the wall, Darleen scooted sideways.

"You're making simply beautiful progress," said Victorine, leaning out a little farther to get a glimpse of the lay of the land. "And now there's another nice crevice for your fingers, just a few inches above the sill. Reach up to the right and you'll find it — *there!*"

For a moment Darleen perched like a four-legged spider (*a half-spider!* she thought a little incoherently) on the side of the wall, her fingers and toes ensconced in the cracks between bricks. The fire escape was just a few more feet to her right. She moved her right hand over and then her right foot.

She was going to have to leap. She felt that knowledge thrill its way through her, fast as a lightning strike. And then, just as all the helpful stickiness vanished from her fingertips — when she realized she *really was* about to fall, which made her heart feel queer and curious — at the last second, Darleen's left foot (thinking faster than the rest of her) pushed very hard sideways, against the wall, to make Darleen's fall slant to the right, and the fall became almost more like a leap, and her right hand found a bar and clung to it, *clung to it.* Oh, that hand had done it! She, Darleen, Half-Spider and Only Sprig, had done it!

Darleen whipped her other hand up so she could cling with both hands. That was better. Now her bare feet could find their way to something more solid than air. She had made it to the fire escape, and she had not even actually fallen.

When she looked back up to that window, above and

to the left, she saw a ghostly pale Victorine staring out at her, her wide eyes glinting a little in the lamp- and moonlight.

"Oh, my!" Darleen could hear her saying. "Oh, my, oh, *my*!"

There was surely not even a second to waste now. Had she herself really climbed out of that window? Oh, but she found she couldn't think yet about what she had just done or about how it had made her feel.

Instead of thinking those thoughts, Darleen took the loose end of their braided-sheet rope back down the fire escape until she was about half a floor below Victorine, and she used the best knot she could think of for tying one end of a rope around a fire escape bar.

Suddenly she looked at this rope traversing the cliff of the brick wall and felt *afraid*. What a strange thing! She could not be properly afraid about cliffs on her own behalf, apparently, but for Victorine she was, all of a sudden, terribly afraid.

She was worried that her face might give too much away, so she tried to make no expression whatsoever. She acted the part of someone with perfect confidence in the ability of her friend to do this mildly impossible thing at a great height over the hard and unforgiving paving stones.

She waved up to Victorine, perched already on the

windowsill and watching Darleen's preparations with great care.

"That's it! Quick, now! Don't think about it—just come on down and over, Victorine!" Darleen said in a shouting sort of whisper. "Think of it like a fireman's pole, only going slightly sideways."

"Oh, *Grandmama*!" said Victorine. "I am deeply terrified of heights, did I tell you that? Oh, well, here I come!"

And then she came tumble-slipping sideways and down, humming rather fiercely, as promised, and following the line of the rope they had made. And a moment later, Darleen was hauling her over the side of the fire escape, and they were hugging each other in terror and elation, such a wild mix of emotions like nothing Darleen had felt before. She had been so sure that she was about to fall and be squashed, and then she had been so terrified for Victorine, *and somehow they had not fallen.* They were unsquashed and alive! Oh, they were so, so very alive, maybe more alive than Dar had ever been in her whole life before. They clung to each other, shaking and laughing and trying not to make too much noise in that brief but glorious celebration.

"That was . . ." said Victorine. "That was . . ."

"That was *incredible*!" said Darleen.

And then there was a sound from somewhere, and they fell silent all at once and realized they were outside on a fire escape, and their legs were bare, and the air was cold, and they needed to get away from this spot as fast as ever they could before those awful kidnappers opened the door and looked into that terrible room and saw the ruined bedsheets tracing a trail out the window. So they untied their end of the rope ("no need to give them any extra help," said Victorine) and pulled their shoes and stockings back on as speedily as they could manage and scrambled the rest of the way down the fire escape (which might ordinarily have felt like an adventure in its own right) and dropped carefully from its bottom landing to the street and then ran and ran, until there were a few streets between their panting selves and the kidnappers they were trying to leave behind.

They didn't pause until they were under the sign for 67th Street, where for a moment all they could do was gasp for air. Then they looked around at the empty city and gasped again from the sheer unlikeliness of their circumstances. Neither one of them had ever been out alone at such an hour. They weren't really dressed for the chill of April, either, despite their coats. The wind was picking up. The sullen, coal-tinged dampness in the air suggested that any moment now it might begin to rain. They could see that, if they paused for long, soon they would feel thoroughly miserable.

"Where shall we go now?" said Darleen, hopping a

little from foot to foot to try to keep just slightly warm. "Where do you live, Victorine? Even if they aren't the tenderest of cousins, those guardians of yours must be frantic after getting a ransom note on their door. Shall we take you right home?"

Victorine shook her head and rubbed her arms to warm them up.

"I think—" she said. "I think, in fact, perhaps we'd better not. Darleen, promise you will not judge me an unreasoning or ungrateful person. It must seem very dramatic, I'm sure—practically a story out of the photoplays—but I've been considering everything, you know, and I simply *can't* go back to the Brownstones."

Victorine took a breath to steady herself, and then they walked on because it was too cold to stand still. (Also, it is easier to have deep conversations when you are both in motion. The motion relieves the pressure somehow and lets your secret heart think about peeking out at the world.)

"Victorine, are you sure?"

"I believe I told you the sad truth," she said. "About my distant cousins and guardians, the Brownstones, not caring for me a bit. I had to come to that conclusion after a few weeks of close observation. They care only about my fortune."

"But how can that be?" said Darleen. She felt sorry

to the core for Victorine, left so alone in the world. She also found it very exciting and new, to be walking in the middle of the night with someone who could use a phrase like *my fortune* so matter-of-factly.

"I'm quite sure of it," said Victorine. "And Darleen, I'm afraid it gets worse: the dreadful Mr. Brownstone and his equally dreadful sister, Miss Brownstone — although the way they behave together, I wouldn't call it, to be honest, *fraternal* —"

"Fraternal?" said Darleen. Perhaps it was because Miss Berryman had spent her life traveling the world, but she did use the strangest words as if they were as ordinary as bread and butter.

"I mean, they are not exactly, to my mind, like brother and sister," said Victorine. "But then again, I have no brothers or sisters of my own, so perhaps I am not a proper judge. But there is something in the tender way they conspire. Well, never mind."

"Conspire?" said Darleen.

"*That,* I am sure of!" said Victorine, with some heat. "They are always conspiring! Plotting and conspiring! And since the moment they swept through the doors of our home, I must be honest, they have not shown me a speck of human warmth. Instead, they seem to spend their time rummaging through Grandmama's rooms, taking the paintings off the walls, and — I do believe, though it's shocking to think of it — *selling them.*"

"How awful!" said Dar. "And just when you needed truly kind people around you. Oh, you poor thing!"

"You understand me," said Victorine. "Darleen, I have to say, that in itself is a comfort. I'm afraid I have been very alone in the world the last few months."

What a horrible story Victorine was telling!

"Oh, and there's more about those Brownstones. When I saw what they were doing with all of Grandmama's dearest possessions, I was — I'm ashamed to admit it — I was incensed. I was angry! So much so that I did something rather unwise. I quite sneakily crept downstairs one afternoon when they were out and called up Grandmama's lawyer, old Mr. Ridge, on the telephone, and I *told him* what they were doing."

"Well, good for you!" said Darleen, impressed that Miss Berryman felt so confident about using a telephone. There was a telephone at the Matchless studios, but only Aunt Shirley dared to use it. "Did he help?"

"Quite the opposite, as things turned out. He came to speak in person to the awful Brownstones, and they denied all wrongdoing, their voices simply oozing with honey. I did not exactly listen at the door of the parlor, mind you. But I heard the tone of their awful voices, and I heard the way Mr. Ridge's words softened and quietened, and it was clear to me that they had managed to pull, as they say, the wool over his eyes. He went away and did not return. Grandmama used to say of him that he was a fine person, within certain strict limits. I'm afraid my telephone call forced him a little beyond his limits. It came to nothing. And then of course the Brownstones were *quite* furious with me. Oh, Darleen, their eyes were simply terrible! And Mr. Brownstone — the 'two-eyed man,' I call him secretly —"

"But aren't *most* men two-eyed?" asked Darleen.

"Well, yes, but the thing is, *his* eyes you can't help but notice because one of them is much lighter brown than the other one — almost as if it belongs to a different person, you know."

"Oh, how interesting!" said Darleen. She had certainly heard before of people having only one eye due to some unfortunate accident — Uncle Charlie told awful stories about how that old Fire-Bug Lukes (father of Jasper) had had a run-in with a poker that left him with an eye patch and a bad temper. But someone with two entirely different-colored eyes! That was new. "I'd like to see that, I think."

"You wouldn't want a *furious* Mr. Brownstone near you at all, I'm quite sure," said Victorine. "He stormed at me terribly for making that telephone call on 'his' telephone, and then he became even angrier and said it was time I *forgot* my poor Grandmama—imagine saying that!—and then he had the servants take my mourning clothes away, and in general he made the most terrible, angry threats. He called me a 'thorn in his side' and even said—I shudder to repeat it—that it would be better for everyone if I had never been born."

Darleen gasped. This Mr. Brownstone sounded as bad as any villain in a photoplay!

"Oh, poor Victorine!" said Darleen with all her heart. "How awfully, awfully frightened you must have been."

"Frightened and very alone," said Victorine. "The disaster with Mr. Ridge was only a few weeks ago, and it was not until Thursday that they so much as spoke to me again, to say that I would be allowed to go to the opening of the Strand Theatre—and we know how that turned out! I'm sure they simply rejoiced to think the kidnappers had rid them of their 'thorn.'"

"So we won't take ourselves to the Brownstones," said Darleen, after a moment or two of trying to sort out all the pieces of Victorine's sad story. "I guess we'd better go right to the police, then."

Victorine shook her head.

"No, but Darleen, don't you see? That won't do either," she said. "The police will feel obliged to follow the Law, and that means they'll send me right back to the

Brownstones. But now you will understand: I don't trust those people an inch, and I don't want anything to do with them. I can't risk being sent back to the Brownstones."

Darleen had to take a moment to digest this last bit of logic.

"You were kidnapped, and now you are *running away*?" she said finally. "Is that it?"

"It sounds strange when you say it right out loud that way," said Victorine. "But perhaps yes. So what shall we do now?"

Darleen didn't hesitate a single wink.

"We head uptown!" she said. "We'll take ourselves right up to the 125th Street ferry, that's what! What time is it, I wonder? We'll get on the first ferry we can, back over the Hudson to Fort Lee."

"Goodness!" said Victorine. "Whatever's in Fort Lee?"

"Oh, just Champion, Eclair, Pathé, Solax, and Matchless," said Darleen.

Victorine tried to look polite. "What are those? Racehorses?"

"No, no!" said Darleen after letting one — only one — wild scrap of laughter escape from her throat. "Not racehorses — studios! The studios that make the photoplays! And anyway, that's not the most important thing about Fort Lee. The most important thing is my own dear Papa. He'll have been waiting for me to get home for hours now, and he'll be so dreadfully worried. They'll all be worried. And I'm sure he'll be kind to you while you decide where you want to run away *to*."

And she pulled Victorine along the sidewalk. They had been going roughly the right direction already, which was *north*. The numbers of New York streets got larger as you headed north, so that was a helpful guide.

"You're very lucky to have a Papa," said Victorine in a musing-and-shivering sort of way as they crossed the streets in the chill of night. The pavement smelled very slightly of water, and of course of all those other city middle-of-the-night smells, some of them not very nice but all of them rather exciting if you're not used to running through the biggest of big cities in the middle of the night.

Dar was so glad Victorine was there with her so that she didn't have to walk through the night alone. And then she thought of how alone poor Victorine had been these past months, with her beloved Grandmama dead and those awful, selfish, *very distant* cousins moving in to take control of everything and be cruel to the one lonely girl left behind.

"I know it," said Darleen with feeling. "I do know

how lucky I am to have my Papa. And I used to have a Mama too, but she flew away from bad lungs years ago. She caught a chill and was gone. And that's why . . ."

She was inching so close to confessing the existence of that feeling inside her. A conversation can sometimes hover right on the edge of a cliff while we wonder whether or not to leap (or climb). What was it about walking in the night with someone that made all your inmost secrets want to come sneaking right out into the cold but interestingly pungent air?

"That's why *I* must never fly away. It would rebreak his heart, you know, and he'd never survive it. We have to get home to my Papa as quickly as we can and show him I'm still here despite everything. Here and with my feet on the ground."

Chapter 8

Bad News for All

It was so late that it was almost early.

"If only we had some money," said Darleen, "we could find somewhere warm to have coffee or cocoa while we wait for the ferry to start running. I don't even care for coffee, but it's medicinal, says my Aunt Shirley. Anyways, it seems like the right thing to drink when a person's as cold as we are. But that's if we had money."

"Of course, we do have a *little* money," said Victorine. "I carry an ironed bill hidden in a special pocket at all times. It's only prudent! You never know when you're going to find yourself standing on the streets of Manhattan in the middle of the night. For instance!"

She smiled.

Although New York City never sleeps, this morning it seemed to be dozing. It was very early, in New York's defense, and it was a Sunday. But finally Darleen was able to pull Victorine in through the doors of a place called Murphy's for some hot medicinal coffee and a fried egg.

"We must look very bedraggled," said Victorine with some satisfaction. She took a nice slurp of her coffee.

The man at the next table startled himself out of a doze, checked the time, and sprinted right out of Murphy's, leaving his newspaper behind.

Victorine leaned over to take a peek at the headlines. "'Sunshine This Afternoon,'" she read aloud. "Well, and thank goodness for that. I'm chilled to the bone already. 'A Rainy Morning Forecast, with Clear Skies Later.' And the rest of the news seems quite terrible. I don't think I want to read about Sing Sing Prison."

"Let's flip the front page over," said Darleen. "See? They put the funnier stories under the fold. Look—the Pope doesn't like the tango!"

Victorine shook her head and tapped the story right above.

"I don't know, Darleen," she said. "This one says there's a poor woman who is ill of mercurial poisoning, and they don't know who she is! That isn't exactly funny, is it?"

"Makes a good story, though," said Darleen. "And look here, some man bid an enormous amount of money for a baby. But the mother said no!"

Dar was so tired she couldn't even exactly remember what a five with five zeroes following it was called.

"Selling babies does seem wrong," said Victorine. "Even for half a million dollars, it can't exactly be the right thing to — Oh, my, look at this!"

A headline was shouting in the lower-right corner of the front page:

"YOUNG BERRYMAN HEIRESS
NABBED AT STRAND!"
"Desperate Search Underway for
Richest Girl in World"
"Guardians Distraught"

"On the first page, too!" said Darleen. Only the most important stories could squeeze onto the front page of the newspaper.

"Shall I read it out loud?" said Victorine, but then they looked around and saw the waitress's beady eyes flicking their way.

"On second thought, I'll use my quietest murmur," she said. "Come close, Darleen."

It was very short, but then again, it must have been

squeezed onto the front page at the very last possible second, since their adventures had started only the evening before.

> *"'The grand opening of the new Strand Theatre was apparently the scene of a terrible crime last night, when Miss Victorine Berryman, young heiress to the Berryman fortune, was kidnapped by bandits who came equipped with brazen intention and a motorcar. The little girl, in the care of guardians since the death of her grandmother, Mrs. Hugo Berryman, had been brought to the theatre by her loving guardian, Miss Brownstone—'"*

"Loving!" Victorine paused to exclaim, but still under her breath. She tapped that last phrase with her finger. "I should say not! But I'll continue."

> *"'—who reported the poor girl had been taken off by bandits in a white motorcar.'"*

"*White!*" whispered Victorine and Darleen together, and they shook their heads. That motorcar had been black as onyx, and anyway, what self-respecting kidnapper would ride around in a white motorcar? Wouldn't that stick out like a sore thumb?

> *"'Guardians Mr. and Miss Brownstone are said to be distraught after the receipt of a ransom note reportedly demanding millions and threatening the worst if their demands are not met in the briefest period of time. There seems little hope that young Miss Berryman's ransom and rescue can be arranged with the necessary haste, since there are still legal barriers to the Brownstones' ability to touch the Berryman fortune. Poor Little Rich Girl, indeed! All New York holds its breath, hoping for a swift and positive resolution to this tragic crime. A massive search is underway. $25,000 reward offered for information.'"*

"Well!" said Victorine, sitting back in her chair. Her eyes were flashing. Perhaps even coffee is not as galvanizing on a damp morning as reading (somewhat inaccurate) news of your fate on the front page of the *New York Times*.

"'Massive search' means everyone will be looking for me, I'm afraid," said Victorine darkly. "So that they can simply *fling* me back into the hands of the Legal Terrors, Mr. and Miss Brownstone. Who will probably try mercurial poisoning next, for all I know. It's indeed bad news for Miss Berryman, I'd say."

Darleen was paging swiftly through the rest of the newspaper.

"Oh, dear," she said. "Bad news for us Darlings too."

"More bad news?" said Victorine. "What do you mean?"

"There's not a peep about Daring Darleen in this whole paper. Not one word. All that planning and arranging for nothing!"

For a moment Victorine looked puzzled, and then it was clear that she understood. She put her hand over Darleen's to show how sorry she was about the failure of the Darlings' clever publicity scheme, just when the Matchless studios so needed a financial boost. Darleen shook her head.

"Oh, don't, Victorine. It's all right. Just our bad luck, is all. *Of course* a real kidnapping should drown out a fake one — that's only what's right. Still, Aunt Shirley and Uncle Charlie will be awfully disappointed."

The good news was that the ferry would be departing soon. Fueled by the coffee, they trotted down the street to the place where the ferry docked.

The ferry was a big boat with a gaping, cavelike mouth — a mouth so large it could swallow whole motorcars! There were a few of those lined up now, waiting to be allowed on the ferry. That was a convenient thing, to be able to take your motorcar right across the Hudson River with you from New York City to Fort Lee or the other way around. There were some horse-drawn carriages waiting, too, of course. The horses stood mostly quietly in the morning air. Maybe they were eyeing the motorcars with some suspicion. (Motorcars can be noisy, explosive beasts.)

Darleen had been on the ferry a number of times and knew that on a weekday, it would have been simply brimming with photoplay people heading to the studios in Fort Lee. It seemed very quiet now, but Victorine was looking around with bright, interested eyes.

"Let's pay," said Dar. "We'll need a nickel each."

Once they had paid their fares, Victorine grabbed Darleen's arm.

"Is there always an enormous, sour-faced policeman at the entrance gate?" she said.

"No, never," said Darleen. "Why?"

But she looked and saw that this time there was. He must have been more than six feet tall, that policeman, and broad as a well-muscled tree. And one eye was screwed almost shut. Maybe that was just the way he liked to see the world, or maybe he had learned over the years of being a policeman that squinting that way made him look scarier.

He stood there, that muscular tree trunk of a man, and seemed to be scrutinizing the people getting on board as he swung his nightstick in thoughtful circles.

Without saying anything to each other but acting in unison, almost like a single four-footed creature, Dar and Victorine found themselves scooting back, trying to be as inconspicuous as possible while they figured out what was going on with this fellow and what it was he was scrutinizing.

A man asked a joking question of the policeman, and he grumbled in response:

" . . . young lady . . . high-toned type . . . gone missing this morning . . . suspicious circumstances . . ."

Dar and Victorine exchanged a worried look and backed away a few more steps.

"There it is," said Victorine grimly. "The 'massive search.' So they can send me back to the dreadful Brownstones."

They stole more glimpses of the setup at the ferry entrance: the gate the passengers went through, and the larger maw that the vehicles used, and that daunting policeman with his nightstick positioned between the two.

"He's like the Cyclops guarding his cave!" said Victorine. "From Homer, you know."

Darleen nodded. In fact, she *did* know: she had seen

the photoplay of Homer's *Odyssey* that had come over from Italy a couple of years ago. The Cyclops was a cruel, one-eyed giant who had eaten some of Odysseus's poor sailors when he had them all trapped in that cave. He had been filmed so well! On the screen he had been twice the size of those sailors, and so fierce!

But then that gave her an idea.

She pulled Victorine away from the police officer, over to the far side of the motorcars and the carriages.

"Victorine," she said. "Do you remember how Odysseus escaped that Cyclops?"

"I certainly do!" said Victorine. "But Darleen, are you suggesting we sharpen a stake and throw it at that man's eye?"

"No, no, I didn't mean the stake," said Dar. "I meant the *sheep*."

And she tipped her head a little, as a way of pointing without pointing at the motorcars.

Victorine considered the motorcars, looked back at Dar, and smiled so brightly that Darleen could see she had understood. In the old story of the *Odyssey* — and in the more recent photoplay — that wily hero Odysseus had blinded the giant Cyclops and then tied his men (the ones the Cyclops hadn't yet eaten — poor fellows!) underneath the giant's sheep, and the sheep had carried the men safely out of the cave. In a twentieth-century city, there might not be so very many sheep wandering about. But there were *motorcars*!

"It will be fearsomely muddy under these 'sheep.'"

"No, no," said Dar. "We don't need to get under the cars. We'll just hop onto the runners on the sides, you know. And cling to the doors."

"Like you did in that episode with the pearl thief!" said Victorine. "When you jumped from car to car! Goodness! That was exciting! You must have been going about a hundred miles an hour. So very brave!"

"Well, actually," said Dar, "the motorcars weren't going fast at all. The cameraman just cranked slowly, so that it would *look* speedy later when the projectionist — Oh, never mind, I'll explain some other time. They're about to push the cars onto the ferry."

"Push?"

"Yes; they can't use the engines or the horses will take fright. Here we go! Let's grab ourselves a motorcar — a nice big one — and keep out of view."

They had to keep out of everybody's sight, of course. But, by some miracle, the only person who spotted anything strange was one of the ferry workers who was pushing the cars onto the boat.

"Hey, now," he said to Darleen. But thank goodness it was Darleen he noticed! She had been on that ferry often enough that he knew who she was. Why, she had even signed his daughter's autograph album once upon a time.

She smiled at him, trying to make her smile as confident as possible, and put a finger to her lips. The ferry worker looked around a little, probably half wondering where the movie camera might be hidden. She could practically see him thinking, *Oh, these photoplay people! Always up to something!*

But then he smiled back and shrugged, and the motorcar-sheep rolled into the belly of the ferry, with the girls safely clinging to its not-very-woolly side.

Once the car stopped, they stayed low for a while, until they felt the ferry churning its way out into the river and heard the driver get out of his motorcar and stride away. Then they squeezed past the other motorcars and climbed up the stairs to the passenger deck. It smelled of smoke and dampness up there — and worse.

"Spitting is *such* a vulgar habit!" said Victorine, shaking her head at the stinking cuspidor.

"Hush," said Darleen, and she hurried Victorine forward into the fresh air at the bow.

Even in damp weather, on the ferry it was better to be outside than in. A small family was hovering by the rail, lovingly braving the wind so that their tiny toddler could point from his nursemaid's arms, as toddlers like to do, out across the waves. The elegant mother held a round wicker picnic basket, and a little girl clung close, picking idly at the latch of the basket as she smiled up into the face of her mother.

A pang leaped up like a spark of electricity right inside Darleen's heart: a girl smiling up at her mother! Oh, there are sorrows that never quite heal, no matter how long ago the loss. But then Dar thought of her new friend, who had lost her Grandmama so very recently, and her heart straightened up and became unselfish. *Poor Victorine!*

Then a lovely thing happened: the moment Dar reached out for Victorine's hand to give it a comforting squeeze, she discovered that Victorine had already stretched a hand out to her. The hands found each other in midair; the two girls glanced at each other, saw the sympathy mirrored in each other's eyes, and almost laughed aloud right there on that windy deck.

Because, to be sure, even though they were two motherless and grandmotherless girls, it was still glorious to be speeding across the river toward the green cliffs of New Jersey. Somewhere out there, behind the clouds, the sun was up now. The morning had begun. It wasn't even actually raining just at the moment, merely drizzling. They had escaped from the evil kidnappers. And they were really, truly on the move, as if the great projectionist in the sky had suddenly started cranking the film forward, just a little faster than normal, so that the wind felt extra-exciting and the water swirled by extra-fast and their hearts beat a bit faster, too.

And then the little girl by the railing gave a cry of alarm and jumped back to hide behind her mother's skirts. Her fingers must have accidentally undone the latch of the picnic basket, because the lid of the basket was rising now . . .

And, oh! What sort of picnic was this?

Black coils were spilling up and over the edge of the basket and now half reaching, now half tumbling toward the deck of the ferry.

In that basket was not a picnic but a snake!

Oh!" said several people at once as four feet or more of snake hit the damp deck of the ferry. (The nursemaid said a lot more than "Oh!" but it was impossible to make out the exact words. *Fear,* thought Darleen, *must be making her babble.*)

"Darleen, quick!" said Victorine. "Oh, quick, quick! Like that rattlesnake in Episode Three!"

But that rattlesnake had been stuffed — a mere prop of a rattlesnake! And then they had pasted in a shot of a real snake in close-up so that the audience would think that the toy had been real.

It turns out that a stuffed snake is very unlike a real snake in certain respects.

A stuffed snake, for instance, will not usually slither across the deck of a ferryboat. It will not render nearly speechless a small crowd of human beings who had just moments before been happily smiling at the Hudson River.

Moreover, in Episode Three, Daring Darleen had used a broom against the threat of the (stuffed) rattlesnake, but here there was no broom.

Nor was there much hope of help from the other people on the deck; the mother was busy trying to calm the little girl, and neither nursemaid nor toddler seemed likely to be of any help in catching a snake when they could hardly even catch their breath!

No broom, no bucket, no zookeeper nearby. Darleen and Victorine looked at each other again in alarm. They would have to handle this snake themselves.

"I'm sure you must know quite a lot about snakes," said Victorine, "since you've filmed with them before."

"Well," said Darleen with some reluctance. Snakes, it turned out, were different from cliffs: no wild thrill blossomed in Darleen's chest when she looked at those mysterious coils. Instead, she was wondering how to go about shooing a snake (that wasn't stuffed) back into a basket.

I don't have to be brave, she told herself. *I am acting a part.*

"There you go," she said to the snake as she shuffled her feet on the deck behind it to encourage it to move along back the other way, toward the basket. "Go on, go on!"

The snake was now a dark scrawl against the pale boards of the ferry deck, like a message in some ancient language written all in loops and curls. It raised its head in what Dar thought was probably annoyance and shook the end of its tail a little, as if it, too, were playing a role, and in its case the role was Rattlesnake. But it produced hardly a whisper's worth of noise (its tail had no actual rattle), and it was so very blue-black.

"Oh, *my*!" said Victorine. "Look at that! Now it's flattening its head at you, Darleen! Well, goodness, the poor thing. I guess perhaps we'd better pick it right up."

And without even seeming to do anything much at all, Victorine got herself behind the snake's range of view and, slipping her hands in low and from the side, gently lifted that snake right up from the deck.

Darleen took a quick breath and followed Victorine's lead, because it did seem too long a creature to rest on only one pair of hands. The snake was heavier than she had expected, and those coils were smooth and cold and strange to the touch. Darleen had assumed the snake might feel sort of limp in her hands, like an enormous earthworm, but in fact it turned out to be a very muscular creature.

"Nicely done. Now don't squeeze it," said Victorine quietly. "Grandmama did always say the main thing about snakes was to stay calm and come in from the side. We want it to feel utterly unworried as we move it back to its basket home."

Darleen managed not to squeeze her half of the snake, and she didn't drop it either.

They took easy, easy steps together across the deck, Victorine keeping the snake's head well away from her own.

Darleen could hear her humming very slightly under her breath. But fortunately the transfer time was not terribly long. The elegant woman carefully opened the basket, and a half second later, they shifted the poor snake back into its home, and the woman shut and latched the lid so that the basket sat innocently on the deck, pretending not to have anything dangerous hidden in it at all. The children (and the nursemaid) were gaping at Dar and Victorine.

The elegant, small woman did not seem like someone who would ever do something as inelegant as *gape*, but she was certainly smiling, and her dark eyes were full of amusement.

"Bravo, *les filles*!" she said, clapping her gloved hands together.

She had quite a lovely accent.

While Darleen kept a wary eye on the latch of the

picnic basket, the elegant woman and Victorine fell into a conversation, using words that weren't English at all, but *French.*

Darleen knew they were speaking French because the movies had been born — nearly twenty years ago! — in two places almost at once — France and New Jersey — and that meant that nowadays, there were quite a few people working in Fort Lee who had come all the way across the ocean from France.

But recognizing that people are probably speaking French is not the same thing as understanding a single word of what they're saying!

Sure enough, one moment later, the elegant woman was already turning midsentence to Darleen to say what was almost certainly a question.

Everyone fell silent and looked at Darleen, who blinked.

Playing a role! she told herself sternly, and she tried to stand taller and to look more like, say, Crown Princess Dahlia Louise. But her words came out of her mouth sounding much more like Darleen than like Crown Princess Dahlia Louise:

"Pardon me?" she said. "Sorry. I don't understand."

"Ah, excuse me, please!" said the elegant woman. "I made the assumption, since your friend speaks such very lovely French, that so must you also. I do apologize.

Thank you so much for helping us with our serpent. But I am forgetting all of my manners. May I ask who you are, my brave snake-conquering girls?"

Dar and Victorine looked at each other in sudden alarm. The elegant woman seemed a kind enough sort of person, but they couldn't risk revealing Victorine's identity to anyone who might go on to reveal it to a cop. And Victorine herself was probably the one most tempted to betray her secrets, with her inconvenient vow to always tell the truth.

Darleen tried to make her eyes say *quiet, quiet, quiet, don't you* dare *tell her your name!* to Victorine, and Victorine clamped her mouth shut and looked like someone wrestling with inner demons.

In the middle of their silent alarm, the woman laughed.

"Never mind, never mind, I see," she said, and a playful sort of fire flickered in her dark eyes. She leaned forward as if sharing a confidence. "Even I, dear girls, enjoy an occasional outing incognita. Moreover—"

And then they were saved by the bell, as Uncle Charlie, who sometimes went to boxing matches in his spare time, liked to say. When a boxing match is going badly, sometimes the bell that ends a round will ring just at the right moment and spare the poor loser from being too terribly pounded.

In this particular case, the bell was a whistle: a ferryboat whistle.

They were already close to the other side of the Hudson River, and the ferry was shrilly announcing that it was almost time to disembark.

The French-speaking family bustled about, getting themselves together and picking up the wicker basket filled with snake.

As the elegant woman shuttled her children and the nursemaid toward the exit, she turned around and smiled once more in the direction of Victorine and Dar.

"I must say, Mademoiselle Daring Darleen, that you were *particularly* good in the serial last night at the Strand. I admire a girl who can dangle with so much expression from a cliff! This little snake you have rescued is also an actor in the photoplays — but not, I think, as skilled as you."

And then she was gone.

Darleen and Victorine stayed on the deck for a moment, just staring at each other in shared relief and surprise.

"Oh, goodness, she recognized me!" said Darleen.

"Well, of course," said Victorine. "You are terribly famous."

"But she had just asked who we were, hadn't she?"

"*That* was sheer politeness," said Victorine. "Thank goodness I'm not famous — well, not as far as my face goes — so she couldn't recognize me. Imagine if she had kept asking who I was! Even staying silent felt like edging *quite* close to a falsehood."

"I think you did a beautiful job staying silent," said Darleen firmly. "I wonder who she was, though. She must have been fetching that snake for a studio, since she said it was an actor too. Perhaps she's married to a properties man at one of the studios. There are quite a few photoplay people from France, you know, working around here. I'm sure Aunt Shirley would have known who she was right away. Sometimes I think Aunt Shirley knows every person at every studio anywhere around here."

They were following the Sunday crowd off the ferry now.

"So this is the town of Fort Lee?" said Victorine, looking around.

"Oh, goodness, no," said Darleen. "This is just good old Edgewater, where the ferry stops. We'll have to take a trolley up the hill to Fort Lee. Over there."

Darleen pointed to the place where the streetcar stopped.

"Oh, and Victorine, wherever did you learn to be so brave about snakes?" asked Darleen as they hurried across the street.

"Brave!" said Victorine. "Oh, my, no. I assure you I'm actually irrationally terrified of snakes!"

"Are you sure?" said Darleen. "You seemed so calm."

"Well, you know," said Victorine, "fear is such an *interesting* thing! My dear Grandmama called it 'an instinct meant to save us,' but then, she did like to add that when our rational brains are telling us one thing, and irrational fear is shouting something else, it is usually best to listen to the quieter voice of reason. And in this particular case, I knew — my rational brain knew — that the snake was *actually* harmless, although I certainly didn't feel that way in my spirit."

"Harmless?" said Darleen with a shudder. "But Victorine, how could you be sure?"

"Because it was an eastern indigo snake," said Victorine. "And that is a nonvenomous species and no danger at all. Of course, it has teeth, but from what I've read, it bites humans only very rarely."

Now Darleen was gaping.

"How do you know all that about snakes?" she said.

"Grandmama was very intent that I should have a well-rounded education," said Victorine, her voice quite sad. "And she did especially love all of the natural sciences. When one travels the world, it is useful to know something of the natural sciences. If you are in Turkey, and a bug the size of your hand is hanging on a tree in front of you and making quite a riotous noise, it is immensely helpful to be able to think, *Ah, a cicada,* instead of flinching, you know. At such a moment, a good scientific education is a boon."

"I guess it might be," said Darleen politely. Aunt Shirley had taught her some arithmetic, but all she knew about insects was which ones to swat. "Your grandma was interested in bugs and snakes?"

"*Very* interested, oh, yes," said Victorine. "We traveled the world to perfect her collection. It was such a disappointment to her that I persisted so stubbornly in being afraid of snakes, despite all of her training."

Darleen put her arm around poor Victorine.

"Well, don't be sad now!" she said. "Your grandma would have been awfully proud of you today, the way you handled that thing, that —"

"Eastern indigo," said Victorine. "*Drymarchon couperi.*"

Darleen shuddered.

"That . . . ugh," she said. "And here's the streetcar coming right —"

Before she could say *now,* Victorine made a surprised sound and pulled Dar back into the shadows of the nearest building.

"Look there!" she whispered into Darleen's ear. "Look at those two! Aren't they — Oh, they are!"

Sauntering toward the streetcar from the opposite direction were two men who must themselves have just come off the ferry, right before the girls, and had been waiting a distance away, smoking cigarettes.

There was no doubt at all about it: one of these men was the very kidnapper who had driven the motorcar. And the other had a shock of blond hair under his hat.

"Oh, no!" said Darleen.

It was him. Jasper Lukes. So he *was* mixed up with these kidnappers somehow!

The men were sunk deep into their coats, like men who did not want to be noticed, and yet they seemed to be bitterly disagreeing about something, to judge from the words that washed back here and there toward the girls:

From Jasper came a mix of complaint and fury: "Just because you messed things up, now you're wanting *me* to get *my* hands dirty. . . . I'm not like the rest of you. . . . I'm *family*."

And from the kidnapper, an icy murmur that left no question who was in charge here: "*Fambly, fambly* — watch me shed a tear! . . . Nah, don't you go waving that at me. . . . Boss says you're the one who knows who's who and what's what. . . . Gotta find the girl, or everyone's gonna pay. . . . Better get some news out of that dame you've been mentioning."

"We'll go see Shirley. I guess she'll know where Darleen's gotten to," said Jasper Lukes, sounding very glum indeed. "If anyone does."

And then they swung themselves onto the streetcar

and out of earshot while Dar and Victorine stayed in the shadows and out of sight as much as they could manage.

"*They* were on that ferry too!" said Darleen. She and Victorine looked at each other in horror, sharing one terrible thought: *How did they not see us?* What a close call!

The streetcar was jangling off up the road, while Dar and Victorine kept themselves flat against the wall, their hearts beating so fast it was a wonder the wall could withstand the pressure.

"Darleen, didn't you say you know that golden-haired man there? The one who came up the street last night? Why is he cozying up with kidnappers, do you think?"

Darleen shook her head. "I'd sure like to know," she said. "That's Jasper Lukes. Don't you recognize him? He plays the villain in *The Dangers of Darleen,* so I guess perhaps even you may have seen him before."

"Oh, but with a mask on!" said Victorine. "I had no idea. Some people look so very different in different disguises, you know. Never mind that. But what do we do now?"

They stared at each other, both trying to think clearly about all of these unclear but clearly awful things.

"We have to get ourselves up the hill right away!" said Darleen. "Oh, where's the next streetcar? We simply *have* to get to my father before that wicked kidnapper does. Papa must already be frantic with worry! And they were talking about Aunt Shirley too. At least if they go to see her, then we'll have a few more minutes to get to Papa. Oh, but Victorine—"

A helpless giggle came wriggling out of Darleen's mouth, taking her entirely by surprise.

"Can you believe we were worried for a moment about a *snake*?"

"A harmless eastern indigo, at that," said Victorine. "Well, we've learned our lesson now."

"I'll say," said Darleen. "Compared with kidnappers, a snake, Victorine, is *truly* a picnic."

Chapter 10

Spiders Possibly Everywhere

On the New Jersey side of the Hudson River, bluffs rose up above the waterway, and the roads that carried people up to the top of those bluffs, where the little towns and the woods and the farmlands and the movie studios were, zigzagged steeply up the slopes.

"So wonderful!" said Victorine, her eyes glowing, and Darleen couldn't quite tell whether it was the view of New York City across the river or the jangling, clattering streetcar itself that most amazed her.

Darleen was too nervous to enjoy the view. The streetcar trundled along the top of the bluff for what felt to

Darleen like some very long minutes, and then finally it turned that last corner.

"Here we are," said Darleen to Victorine. "Quick! Let's get ourselves to my Papa."

"Yes, indeed," said Victorine, looking around at sleepy little Fort Lee with its unpaved streets. "Don't see any kidnappers either. Although, honestly, Darleen, it doesn't seem like the sort of place that would *ever* have kidnappers!"

Darleen could appreciate that to someone who had not been here before, Fort Lee might seem an odd sort of place. There were little houses around, such as you might see in any small town, but they were interrupted here and there by large, square, barn-like structures eating up most of a town block. And it was quiet here, apart from the sound of chickens coming from somebody's backyard coop.

All in all, it was hard to believe it was just a river's width away from the modern bustle of New York City.

"Come this way," said Darleen, leading Victorine rather quickly now, toward—oh, her inner eye was squinting a little, trying to imagine what this place must look like seen through Victorine's eyes—one of the smaller and shabbier little houses on that street. It could not brag, that little house, about the condition of its paint, which was ancient and flaking off, leaving dark patches and streaks on the white walls. It could not boast about its structural soundness, because there was a distinct sag in the wood of the front porch. It could only claim that once a very happy small family had lived there, and now the shipwrecked remnants of that family did the best they could under this slightly leaky old roof. And that it was very conveniently located for people who spent many daylight hours working at the Matchless studios, just right there, a stone's throw away down the street.

"Goodness, what will we say to him?" said Darleen, hurrying Victorine up the path.

"The plain truth, if we can," said Victorine, as if that were the obvious answer to everything.

"Hmm," said Darleen. "Since we don't want to frighten him too much, perhaps I'd better do most of the talking. He'll have been worrying terribly."

It was oddly quiet inside Darleen's house, however, and Victorine's face became solemn as she looked around.

"This is your home?" she said.

"Well, um, yes," said Darleen, as her inner eye noticed the way the wallpaper in the front hall peeled and curled. And, yes, her inner ear immediately heard the defensiveness peppering her voice, but once one is growing defensive, it is very hard to change course. "Actually, Papa and I are very happy here."

"Of course," said Victorine sadly, and oh, Dar's heart smote her! Because Victorine sounded not at all like an heiress looking down her fine nose at the way people live in Fort Lee when they are not heiresses in any respect. Victorine sounded like someone thinking it must be lovely to have a father.

Papa! Where was he, though?

"Oh, Papa!" called Darleen. "I'm home!"

But the words bounced aimlessly down the hall: the little house stayed silent.

"Maybe he's asleep," said Dar. "Wait right here, Victorine."

She peeked into the kitchen: nobody. (She popped a couple of apples into her pockets, though, because you never know when apples will come in handy.) Then Darleen ran up the stairs and looked in her father's room and in her own little attic corner: still nobody. And finally she came back downstairs to where Victorine stood on tiptoe, examining the decrepit old grandfather clock in the shadowy hall.

"That's strange," said Darleen. "He's not here, and it's Sunday. We always take the morning so nice and slow when it's Sunday."

"But you weren't at home," Victorine pointed out. "He'll have gone somewhere to look for you."

Of course!

"Aunt Shirley's house!" said Darleen. That was where any and all Darlings went whenever there was trouble of some sort. "Oh, my! But that's where those villains have gone! We've got to get ourselves to Aunt Shirley's place right away. Come on. Fast!"

The clock was muttering along happily now, *tick tick tick*. Victorine must have wound it, Darleen realized, while she was looking for her Papa upstairs and down.

"What if the kidnappers see us coming?" said Victorine.

"They won't," said Darleen. "This is my town, and I know all the sneakiest ways from everywhere to everywhere. Just you follow me."

Impatience was springing up in her: she wanted to hurry, hurry. What must her father be thinking? He would be thinking . . . Well, whatever he was thinking, it was probably both better and worse than the actual truth.

They slipped like shadows out into the streets of Fort Lee — or rather, alongside those streets. Early on a Sunday morning, there was no one about to see them, but that also meant they themselves would be more obvious to anyone who happened to look their way, so Darleen made sure they stayed behind fences and the trunks of trees as much as possible, and of course they kept their eyes peeled for villains.

There was a pleasant smell of wet grass and of woodsmoke from kitchens where people who had not been running from kidnappers all night were cooking up nice breakfasts.

The earlier, braver birds were chattering about how glad they were the snow was all gone: spring, spring, spring!

"There's Aunt Shirley's house," said Darleen quietly as they hovered behind a chicken coop nearby. "Oh, but look!"

Jasper Lukes had just popped out the door of that house and was walking down the steps. While the girls froze in place, the hens inside the coop began commenting to one another, probably wondering (as Darleen and Victorine were also wondering), *What is going on here?*

"Where's the other one?" said Darleen. It was like seeing a spider wandering in your room and then looking away for a moment, only to discover that the spider has moved to somewhere your eye has not followed. A spider that might be anywhere was a spider that was more or less *everywhere,* as far as Darleen was concerned.

But in this case, the missing spider came out of hiding quite fast; the kidnapper emerged from where he had been lurking behind the house on the other side of Aunt Shirley's place, and Jasper Lukes and the kidnapper walked rapidly away together and eventually turned a corner out of sight.

"You'd better stay here," said Darleen to Victorine.

"Stay out of sight while I go in. Maybe Papa's there. I hope! Anyway, I'll come back out as soon as I can and fetch you."

Victorine hummed and nodded, but her hum was about as quiet as a hum could possibly be.

Darleen slipped around behind Aunt Shirley's house and sneaked right in through the back door that she had skipped through so many times before. It was then easy enough to follow the voices to where her Aunt Shirley and her uncles were having sort of wild and desperate conversation, the kind one has when it looks like your niece and Only Sprig has gotten herself into some serious trouble.

"Better tell Bill," Uncle Charlie was saying in a voice stretched very thin, as Darleen came tumbling into the room. Her aunt and uncles variously sprang to their feet (Aunt Shirley and Uncle Dan) or fell into an armchair in apparent shock (Uncle Charlie), and all of them said out loud, *"Darleen!"*

"Where's Papa?" said Darleen, finding it hard to catch her breath. "Is my Papa all right?"

"Worried to death about you, you thoughtless girl!" said Aunt Shirley, folding Darleen into arms that were a good bit kinder than her words. "How could you frighten us this way? Why, that Jasper looked so fretful! He was saying such upsetting things—wanting to know where you were — questions to ask you — saying that you didn't get kidnapped by the right people at all and might have gotten mixed up in a crime. What can any of that mean? And when we went to the police, they *laughed*!"

"You went to the police?" said Darleen. "And where is my Papa? Isn't he here?"

"He went home," said Uncle Dan. "I guess. Or to the laboratory."

The laboratory! Oh, why had Darleen wasted time coming over here?

"We certainly did go to the police," said Aunt Shirley. "When Dan and Charlie got back, and there was no sign of you, and they said something strange had happened at the filming, that the actors had shown up late, and yet you were already gone with who-knows-who — Darleen! How could you make such a mistake? You've taken years off my life, I do promise you. But the police laughed. Not nicely either. They said we *told* them to stay away, didn't we? Said it was just a stunt we were pulling, they knew."

"Well, to be fair," said Uncle Charlie, "it was supposed to be a stunt, wasn't it? But what did happen to you, Darleen? We were setting up to film you, and there was all sorts of commotion at the side entrance, so we thought maybe you had gone to the wrong place. And then when we came back, there you were, and the kidnappers too, and Dan caught it just fine in his camera."

"I hope I did," said Uncle Dan. "Tricky lighting."

"But then you were gone, and another car came by, with *our* kidnappers — the actors, you know. They were a little late, so they missed you. So there we are, beginning to worry, and then —"

"Police," said Uncle Dan. "Lots."

Uncle Charlie put his hand on Darleen's arm as if to steady her.

"Because — I don't like to be the one to break bad news to you, Darleen, but there was another girl taken, poor thing."

"Well, yes: Miss Victorine Berryman!" said Darleen, absolutely glittering with impatience. "Oh, I *know.* That's why they took me, those other kidnappers — because they thought I was *her.*"

"Richest girl in the world, say the papers!" said Aunt Shirley. "The same papers that won't write a peep now about Daring Darleen being kidnapped, just because that spoiled rich girl had the bad manners to go missing at the same place and the same time. Guess *she* never worries about where the money's coming from to pay the next round of wages!"

"*Big* ransom," said Uncle Dan. "Millions."

"More or less her weight in gold, hmm?" said Uncle Charlie, running a hand through his shaggy red-gray hair so it would stick up from his head the way he liked it.

There was a momentary hush, in which most of the people in that room were thinking about how much money a million dollars was. It was too much money even to imagine, to be honest. A million dollars didn't even seem like an actual real quantity; it felt like something more extravagant than a number. Like the very spirit of exaggeration itself turned into a couple of words. The hush crested over their heads like a wave and then suddenly broke.

"Wait!" said Aunt Shirley, spinning back to Darleen. "They took you, thinking *you* were the little rich girl? But then, where is she? Did they give you even the slightest clue where she might be? Because you know there's a big reward out for information."

"Twenty-five thousand dollars," said Uncle Dan. "The papers said."

"Can you imagine?" said Aunt Shirley. "Twenty-five thousand! That would be like a miracle for Matchless studios, wouldn't it now? All our debts paid off just like that! So think a moment: Did you see any sign of that girl, Darleen? She'd be worth a whole lot of money to us."

Darleen felt a flicker of fire in her that wasn't entirely unlike what she had felt the night before on the face of that building, and what she had felt not so long ago on the Palisades above the Hudson. How strange that joy and fury should feel so similar when they sprang up in your belly!

"But, Aunt Shirley," she said, with a voice that was already slightly on fire. "What if that girl's guardians are wicked, greedy people who just want her fortune? We wouldn't send someone back to people who don't care one whit about her. And who might be evil to boot. Would we?"

There was a stunned silence in Aunt Shirley's parlor, and then Aunt Shirley actually laughed.

"Don't be absurd, child!" she said. "That's none of our business, any of it. You're spinning nonsensical stories."

"So you're saying, even if you knew her guardians were wicked people, you would ship that poor Miss Berryman right back to them?"

"For twenty-five thousand dollars," said Aunt Shirley, with utter and complete conviction, "I certainly would."

Chapter 11

Unexpected Angel

Darleen gulped some air; her uncles shifted slightly; Aunt Shirley looked very stubborn and determined. Darleen considered saying something more and then decided she'd better not.

"Well, I'll go find Papa, then," she said instead. "Don't want him worrying more than he has to."

And she turned on her heel and ran into the hall, ignoring the voices that trailed after her, saying things like:

"Wait!"

and

"Darleen!"

She sprinted out the door and then sped to the back

of the house to get to Victorine before her relatives could make her any angrier than she already was.

Victorine, waiting behind the chicken coop, took one look at Darleen's face and shook her head.

"Oh, dear. You look like you have just been having a very heated discussion with somebody," she said.

"We have to go find Papa in the lab," said Darleen, fidgeting from foot to foot and desperately trying to think. "Oh! Who even knows what kind of nonsense that Jasper Lukes was just saying to my aunt, and now she's got her mind set on the stupid reward money, so they can't know you're here. We've got to hide you safely away. And I'm sure you are tired and hungry both. I'm so sorry, Victorine. I love my Aunt Shirley, but sometimes she's impossible."

And then Victorine put her hand on Darleen's arm.

"Ah, Darleen, I've been thinking," she said. "I've been wondering, while I waited for you out here, whether perhaps I should simply move on out West somewhere, you know, beginning right now, this very minute."

"What kind of a plan is that?" said Darleen. "What do you think you're going to do out West?"

"What do people do when they're left alone in the world? They go somewhere new to make their fortune. I suppose I don't have many useful skills yet, but I can read and write and ride a horse, and thanks to Grandmama's strong interest in the biological sciences, I do know a little something about insects —"

"Not to mention snakes," said Darleen, and then she suddenly had a plan of her own. "But Victorine, hush. Don't you be silly. You can't go out West where you don't know a soul and when you haven't even had any sleep yet today. Not to mention not much to eat. I know where I can hide you, but we have to be even sneakier now than we were before, because I don't know where Jasper Lukes and that awful man have gotten to, and they mustn't catch even the slightest glimpse of us."

So they sneaked very sneakily indeed from house to house and tree to tree, until they were across the street from a building that was half glass cliffs and half ordinary wood and brick. This was Matchless Photoplay.

"Isn't that beautiful!" said Victorine (looking at the glass).

"If Papa's not at home, and he's not at Aunt Shirley's, he is absolutely for certain here, in his laboratory," said Darleen. "And Matchless is the perfect place to hide you too."

But spiders, spiders, everywhere!

Darleen hesitated for a moment, wondering where the spiders were hiding in this picture, and it's a good thing she did, because a second later, human-shaped shadows flickered across the low windows of the laboratory.

Someone was in there. At least two someones, and the shadowy profile of one of them very much resembled Jasper Lukes.

Oh, Papa! thought Darleen.

She had to get in there right away to help her Papa, but she couldn't risk letting the villains get a glimpse of Victorine.

"Quick! Around the other side," she said to Victorine, and they got themselves out of view and to the opposite corner of Matchless, where the amazing glass-covered studio backed right up against a more ordinary two-story building. And next to the ordinary, nonglass part of the building grew a wonderful old tree, probably quite surprised by the sorts of things all those quick-living two-footed creatures had been getting up to around its feet over the last few years. To think that only a blink ago, in tree time, all of this busy place had been farmland, quiet and calm!

Darleen knew this oak very well. They were, you might say, old and secret friends. Her Papa had never *directly* told her not to climb trees, after all, and the trunk of an old oak is surely as solid as any patch of ground.

"The dressing rooms are right up there," said Darleen. "Will you mind very much, having to climb a tree? It's perfectly safe."

Victorine looked at the tree. Her eyes grew wide.

"I guess I can try," she said. "But I don't know how to —"

"Quick, quick!" said Darleen. "I'll give you a boost up to that first branch. Like getting on a horse, I guess. Then it's as easy as the back stairs from there. Here —"

And with her hands she made a step for Victorine's foot. "Up you go!" she said.

"Like mounting a horse," said Victorine in the stern tones of someone telling herself an impossible thing is actually completely possible after all, and she clenched her jaw and began to hum, and two minutes later she had successfully hauled herself up onto that great lower branch and was already reaching for the next.

Darleen didn't need a boost, of course. She knew every barky wrinkle of this tree's old trunk by heart, and before you could say Jack Robinson, she had passed by Victorine and was already a few branches above. Her heart had only time enough for one wild and joyful twitch, and then she was already reaching out to open the second-story window and slipping right through it, into the studio building's upstairs hall.

Victorine's humming grew louder as she climbed.

"Almost there," said Darleen, leaning out to give the novice tree climber some encouragement. "Take my hand!"

When Victorine finally scrambled through that open

window, Dar said "Hush" again, first thing, and led Victorine on speedy tiptoe down the hall to the simplest of a series of simple doors, those of the storerooms and dressing rooms that were squashed under the roof up here.

"You can hide out here," said Dar, mouthing the words more than speaking them. "That's my dressing room. I'll be right back. I've got to go down to the laboratory to see what's going on with my Papa."

The laboratory was in another part of Matchless entirely, on the far side of the glassed-in studios. The whole effect was very higgledy-piggledy, one building suddenly tacked on to the next. But the builders did try to keep the most flammable part of the operation relatively far from the little rooms up here.

"Coming with you," said Victorine, also with barely a sound.

"Careful," said Darleen, more through gestures than actual words, and then, on second thought, she put her finger to her mouth to warn: *No humming.*

At that moment, there was a strange set of sounds from somewhere below them: a shout, a crash, and something that might have been a door banging shut.

Darleen was already racing down the stairs. Inside, her mind was saying something like *Oh, no! Oh, no! Oh, no!* Nothing more coherent than that.

There were no more shouts or crashes assaulting her ears, but as she opened the door of the great laboratory room, where they put the film through its chemical baths and made the pictures come out into the world, she heard something worse than a crash. It was a moan.

She came running around a worktable, and there lay a figure, sprawled on the floor.

"Oh, no!" she said aloud now, even before she was close enough to see for sure who it was.

Sometimes our heart sees many feet ahead of our eyes. It does happen. Darleen's heart looked ahead and contracted with pain and distress.

"Oh, no!" she said again, as she flung herself down by the body on the floor. "Oh, Papa!"

A half second later, Victorine had her fingers resting gently on his wrist. "How dreadful! Poor man! He's breathing, but his pulse is awfully quick."

"Papa!" said Darleen. It was so horrible, seeing her strong, quiet Papa collapsed on the floor this way.

"Look, he's opening his eyes! I'll go for help."

Dar looked up at Victorine, and her head was swimming in the murky places a bad shock will heave us into. For a moment she couldn't think clearly at all. Then she said, "No, you'd better stay here with him, Victorine. We can't let them see you. I'll run back to Aunt Shirley's place and get help. It will only take a moment. Oh, Victorine, don't let anything more happen to Papa. And maybe don't tell him we were just climbing a tree."

"Go now," said Victorine. "Run fast! I'll take good care of him. And when I hear you coming back, I'll just float away upstairs, and no one will see me at all. Oh, Darleen, go!"

So Darleen went, fast as the wind (if the wind were a twelve-year-old girl with fear in her heart and with quick, trembling feet), right back up the street again. That was the start of a bad half hour that was all running and stammering and watching her aunt's face flush with alarm and seeing an uncle (Charlie) sent off to call the local doctor, and then a breathless swift trek back to the Matchless laboratory.

They found Darleen's father still lying on the ground, but with his head more comfortably cushioned on a soft wrap. And most important of all, his eyes blinked in recognition as Aunt Shirley and Darleen rushed toward him.

A sob of relief escaped Darleen's throat. She had thought . . . she had thought . . .

"Now, now," said her Papa, squeezing Darleen's hand. "Don't worry so. Look, Darleeny, I'm quite all right. I could sit right up, you know."

"No, don't!" said Aunt Shirley and Darleen, both at once.

"Not until Dr. Jones takes a look at you, Bill," Aunt Shirley added.

"That's what the angel kept saying," said Darleen's father, and Darleen and Aunt Shirley both fell immediately silent, though for very different reasons. "'Not until help comes,' she kept saying, and she had the sweetest hum, just like an angel should have. 'Stay calm, stay calm,' she said, 'and help will be here in a moment, surely.'"

"Oh, Bill," said Aunt Shirley, almost tenderly, which was not her general mode. "You really *have* been hit on the head."

"As if I didn't know it! Ruffians in the laboratory, pawing at the reels."

"Papa!" said Darleen. "Was it Jasper Lukes?"

"Jasper Lukes? Well, I didn't exactly see — they had scarves wrapped around their faces, so I didn't get a good look at them. But why would Jasper do such a thing? No, a couple of scoundrels, I guess."

"Two scoundrels, and one of them Jasper Lukes," said Darleen.

"Hush, really, Darleen," said Aunt Shirley. "That's enough. But then what happened, Bill?"

"Their voices were all muffled," said Papa, pausing to cough a little. "Because of the scarves, you know. But one of them kept talking about the Strand, wanting Dan's reels. When I told him to leave, he just up and whacked me, and out I went."

"How awful," said Aunt Shirley. "What were you doing in here all alone?"

"Fretting about our Darleen, I was. She hadn't come home, and there was that stuff in the paper about the other kidnapping and nothing about ours, and I didn't know what to think. Thought I'd develop a test strip from the reel Dan filmed at the Strand, you know, so I could get a little glimpse of my girl. I thought it would be comforting. Had it drying on the wall when that bandit surprised me. Those thieves will have pinched the rest of the reel, I guess. Is that really you, Darleen? All safe and sound?"

"It *is* me, poor Papa!" said Darleen, her heart very full.

"Shiny as a new penny and perfectly fine," added Aunt Shirley. "So you see how foolish it was of you to be fretting that way."

"Yes, but —" said Darleen, but then she stopped short. When Aunt Shirley pinched your arm that hard, speaking became difficult.

"Dear child. The angel said you were fine," said Darleen's father. "And look, she was right. Here you are and . . . and . . ."

His voice was beginning to grow faint. Aunt Shirley put her practical hand very gently on her brother's shoulder.

"Now, Bill, do be sensible and save your strength," she said. "The doctor will be here any second, and then we'll take you home to my place, I think, where I can be sure you're being properly looked after. Don't you worry yourself about the missing reel. It's not as important as your head! Oh, and here's the doctor now!"

It was a relief, really, to have Aunt Shirley there and taking charge as Aunt Shirley so liked to do. It was a relief, too, when good old Dr. Jones examined Darleen's Papa and declared that his neck wasn't broken and his skull was still in good shape, and that, with a couple of quiet days of good nursing and rest, he should be back to full strength.

Aunt Shirley and Darleen hugged each other, they were so glad, and the uncles fitted up an impromptu stretcher and carried Darleen's father down the street to Aunt Shirley's house. "I'm going to nurse him properly, so I guess the studio will have to do without the both of us for a few days," said Aunt Shirley, and the dark tone in her voice suggested she wasn't entirely confident that Matchless would be able to manage. But it couldn't be helped. Darleen was given the task of fetching supplies from her house for her father and then was told it would be better, after all, if she didn't mind sleeping in her own bed at home.

"Unless it's too lonely there," said Aunt Shirley. "We

could put you on the sofa here, I suppose, but I want you to get some actual sleep."

"Oh, no!" said Darleen quickly. "I'll be fine on my own, really!"

She did not speak aloud the rest of her thoughts on the subject, though, which included some worry that Aunt Shirley might want to ask her questions that would be very awkward, as far as Darleen could figure, to answer, such as:

— What exactly happened to you last night?

— Where do you think that Berryman girl might be?

— Why do you keep saying those quite peculiar things about Jasper Lukes, anyway?

I'll have to figure out a plan, as soon as I have a moment to catch my breath, Darleen told herself over and over as she lugged a box of clothes for her Papa from her house to Aunt Shirley's (keeping her eyes peeled for any lurking spiders). *I'll make this all right, somehow. I will.*

Chapter 12

Not an Onion After All

And Darleen repeated that promise to herself — *I'll make this all right, somehow. I will* — as she pocketed bread from Aunt Shirley's pantry, filched a piece of cold chicken from the kitchen to share with Victorine later, and clambered back up her friendly tree. She considered smuggling Victorine back to her actual house, but there were the spiders to worry about. And at least in a photoplay studio, there are always extras around and about, so at Matchless, Victorine could hide in plain sight.

As Darleen came up the stairs to the floor where the little dressing rooms and supply rooms were lined up like broom closets, she suddenly felt tired to her very core. So when she opened the door of her dressing room, at first she hardly recognized the space. Victorine had been at work while she was gone, heaping up whatever blankets and soft coats she could find to make a most comfortable little nest for people who had been cheated of sleep by adventure and mishap.

Victorine herself was curled up in that nest, below the mess of old photos tacked to the wall. In one, the members of the old Darling theater company (before their moving-picture days) were lined up like schoolchildren on risers. All those strange but familiar faces! There is something mysterious about old photographs, the way they promise to tell you secret truths about the people they capture. But they don't always exactly keep that promise, do they? Darleen knew that from experience: stare at any picture long enough, and the souls in it, instead of coming into focus, begin to waver and fade farther away. Her mother's sad eyes, for example, in the old photograph at home. What were those eyes trying to say? And what secrets were hiding in the photograph here? Darleen never knew quite what to make of that infant Jasper Lukes, looking deceptively angelic at the end of the second row as he dozed in the arms of his mother, or, next to them, Jasper's no-good father, who seemed to have turned his head away right when the camera was taking the picture.

As soon as Darleen came through the door, Victorine jumped up, all worry and concern.

"How is your Papa doing? What did the doctor say? He's such a sweet man, your father! I can't believe someone was wicked enough to strike him down."

Darleen rattled through everything she could think of: what Aunt Shirley had said, what the doctor had said, how her Papa would be staying at Shirley's house for a little while for the sake of the nursing. And then she remembered the funniest part of that not very funny adventure:

"And, oh, Victorine, imagine: Papa kept saying you were an angel! I think Aunt Shirley was about ready to faint when he said that. She thought, you know, that he must be awfully close to the heavenly gates if he was seeing angels."

They both laughed a little at that, the rueful kind of laughter that is mostly relief that something worse didn't happen.

"One more thing, Darleen," said Victorine. "Your Uncle Dan is the one who takes the moving pictures, is that right? The cameraman? Well, those villains were after the pictures he took. The pictures from the Strand. That's what your Papa told me, poor man."

"Because they were pictures of *them*!" said Darleen. The light was going on in her mind.

"Evidence, then," said Victorine. "Like in the Sherlock Holmes stories. And now it's gone."

"I don't think so!" said Darleen. "Papa developed a test strip—he said so himself—and hung it up to dry." She clapped her palms together. "Victorine, let's go see."

Victorine was already on her feet, ready to go. So Darleen led the way back down the stairs and through the door separating the laboratory building from the rest of the studio, the door with the warning posted on it. Darleen gave the sign a friendly tap as they passed by:

REMEMBER!

MATCHES, CIGARETTES, CIGARS,

AND

FIRE OF ANY KIND:

FORBIDDEN ALWAYS!

LET'S STAY SAFE AND STAY ALIVE.

"I forgot to warn you not to smoke your pipe or cigars!" she said to Victorine, who laughed.

"Not too much danger of that," said Victorine. "And I've read about fires in the picture theaters. It's a danger, isn't it?"

Darleen nodded.

"Photoplay studios are an awful lot like the Scarecrow in *The Wonderful Wizard of Oz*. Not afraid of anything but a lighted match, I mean."

"For good reason," said Victorine.

"For very good reason," agreed Darleen. "A few weeks ago, there was an awful fire that burned the laboratory over at the Eclair studios. My family's always been frightened about fire, at least since that old theater of ours burned down all those years ago. And there's so much that's flammable at a photoplay studio: the celluloid that the film is printed on, the wood everywhere, not to mention all the chemicals they use."

In fact, the smell of the chemicals in here was enough to make a person's eyes water. Darleen had been raised to admire the tough lungs of the laboratory workers — like her Papa, who claimed not to be bothered by any of it, even though Darleen could hear him coughing sometimes in the middle of the night.

"Hey, now, Darleeny. Don't you worry. Pickles last longer than cukes," he liked to say about that. He figured he had been brining in photoplay chemicals for years now.

A person like Victorine probably had delicate and tender lungs, though, thought Darleen, the kind that weren't used to bad air and chemicals. She would surely be wanting to get out of this room as fast as possible. But when Darleen turned around to look at Victorine, she caught her spinning around slowly, taking in all the interesting chaos of the laboratory: all the equipment, the vats of chemicals, and the long strips of celluloid film that were draped along the walls to dry. She did not look like someone desperate for cleaner air.

"What a *wonderful* place," said Victorine, and Darleen couldn't help but smile. "You can certainly see how much work goes into making a photoplay."

"All kinds of work," said Darleen. "Papa does the chemical developing and some of the editing and all sorts of things. Everybody knows more than one thing around here, I guess. Why, Uncle Charlie, years back, had a job in the lab as a *perforator*! Do you know what a perforator used to do?"

"I certainly don't," said Victorine.

"That was the person who put the holes in the sides of the celluloid filmstrip so that the film could be run through a projector. See?"

There was a strip of film stretched out to air-dry, and she showed Victorine the sprocket holes, running along either side of the celluloid.

"Perforator! Can you imagine a job duller than that? But now they don't need a special person for that. I guess the strips of film come with the little holes already made."

She led Victorine to the far wall, where a few strips of celluloid were hanging on a kind of clothesline.

"And, yes! Here it is!" said Darleen, holding the edges gingerly. "Just what we were looking for. See?"

"So that's what a film looks like up close," said

Victorine. "How interesting! All those little tiny pictures of *you*, Darleen. And of that awful man, too, the one who wasn't driving the car."

Indeed, there he was: the side-winding man, looking around over his shoulder toward the cameraman, every inch of his face beautifully caught in miniature.

"Perfect!" said Darleen. "We can hide this safely away, and it will be, you know, a guarantee. Insurance, in case the thieves come sneaking back."

They were glad to leave the fumes of the laboratory behind. But instead of going right back upstairs, Darleen nabbed a handbill from a desk outside Aunt Shirley's office and then led Victorine through an entirely different door.

"Look at this!" said Darleen, gesturing into the great space where the photoplays were filmed.

Victorine followed her, her mouth falling open in amazement. Darleen felt a surge of pride. The Matchless studios were really *something*!

"But it's like . . . it's like . . . the largest hothouse in the world!" said Victorine.

They were in a huge building made of a thousand glass panels, so yes, it was quite like a hothouse.

"In fact, it's boiling in hot weather, that's for certain," said Darleen. "But the glass lets the sunlight through, and that's good, because it takes a lot of light to photograph a moving picture."

"Look, a piece of a parlor," said Victorine, looking around in awe. "And over there — a Wild West saloon. Is that a photoplay set?"

"Surely is," said Dar. "We can be filming three or four different photoplays at once in here, it's so big. Tomorrow you'll see it in action, I guess."

Victorine spun around slowly, taking it all in.

"Do you like it?" said Darleen.

"I love it," said Victorine. "Oh, Darleen. It's so unlike my world — my world in recent months, I mean. Anything must be possible here. *Anything*!"

When they got back to their hideaway upstairs, they collapsed into their comfortable nest.

"Suddenly I don't know whether I'm mostly ravenous or mostly exhausted," said Victorine.

"Well, we were up pretty much all night, weren't we?" said Darleen. "I say, let's have a bite of something, and then I'll tell you my next idea."

"You are so wonderfully full of ideas, Darleen!" said Victorine. "But a little bite of something sounds lovely. My Grandmama used to say that an escape from danger is better than medicine for increasing the appetite."

So they ate two of the apples and the piece of chicken

and then settled comfortably into the nest Victorine had made, with their backs leaning against the wall, and with overcoats from the costume closet pulled up over their shoulders like blankets.

"Now take a look at this!" said Darleen, giving Victorine the handbill she had grabbed downstairs. "This is part of my new secret plan for you!"

Victorine took a glance and then looked up with such a puzzled expression that Darleen couldn't keep from laughing right out loud.

"It's a kind of list?" said Victorine.

"It is!" said Darleen. "That's the 'I CAN' list, the studio questionnaire for the actors applying, you know. To see what talents they may have. Oh, but Victorine, don't you see? You're going to become an actress! It will be the perfect disguise around here. We'd better have you go through the list properly, and then you'll just hand it in at the office tomorrow morning, as if you were the most ordinariest extra actress there ever was."

They studied the list together:

WHICH OF THE FOLLOWING ABILITIES
DO YOU POSSESS? PLEASE CHECK:

☐ I CAN RIDE A HORSE

☐ I CAN SWIM

☐ I CAN BOX

- ☐ I CAN DANCE
- ☐ I CAN DRIVE A MOTORCAR
- ☐ I CAN CLIMB ROPES
- ☐ I CAN STAND ON MY HANDS
- ☐ I CAN WRESTLE
- ☐ I CAN WALK ON A TIGHTROPE
- ☐ I CAN PLAY A MUSICAL INSTRUMENT:

  ____

- ☐ I CAN DIVE FROM CLIFFS INTO A WILD, CHURNING RIVER

"Oh, dear," said Victorine. "I've never wrestled anyone. *Nor* sprung from a cliff into a river."

"That last one is Uncle Charlie's little joke," said Darleen. "Never you mind about it. And anyway, all the actors just check them all if they really want the job."

"They *lie*?" said Victorine. "But Darleen, what then happens when a photoplay director tells them to stand on their hands?"

"I guess they learn fast," said Dar, and when Victorine looked up in horror, Darleen had to try very hard not to giggle.

"Now, really," she said to Victorine after a moment. "How often do photoplay actors actually have to stand on their hands? That would be just about never."

Victorine sighed.

"It's a daunting list of abilities," she said. "I'm afraid I fall quite short. I've had such a mixed-up education that sometimes I think the only path in life I've trained for, after all, is that of a World-Wandering Librarian. And I'm afraid they aren't very much in demand."

"But I'm sure you can dance," said Darleen. "Can't you? Of course you can. And I myself have seen you slither down a rope to a fire escape. And cling to the side of a moving motorcar. And capture snakes. And climb trees! Very recently!"

"Not on the list," said Victorine, but a smile flickered across her face, and she brought out a pencil end she had found somewhere. With that pencil, she put the most elegant imaginable checks next to riding a horse, swimming, dancing, and playing a musical instrument: PIANOFORTE.

Then she looked up at Darleen with a troubled expression.

"But Darleen, when they read my name on this form, I'll be sent back to the Brownstones quick as quick, won't I? Or at least certainly I will as soon as anyone reads the newspaper, which I guess they already have done, to judge from your conversation with your Aunt Shirley."

Darleen took a deep breath.

"I've been thinking about it, Victorine, and I think you'd better do what everybody does around here: use a stage name. I bet we can come up with a really good one."

Victorine gave her a long and skeptical look.

"You mean simply make something up?" she said. "But what about *the truth*? You've forgotten entirely about telling the truth."

"Well, the truth is important," Darleen hurried to say. (The expression on Victorine's face had her worried.) "But so is keeping you safe. And anyway, stage names are *completely* normal and ordinary and not at all the same as lying," said Darleen. She was proud to discover that she could be as stubborn as the Berryman heiress when circumstances required. "Your stage name is who you truly are when you're at work. On the stage. Right? Many, many very good people have them. Now you give me that paper right now!"

Darleen took the pencil, too, and paused a moment for a thoughtful squint: What would be a name as different from Miss Victorine Berryman as possible?

"We'll call you Miss Henrietta Hankins," she proposed. "There! How do you like that?"

"Absolutely not," said Victorine sternly. "Henrietta Hankins must be about the worst name I've ever heard in my entire life. Here, I'm taking back that pencil right this minute."

There was a brief tussle, which Victorine won. And then, somewhat to Darleen's surprise, instead of flinging the pencil to the far corner of the dressing room, Victorine wrote *Bella Mae Goodwin* on the form, in a lovely, flowing hand.

"And *that,*" she said, "happens to be actually, *truthfully,* my name. Parts of my name, anyway. The parts nobody remembers but that were given to me long ago. Yes, Darleen, you are actually at this moment sharing a room with someone named Victorine Charlotte Bella Mae Goodwin Berryman. Hard to believe, isn't it?"

So many names for only one not-very-large person! Darleen was impressed.

"Finally they come in handy, all those middle names of mine," said Victorine. "I'll put them to work as my stage name, and I will still be telling the truth. Ha!"

She paused for a moment, stricken with another distressing thought: "But *acting*! If I'm an actress, I'll be acting! Oh, dear, I—"

"Victorine Berryman, don't start fretting again!" said Darleen. "Acting is *definitely* not the same as lying."

Victorine tipped her head to the side. "Is that true?" she asked. "Maybe it's true. I don't know. I thought I had everything so clearly sorted out, but now I wonder. Grandmama used to laugh at me, now and again. She said I was an onion sort of person, and she loved me for it, but she wondered whether it might be hard for me sometimes, you know, being an onion."

Darleen stared. *An onion?* "Why would she say such a thing? Did you make her cry a lot?"

Victorine laughed right out loud.

"No, no!" she said. "Oh, dear, that's not what she meant by it at all! She meant I'm just layer after layer of the same thing—consistently Victorine all the way down. Like an onion. I thought it was a compliment, but now I see it might be seen as rather dull, being an onion. Though what's wrong with being an onion, really, when you think about it? But anyway, Darleen, what would you be, do you think, if you were a vegetable or a fruit?"

"I don't know," said Darleen. She had never been asked such a question before. What fruit is the one that just wants to keep its Papa happy and his heart unbroken?

"Well, I don't think you're an onion," said Victorine. "If you don't mind my saying so, I think you may be quite different on the inside from what you seem on the outside, like one of those fruits my Grandmama showed me in South America: purple skin and crinkly on the outside, but inside, full of surprising pulpy seeds that are the sweetest, wildest things you ever tasted. Oh, and they grow on vines. They like to climb freely, you know—like you! They are quite wonderful, I think. Why, if they could simply grow wings and fly away, I'm sure they would!"

It took Darleen by such surprise that she felt as though flames had suddenly kindled right under her skin. How did Victorine *know*? It was like she had looked right into Darleen's soul and seen the wildness hiding there.

"But I can't," said Darleen, her heart now ablaze with longing and pain. "I *can't.*"

"Can't what?" said Victorine in alarm. "Oh, Darleen, I've gone and upset you somehow! How foolish I am! What is it you can't do?"

"I can't fly away! I mustn't fly away! I promised Papa I wouldn't. Because my poor Mama—"

"Your mother? But I didn't mention your mother, did I?" said Victorine. "Oh, dear. Oh, dear. We were talking about *fruits,* weren't we? Fruits on a South American vine."

Darleen just shook her head. The feelings had come first, but now the image followed: *bright wings on a roof, reaching for the moon.*

Oh!

It was that *dream* of hers that came back to her now, that took her by surprise at this moment when she was awake. (Dreams are like that—they fade to whispers and shadows, but every now and then, a sliver's worth will cut right through the haze of the everyday and startle us into seeing something new.)

And when the old dream came flooding back to Darleen now, she saw something the sleeping-and-dreaming Darleen had never been able to see before.

It had never been *just a dream* all those years. It was — it had always been — a *memory* dressed up like a dream. How had she never seen that before? How had she not known?

"Mama used to dance on the roof!" Darleen said. And then she surprised herself by bursting into tears. "It was Mama all the time! She danced on the roof — and then she died!"

Chapter 13

Butterscotch Is Helpful

Darleen knew how to make tears appear when the camera thought tears were necessary, but she had almost no practice at all with sobs that simply welled up in her of their own accord, that shook her all the way through and made her unable to speak sensibly or even move. She was aware of Victorine patting her on the shoulder and keeping a steady stream of words flowing over her, because calm words are reassuring when the world inside you has split right open.

And eventually she realized that Victorine had something in her hand that she was offering to her, a small lump wrapped in waxed paper.

"Have a butterscotch, do," she was saying. "They are *so* restorative in times of trouble. Here, I'll have one too."

It was true; the sweet richness of the butterscotch seemed to quiet something down inside Darleen. Soon enough, she could think again — and then, of course, she was horrified to realize she had given way and fallen apart when Victorine must be counting on her to stay steady and keep them safe.

"Oh, no, I'm so sorry . . ." she began, but Victorine would have none of it.

"Dearest Darleen, think about it! We've had no sleep in I don't know how many hours," she said, using her fingers to tick off the reasons a person might need some butterscotch. "And you've saved my life several times over, and then you had the terrible shock of seeing your father hurt! My goodness, Darleen, I'd be surprised if you didn't feel a bit wobbly in the knees now that we're not actually running from danger. I just blame myself for not remembering about the candies earlier. Grandmama was always a believer in having a Reed's Roll tucked away somewhere safe for emergencies. But then I forgot all about that particular pocket, so you see, you mustn't feel the slightest bit apologetic."

Victorine's kind voice was as butterscotchy as the butterscotch, and Darleen found she was beginning to feel the way one does once the fever (or strong feeling) has passed: weak, but relieved. Comfortable. Convalescent.

"You know," said Victorine, "I think you are very lucky to remember your mama at all. I have seen pictures of my poor mother, but that's not exactly the same, is it?"

"But I didn't *know* that I was remembering," said Darleen, hiccuping a little despite the butterscotch. "I thought it was just this old dream I have sometimes, coming again and again and making me sad."

Victorine listened to Darleen's description of the dream that wasn't a dream—the child looking out the window at some magical creature dancing on the roof, and reaching out to her with arms that would never be long enough to keep a fairy, a butterfly, or a mother from flying away.

"I couldn't keep her," said Darleen. She ordinarily wouldn't have been speaking these secrets aloud, but she was so tired and comfortable, and the butterscotch was so sweet. "I was supposed to be the one to keep her feet on the ground, but I couldn't. Something in her wanted always to climb and dance and fly. She would tuck me in and sing to me, and then—"

Why hadn't she seen it before? That the dream was just the plain truth, wrapped up in dream clothing?

"It's all come back to me this minute, clear as clear: sometimes she would slip out my window and dance in the moonlight, right there on the spine of the roof. I was so little, but I knew she wasn't supposed to do that. She had promised Papa to keep her feet on the ground. I knew that. But she was so lovely out on the roof! Sometimes she would even wear her beautiful billowy wings."

"She had wings?"

"Wonderful silk wings," said Darleen. "From when she was Loveliest Luna Lightfoot and did her butterfly dances, you know."

"*Moth* dances, I suppose you mean," said Victorine.

Darleen looked at her, not understanding, and Victorine blushed.

"Sorry, sorry," she said. "Ignore me, do. The luna moth is just so beautiful, you know. More beautiful than almost any butterfly. What color were your mother's silken wings? The color of a glacial tarn, I'm guessing? Palest green, so lovely?"

"Yes!" said Darleen. "How'd you know that? And what's a tarn?"

"A steep-banked mountain puddle, more or less. They're the most beautiful color because of all the minerals in the water. But never mind that. It sounds wonderful, your mother's dancing. Like a lullaby, but without the singing."

Darleen thought about that, settling even more

deeply into the blankets and coats. Dancing as a lullaby! Victorine didn't seem to understand what was frightening and sad about it all.

"But she had promised not to. You can't have a baby and still be dancing on tightropes and roofs, can you? I was supposed to—*supposed to*—keep her feet on the ground. But I couldn't do it, and she kept dancing me to sleep, you know, until one night it got her."

"Oh, Darleen. . . . Are you saying . . . she fell?" whispered Victorine, and that whisper shook a little, from horror and sympathy.

"Oh, no, not like that," said Darleen. "She didn't fall down, she fell *ill*, and all because her feet kept taking her out to those dangerous places. I didn't stop her. I couldn't stop her. And a chill from the night air caught her, and she died of the pneumonia, and our hearts were broken, and Papa's never really been the same ever since."

"This may sound like a strange question," said Victorine, and she doled out another butterscotch for each of them. Butterscotch slows down a conversation so well, like a sweet and melting pause opening up right there in the middle of too many emotions. "But you know I'm an onion sort of person, the same thing layer after layer after layer, and so sometimes I can't help but be very literal-minded. Anyway, I'm wondering: How were you supposed to keep her from dancing out on the roof when you were so very small? Were you supposed to hold on to her skirts somehow? I guess she would have been much stronger than you, being so much older."

Darleen shook her head.

"I don't mean that. I mean that if I had been — I don't know — the right sort of daughter — easier to love — she wouldn't have wanted to fly away. She would have been able to keep her promise, and keep her feet on the ground. But I wasn't enough, somehow. I couldn't keep her."

They each sucked on their butterscotch candies for a thoughtful moment.

"Goodness," said Victorine. "Mothers must be very complicated things. When I was little, I was sad not to have one, but mostly because my father and grandmother missed her so much. I didn't know her long enough (only three days, after all) to develop a personal impression, or to feel I ought to have behaved differently somehow."

Then Victorine shifted a bit in their nest so that she could turn her clear gray eyes right on Darleen.

"What I mean, dear Darleen, is, I don't have experience with mothers, *exactly,* but I've never ever heard of a child being able to cure a parent from pneumonia. Have you? So I don't think even you could have done it. Or kept her from dancing out on the roof. And now —"

She smiled and then covered her mouth with a hand, because the smile had turned into a yawn.

"Oh, you're tired!" said Darleen. "Poor Victorine! Everything you've been through, and here I am, talking your ear off when you're tired as can be!"

But yawns spread fast, so Darleen was already yawning, too, and that meant they found themselves wobbling back on the edge of laughter — and then tipping right over that edge.

"Oh, Darleen," said Victorine, wiping her eyes. "Imagine. Soon the world will have spun itself around one whole turn since we first met in the back of the motorcar."

"Gosh," said Darleen. She thought back to that surprising moment when the large bundle had turned out to be an actual girl. "I guess you're right about that! Almost twenty-four hours."

"I do believe," said Victorine after a silent moment, "that my life, since meeting you, Darleen, is now irreversibly changed. How lucky for me that we met! I think some of your daring may be rubbing off on me, you know."

"I'm not really —" said Darleen, and then she stopped.

Maybe it was true that what they had done, over that long day and night, could be called daring for real. Did that daring come from being the kind of fruit that is not one thing all the way through? A fruit that has a rind that makes it seem like one thing and yet holds something completely different inside?

She wasn't sure. That feeling that sometimes fluttered inside Darleen, that was always threatening to break out into the world, might or might not be like the sweet insides of a purple fruit. It felt sometimes like a living thing, stretching its wings and wanting to be born. A monstrous something, maybe even.

What if it broke out and then kept on breaking things?

Her father's poor heart;

Her own dreams;

The world.

Chapter 14

The Prisoner in the Attic

Darleen started the next morning by running over to Aunt Shirley's house to see how her Papa was doing and to pilfer some breakfast supplies for herself and Victorine.

"Are you *sure* you'll be all right here if I leave you alone?" she had asked Victorine several times over. "All the studio people will be arriving in an hour or so, and then it will begin to get properly lively around here. Just pretend to be one of them. There are always new people, you know, so you should be able to blend in."

It seemed such a terribly huge thing to Darleen, to be facing a studio full of people you didn't even know! Why, she knew practically everybody at Matchless, and she still sometimes felt tongue-tied around them (when the camera wasn't cranking away).

"I'll be entirely fine," said Victorine, looking the picture of composure and confidence. "Now, go along quickly, or I guess you'll be late for your own picture!"

Darleen ran.

In fact, she ran so fast that Aunt Shirley laughed out loud when she saw her.

"Darleen! Why, you're panting like a poodle! You'll be in rotten shape for your scene this morning if you run yourself ragged."

"How's Papa?" said Darleen, trying to breathe a little more quietly.

"*Perfectly* all right," said Papa himself, and Darleen whirled around to see him sitting up in Aunt Shirley's most comfortable armchair and smiling at her.

Darleen ran and flung her arms around him (gently) while Aunt Shirley smiled and tut-tutted:

"Now, Bill, you must not stir an *inch* from that chair — except to go back to bed. I've told everybody the rules. Absolute rest today and tomorrow for you. An actual nap lying down in the afternoon. Darleen, be gentle with him, child!"

Darleen was actually being very gentle, of course. But it was so wonderful to see her father on the mend that she grinned and grinned and grinned at him.

But after she had kissed her Papa and said goodbye, Aunt Shirley drew Darleen into the hall and pointed at something in the newspaper.

"He mustn't see this, Darleen, dear," she said. "No more sad shocks for him while he's mending."

Looking past Aunt Shirley's tapping index finger, Darleen saw a set of headlines that made her feel very strange inside:

"BERRYMAN GIRL FEARED DEAD"

"Shoes and Hat Wash Up"

"Guardians Grieve"

"No Trace of Kidnappers"

"Poor little rich girl, indeed!" said Aunt Shirley, shaking her head. "Looks like she's been drowned after all, poor chick. We can't let Bill hear about this — I doubt his heart could withstand the thought of it." She sighed. "Well, that's that, then, probably. No one will be getting that twenty-five-thousand-dollar reward now. Too bad."

When Darleen left Aunt Shirley's, she felt quite proud of her achievements. She had not gotten into a single argument with her aunt. She had learned that her Papa seemed to be well on the mend. And she had left Aunt Shirley's with several warm and savory biscuits, wrapped up in the offending newspaper.

She went skittering back to the Matchless buildings, where the atmosphere was nothing like it had been the evening before. If in the middle of the night the studio had felt like an abandoned city or a graveyard, now it was a factory, an anthill, a military camp, a chaotic town on carnival day. All of those things and more all at once!

"Hurry, hurry, hurry!" said one of the director's all-purpose assistants as Darleen came speeding by. "Your Uncle Charlie wants to have things going in thirty minutes! Prisoner in the attic, remember!"

"I know, I know," said Darleen, and she sped on up to her dressing room, where there was, to her surprise, no sign of Victorine. Even the blankets and coats in the corner had been folded up so neatly that they had practically become invisible.

But there was no time to worry about where Victorine must have gotten to. Darleen admired the rather battered look, of course, of her dress from yesterday. Appropriate for a prisoner in an attic! She checked in the mirror, and her hair was also a little battered-looking. All right.

She put the biscuits and newspaper on a shelf and marched herself downstairs.

Stepping out into the huge expanse of the glass-roofed and -walled studio meant walking out into din and chaos. There were at least three different pictures in production at the same time, and the set for each one had its own crew, who were shouting instructions, questions, and suggestions. It was extraordinary how much noise went into making silent films! Darleen was mostly used to the din, of course, since she had been working on film sets as long as she could remember, but today she was scanning the hall for any trace of the missing Victorine, and that made her imagine what this place must seem like to someone seeing it for the first time. It must seem as raucous as Palisades Amusement Park at the end of the trolley line.

She saw technicians down at the far end putting the final touches on what was recognizably a saloon, with a bar counter on the right and swinging doors on the left, as every movie saloon in every Wild West picture always had.

At the other end was a backdrop with arches and a garden painted to fool the eye (well, to fool the not-very-clever eye; the painting wasn't very good — even Darleen could tell that). They were most likely going to film a historical picture there, Darleen thought, something with enormous costumes and lots of the wooden "marble" pillars that the props and scenery men kept stacked in one of the back storage rooms.

In the middle of all this bustle, Uncle Charlie was noisily consulting with some of the carpenters. He was standing next to a cutaway of an attic, with the ceiling angled up so that an improbably large skylight could be seen. The whole room had been lifted up on short stilts so that a few steps' worth of a staircase could be squeezed into the foreground. A few feet away, the camera was set up on a little loft structure of its own to film the attic from straight on.

"Darleen!" shouted Uncle Charlie as soon as he saw her. "How good of you to join us!"

Uncle Dan added, "How's Bill?"

"Papa's much better this morning, thank you," said Darleen, and even Uncle Charlie softened for a moment.

"It's a terrible thing," he said, shaking his head. "Can't believe anyone would have a go at Bill. Now, Shirley on a bad day — I could see someone wanting to clonk her over the ears. But *Bill*?"

They all thought good thoughts about Darleen's Papa for a moment, and then Uncle Charlie went back to his usual mode, which was impatience.

"Where's that Jasper Lukes? We're missing our villain."

A shudder went right through Darleen then. Villain, indeed! Little did they know! She had been fretting about this privately all morning: What would she do if Jasper Lukes turned up on the set today? What could she say? What would he say? *He can't hurt me, not with all these people around,* she told herself, but her self only half believed her.

She wanted to warn them all, but she couldn't quite figure out how to talk about the details of yesterday without bringing up Victorine. She couldn't say a word to her family about an undrowned Victorine now that she knew they couldn't be trusted when it came to large rewards.

"Maybe he won't show up at all," she said, and really she hoped he wouldn't. "Didn't he say he wanted to quit?"

"He's said that a thousand times," said Uncle Charlie. "Doesn't mean a thing."

"Start without him," said Uncle Dan, checking his camera.

"I guess we can film the bits where Lukes isn't needed," said Uncle Charlie. "All right, Darleen, do you recall what we're doing today?"

"Um . . ." said Darleen. It had been a distracting thirty-six hours.

"I'll refresh your memory: the Salamanders nabbed you at the theater. Remember that?"

"Oh, yes," said Dar. She certainly did remember that.

"So, even though your actual kidnapping stunt over at the theater went sideways — with no helpful publicity for us — we're pretty much keeping to that story we had planned in the episode this week. Means that for today, here you are in the attic of the Salamanders' den. Prisoner. Lukes — if he ever bothers to get here — will be threatening you because . . . because . . . Dan, what's the *because* here again?"

Uncle Dan wasn't just clever with cameras; he had the kind of head that could hold on to the plot of a story and never let it go.

"King's head got clobbered," he said. "Amnesia."

"That's right," said Uncle Charlie. "It's all coming back to me now: Your poor Royal Father, who is imprisoned by those Salamanders at the moment, got hit over the head and doesn't remember a blessed thing, including where that Black Sapphire may be. So our villain Lukes wants *you* to give up the Sapphire, but you are a brave girl, of course, and refuse. And then they leave you to starve to death or change your mind in the attic, and a mysterious balloon comes and rescues you."

"What?" said Darleen. That was new! She hadn't heard anything about any balloon.

"An idea we had yesterday. Good, right? We can film exteriors out at the Palisades. There's a balloon at the amusement park that they'll let us borrow. It'll be nifty. Pulling out the stops for Episode Nine! Now get up there. Why don't we do the closer-in shots, hey, Dan?"

Darleen scampered up the narrow half stairs at the front of the set, and Uncle Dan pushed the little platform holding the camera a few feet closer to the set. Uncle Charlie had a list of the pictures they needed, and they checked them off as they went.

Darleen had learned as a little, tiny tot that photoplays

aren't always filmed in regular real-life order; sometimes the end is filmed before the beginning. That is one helpful way to check whether what is happening to you is real life or the filming of a movie: Did lunch come before breakfast today? Did you shout and smile *after* the new puppy appeared at the door, or *before*?

Darleen was supposed to be a prisoner at this point, so an assistant tied some rope around her wrists and another length of rope around her and the chair.

"Here we go. First up is some agonized worrying if you don't mind, Darleen! The Salamanders have just left you to rot in this attic room and have threatened to hurt your Royal Father. Ready . . . steady . . . off you go, Dan. Crank away."

Darleen wrung her hands, widened her eyes, and made a show of pulling against the ropes.

A messenger boy came by, mid-hand-wring, and asked rather loudly whether any fiddlers were around, because the players over in the Western picture were complaining that they couldn't get into a properly jolly mood for their saloon scene without any music.

Uncle Charlie, annoyed, said, "*Stop for now, Dan!* Could you people give us a little consideration? Our Darleen's trying to agonize up there, don't you see?"

"Oh, sorry," said the boy. He didn't seem very sorry.

"For the sake of Pete," said Uncle Charlie to the boy.

"Go tell them to look at the 'I CAN' forms. There's got to be a musician in the pool somewhere. Now, scoot!"

They filmed close-in shots of Darleen loosening the bonds around her hands with her teeth, and then they moved the camera's little perch back again and filmed those actions over again, from a distance. The balance between distance and close-in shots was a delicate thing, Uncle Charlie always said: *like knowing when you're hungry for a banquet and knowing when a single dumpling is just what you need and want.*

Jasper Lukes still hadn't shown up.

Uncle Charlie said some choice words about that. Then he said, "Well, let's do the balloon bit now, then, shall we? All right, Darleen, here's how this is going to work: the rope from the balloon is going to come into the attic through the skylight, and you'll naturally just climb right up it. Got that?"

"I guess so," said Darleen, who might possibly have the strongest arms of any twelve-year-old girl in all of New Jersey. (Serial heroines climb a lot of ropes. Up ropes and down ropes, all day long.) "Who is supposed to be flying the balloon?"

"Don't quite know yet," said Uncle Charlie. "A mysterious friend come to help you out. Something like that. We'll figure it out before tomorrow, don't worry. Hey, you there with the rope! Let's get this scene moving!"

There was a scaffolding platform built right above the attic, and some technicians in overalls were fastening one end of a good, thick rope to the sturdiest part of the platform.

Darleen scooted back down the narrow half stairs so she could see the arrangements for the rope. The balloon was not in evidence at all, not for this shot. The rope would represent the balloon all on its lonesome, and then the ones who cut the film into shape (including her dear Papa, once his head had stopped aching) would simply insert some images of an actual hot-air balloon with some sky behind it. The astonishing thing was how willing a photoplay audience was to be deceived! It didn't take much to make them think, *There goes Darleen in a lighter-than-air balloon!*

But climbing up the rope, even if it was just through the skylight and up to the scaffolding platform, was real enough. Darleen flexed her hands and thought strong rope-climbing thoughts.

"Let's keep your feet tied together," said Uncle Charlie, cruelly enough. "That will look extra nice, don't you think? Daring Darleen climbing up the rope, using only her hands!"

"Thanks so much, Uncle Charlie," said Darleen.

"We'll cheer you on," said Uncle Charlie. "All right, are we ready? Let's go, Dan! Crank away!"

The fellows on the scaffolding above let the big rope down through the skylight and then twitched it back and forth to suggest it was tied to something large and round and buoyant.

"Go on, now, Darleen!" said Uncle Charlie. "Up you go!"

Darleen grabbed the rope. One hand up . . . the other hand up . . .

"That's good!" said Uncle Charlie. "Go ahead and look up at the balloon — it's up above your head. Keep climbing!"

The men on the scaffolding grinned down at Darleen.

"Come on, come on!" they said. "There will be a ginger beer for you when you get up here!"

It took every single last ounce of Darleen's strength to make this trick work, because it wasn't really a trick at all, was it? It was one hundred percent genuine rope climbing. The only thing in this shot that got off lightly, thanks to tricks, was the foolish balloon itself! It didn't even have to show up at all. All things considered, Darleen was quite jealous of the balloon.

Hand over hand over hand.

"Keep it up, Darleen!" "Come on, Darleen!" "Go, go, go!" It seemed like everyone anywhere near the set (and a bunch who had wandered over from the other two photoplay scenes, too, just to see what was going on) was staring up at her and shouting encouragement. All that cheering and hullabaloo did give Dar's arms another boost of strength.

Up! Up! Up!

She was closing in on the scaffolding now; her dangling feet must be the only part of her that the camera could still see. One of the fellows on the scaffold was kneeling, reaching down to help Darleen along as soon as she was just a few inches farther up the rope.

And then there was a change in the sound of the studio ruckus, and the eyes of the men on the scaffold left Darleen and looked down over the top of the set toward the uncles on their loft. The helpful hand that had been stretched down to help Darleen forgot what it was intending to do and floated away out of reach again, and poor Darleen was left dangling from the rope by herself.

"JASPER LUKES!" Uncle Charlie was saying. Followed by "Stop cranking, Dan."

It is hard to keep dangling after your body has happily reconciled itself to being rescued and relieved by someone else's strong arms. Darleen tried very hard to hang on to that rope, to make her hand fly up another few inches, but it was no good.

So instead, she let herself slip and then fall — not far, just onto the slanting roof of the set. It held her weight for a moment and then remembered it was just a set, not a real roof, and started sagging and cracking.

Uncle Charlie would not be pleased if she managed to destroy his set. With a last effort, she rolled herself over to the skylight and, falling back through it, landed with a *whomp* on the sturdier planks of the attic floor. Darleen huddled on the floor there for a moment, counting her new bruises and bracing herself for a volcano's worth of Uncle Charlie's angry words.

But that lava was already flowing, and in a different direction:

"Jasper Lukes! At the crack of ten a.m.!" (When Uncle Charlie was really in a lather, his words could make even a bystander flinch.) "SO! What have you got to say for yourself, you hopeless character?"

Chapter 15

More Frightening Than Cliffs

What Jasper Lukes had to say for himself, at least at first, was nothing.

Darleen rolled into a less awkward sitting position. Now she could see the face of Jasper Lukes, and it rattled her more than any mere tumble from skylight to floor.

He had always been what she considered conceited, full of thoughts about himself and rather lacking in thoughts about anybody else. But hanging out with actual kidnappers had done something to him: his eyes were angry and resentful and tired and cagey all at once. *Villainous* eyes.

He can't do anything to me here, Darleen told her gasping inner self. *He can't! Not with all these people right around us!*

And the other thing she told herself: *Don't let anything slip about Victorine!*

"Let's get this thing rolling," said Uncle Charlie in disgust after waiting a moment for an apology that apparently was not going to materialize.

Those words unfroze everybody all at once; technicians and carpenters and cameramen leaped into action. The place became noisy again in the usual way, with cheerful shouting and things being dropped and a piano being played rather nicely at the end of the studio, where, Darleen realized, they must have found a musician among the extras.

"Don't you worry about the roof," said one of the carpenters quietly to Darleen, as he punched the canvas and thin board back into position. "As long as nobody lands on it a second time, we'll be fine."

"We need the ropes back on Darleen!" shouted Uncle Charlie. "So our heretofore missing Salamander can shake his worthless fist at her!"

While they bound Darleen's hands together and tied her to that chair again, Dar found that unexpected emotions were bubbling up inside her—that is to say, emotions she was not used to feeling on the set of a photoplay, although she certainly had felt them many a time out and about in everyday real life. She felt *angry* and *anxious* and even—embarrassing though it was to admit it — *afraid.* What she did not feel like, just at the moment, was an *actor.* And that was strange too.

She wanted to catch another glimpse of Jasper Lukes's face, to see what he might be thinking, but of course she also really didn't want to see him at all, not now and possibly not ever.

People were so much more frightening than cliffs.

"On the count of three, Lukes, you'll come up those stairs with that envelope. Darleen, I'd like a nice reaction from you. You're terrified but being brave, of course. One . . . two . . . three, and crank away, Dan!"

Jasper Lukes came stomping up the half staircase, an envelope crushed in his angry hand, and as Darleen saw his face this second time, her heart began to pound in some alarm.

"Look menacing, now, Lukes!" called out Uncle Charlie. "Oh, very nice! Good work, Darleen. Now Lukes, ask her where that Black Sapphire thing is. You've got a photograph of that father of hers, that exiled King. Lay those threats on thick!"

Darleen hardly heard these words, however, because Jasper Lukes was looming over her now, and anger and barely contained violence were practically popping out of his skin. Darleen had never seen him in such a state. She actually yelped and tried to lean away.

"Looks fine," said Uncle Dan, cranking steadily away. "Looks dandy."

Jasper Lukes leaned forward, turning his head just an inch so that the camera wouldn't play any lip-reading games with him.

"Listen, Darleen," he hissed at her, quietly enough that only she would hear what he was saying. "What are you up to? How'd you end up back here? They say you know where she is. *Where is she?* You better get this clear, stupid girl: if they don't get her back, you're all in hot water."

He wasn't talking about the Black Sapphire, that was clear.

"Rip that envelope open and show her the photograph now, Lukes!"

Jasper Lukes tore the edge of the envelope off as if he wished he could make something suffer.

Then he grabbed Darleen's wrist and twisted it a little as he waved the photograph in her face. She gasped. Uncle Charlie called out something encouraging (the uncles must have thought Dar was acting). Darleen's heart was pumping away so fast that she couldn't pay proper attention anymore to anything Uncle Charlie was saying, because the awful, villainous Jasper Lukes was hissing at her:

"Tell me where she is. *That Berryman girl.*"

"She—she went home, I guess," said Darleen, her teeth chattering just a bit. "To wherever she lives. Anyway, I don't know where she is right now."

Maybe it was the subtle influence of Victorine at work, but Darleen actually felt a little proud that that last bit of her fib was technically true. She didn't know *exactly* where Victorine was at the moment, did she?

And then, a few seconds later, even that little scrap of truth turned, retrospectively, into a lie. Because she couldn't help hearing that piano playing for the Western picture, way at the other end of the glassed-in studio. She had noticed, but only idly, that the music seemed a little fancier than the usual amateur keyboard banging. But now it struck her: the pianist was playing on the out-of-tune studio piano with extraordinary accuracy and refinement. And playing some sort of high-class music, too, probably a sonata by one of those old fellows in wigs who used to write all the fancy music.

She blinked. That was all. She certainly didn't turn her head or say anything aloud. But that blink caught the attention of Jasper Lukes, who was apparently pretty desperate.

"You're lying to me!" he said. "You are *lying*! Don't think I can't tell!"

What could she say to that? Not much. All she could do was flinch under the pressure of his anger and his threats.

"You're messing with things you don't understand, you little fool," he said to her in that venomous whisper of his. "You couldn't even manage to be kidnapped by the right people! And now you're ruining everything. But let me tell you, if you don't hand over that girl, it's not just your daddy they'll be hitting over the head. It's you and everything here that will suffer—"

"Stop! Stop! Stop!" Uncle Charlie had apparently been yelling at Jasper Lukes for a while already.

"How can you possibly even *think* about handing any person over to kidnappers?" whispered Darleen anyway, she was so angry with him. "Especially a poor girl who has lost her grandma and is all alone in the world. Give her to people who might just drop her in the river? Are you a monster? Or just working with monsters?"

"Don't talk about things you don't understand. She belongs to them. That's what the law says, doesn't it? So tell me where—"

"STOP!" said Uncle Charlie, and then he started laughing so hard, he almost choked. "You two! That was the best scene you've ever done, and you just won't quit! But we can stop now, really!"

Jasper Lukes sprang away from Darleen.

"Stubborn girl! People are going to get hurt, just you wait and see," he snarled at Darleen, and then he turned toward the uncles and increased the volume of his angry words. "I should have quit this long ago. Well, now I am! I'm done with this and with all of you. This time, I'm really gone, and for good!"

He looked around with wild eyes, and then he sprinted down the cutaway half staircase and ran through the studio, everyone gaping after him.

"Don't we need him to drop the letter?" said Uncle Dan mildly from behind his camera.

"Oh, rats, yes! LUKES!" called out Uncle Charlie. "Come back and do the letter-dropping scene properly!"

But Jasper Lukes was gone.

Darleen slumped down into the chair for a moment while, with trembling hands, she freed herself from all of those ropes. She felt shaken, right to her inmost marrow. It was a shock to her system to see that something had broken inside that awful Jasper Lukes. He was capable of much more wickedness than Darleen had ever suspected. When one realizes that about a person one has known a long time—even if it's a person one hasn't particularly liked—the world tilts back and forth on its axis for a while, and all a person can do is hang on and feel seasick.

"What was that?" said Uncle Charlie. "Can someone explain to me what just happened here?"

Darleen, who could have explained but for good reasons thought she'd better hold her tongue instead, said nothing. Plus, there were parts of what he had said to her that didn't seem to make any sense. Who was Jasper Lukes working for, anyway?

Uncle Dan shrugged.

"Time for lunch," he proposed instead as a distraction.

Uncle Charlie rallied.

"Right, then," he said. "We're doing the big party scene this afternoon, so, Darleen, we'll need you tidied up nicely. And I'll have to get the extras into place if your aunt still isn't able to come help us."

Darleen said, "Party, Uncle Charlie? Wasn't I getting into a balloon just now?"

"Balloon exteriors tomorrow," said Uncle Charlie, checking through more pages of notes. "And a train to shoot too. All I can say is, Shirley'd better get back here to Matchless soon, or we'll be dropping scenes right and left."

They all depended so very much on Aunt Shirley's organizational genius.

"But the party?"

"That's where you get to at the end of the episode, yes? Your dear Royal Father — with amnesia, remember! — is being held prisoner by a mysterious wealthy family. All Salamanders actually, of course. Anyway, a ball. And a poignant encounter in which the King doesn't recognize his own child. The usual menu. Dan and I are going to hole up now and organize. You all right, Darleen?"

"Fine, fine," said Darleen.

Darleen moved along down the length of the studio, keeping alert in case Jasper Lukes or any other spider was anywhere in this building.

Exciting things were happening in the saloon at the far end: bandits ran through, brandishing their pistols and shouting quite a bit. And underneath the shouting was the intricate roar of whatever that fancy piece was that someone was playing on the battered old studio piano. Darleen circled around behind the pianist so as not to accidentally catch her eye, and, sure enough, it was the very elegant-looking, straight-backed Victorine, her hands rippling over the keys while some of the extras who weren't wanted on set hung around behind her, admiring her skill.

"Stop cameras!" cried the director on this film, and Victorine dutifully stopped as well, folding her hands in her lap and looking around.

"New girl sure can play!" said one of the boys who ran messages back and forth from Uncle Charlie to the office and back again. "What's your name, new girl?"

"Why, here they call me Bella Mae Goodwin," said Victorine with the confidence of a person stating the simple truth.

And the amazing thing was this: even under the name Bella Mae, Victorine still managed to seem entirely and completely *herself*, layer upon layer, all the way down.

Chapter 16

Many Stories, All at Once

It was quite wonderful to witness what a few hammers, a good supply of backdrops and fake walls, a properties room kept by pack rats, and five or six pairs of nimble arms could put together over lunch: in this case, the majestic mansion room where a masquerade ball would soon be underway. A woman from properties and scripts was briefing the extras, all wearing fancy clothes and holding masks in their hands. Among them was Bella Mae, looking believably aristocratic in her silk frock (which was in remarkably good shape, given everything). "There's a dance going on in this scene, yes? So your job is to not look at the cameraman and to make us all believe that this party is real, while Daring Darleen — oh, there you are,

Darleen! — winds through the lot of you, looking for her poor Royal Father."

"What kind of dance?" asked one of the extras, looking swell in his suit, which he had almost certainly rented for the day. (Extras had to rent their own suits, it's true. And pay the ferry fare over from New York and buy themselves meals and everything. Being an extra in a photoplay wasn't anybody's best get-rich-quick plan, that was for sure.)

"You all can waltz, yes?" said the woman from properties and scripts. "So you'll waltz. Listen, people. I want a nice, *controlled* little waltz. No grand gestures. No falling into the scenery and bringing it down. No bumping into one another, despite all these masks, or stumbling into our Darleen. Got that?"

The extras agreed with very good cheer.

Uncle Charlie and Uncle Dan, meanwhile, were setting up the camera for the first pictures. They had the carpenters change the angle of the mansion room's right-side wall so that the door could be more prominent.

"Darleen!" said Uncle Charlie. "You'll be coming from over there and snaking your way over here. Fresh from your balloon adventure, remember — we'll film that tomorrow. All right. Get yourself to the front so we can see you, and then you'll notice that door, peek through it, and in you go. Into position, everyone!"

It was an odd thing, how the world looked from a photoplay set. Darleen was at the rear of the scene to start. She could look back and see the painted garden outside the French doors she had supposedly just come through. She could see all the flaws in the thin, painted walls that would look like the solid walls of a rich man's house once the camera captured them, and strangest of all, of course, she could look out past the shoulders and arms of the dancing extras to the place where the fancy room suddenly ended, to Uncle Dan and his camera, to the guys with white sheets casting yet more light onto the scene, to the glass panes of the studio wall and roof farther beyond. It was really like being in two worlds at once.

No, three. Because if a world meant a story, then there was also the story Uncle Charlie didn't know and couldn't direct: the story of Victorine, who had become Bella Mae for the day and was now standing very elegantly with one of the suit-renting extras, waiting for the music and the filming to begin. She was right near Darleen but knew better than to let that affect her or make her give herself away. Anyway, a number of the female extras were rather short, so Victorine blended in surprisingly well, even though she was so much younger. In fact, she had an elegant way of standing that made it seem like she belonged at an aristocratic ball.

And then Uncle Charlie did some shouting and

waving from up front, and Joe from scenery pounded out the worst excuse for a waltz that Matchless Photoplay had ever heard, and most of the extras fiddled with their masks a little, and then they were off.

Darleen made her way through the dancing extras, who weren't supposed to be chatting but were saying occasional things anyway like "That's my foot you're on, buster."

"Look into those faces as you go by! You're looking for your father! But keep moving! You lot, don't be gawking at Darleen!"

She moved forward until she was in front of the dancers, raised her mask, and looked dramatically from side to side.

"Over to the door!" said Uncle Charlie. "Check over your shoulder that nobody's paying attention to you. All right, fine, open the door and slip on in."

But of course the door in the set wall did as stage doors will do: it got stuck.

Darleen paused for a while with her hand on the knob. She knew better than to yank too hard at the doorknob, because she'd seen set walls come tumbling right down that way. (And even if the wall doesn't come down exactly, a smaller but still illusion-destroying ripple can run across the canvas of the set, or a "house" can begin to shake because someone is pulling too hard on the door.)

"It's stuck, Uncle Charlie," Darleen said, and she tried not to let her lips move as she spoke, in case they would need to use these images.

"Stop cranking, Dan," said Uncle Charlie. He did a little cussing, and the piano stopped, too, partly because the dancers didn't need to be dancing, and partly because Joe was the nearest scenery man and was hopping over to fiddle with the door handle.

"Got it!" said a voice from the other side of the door, which was a large one, and Joe popped a smiling head around the edge of the door, just to show that it really, truly worked.

"All right, then," said Uncle Charlie. "We'll patch this up afterward with a little hand-on-doorknob shot. Let's get ourselves into that foolish room now. Count of three . . . two . . . one — and crank away, Dan!"

Darleen pulled the door open, peeked inside (a couple of crew members were waiting there, out of the camera's sight), pretended to see something that caught her interest, and slipped in through the opening, closing the door behind her.

"Stop, Dan," said Uncle Charlie. "Well done, Darleen! All right, now we're going to try something ambitious here, at Dan's request. Stand aside, people, if you don't want to risk death by scenery."

The scenery people were shifting things around at the

front of the set. A whole new set was rolled over in front of the first set, and Uncle Dan's camera on its little square perch moved back to make some room. The idea was that beyond the door Darleen had just come through (in actual fact, this was an entirely different door, somewhat larger than the first one), the camera would catch a glimpse of extras dancing.

"Something fancy for Episode Nine!" said Uncle Charlie with pride. "We are pulling out *all* the stops this week here at Matchless!"

Darleen's job now was to slip behind a curtain and peer out.

At the desk on this set was none other than Mr. Williams, of course, who played Darleen's Royal Father in the serial. He had been missing from Matchless for the last few weeks while supposedly he was imprisoned by the Salamanders. (Mr. Williams, the actor, had in fact taken a break to go to see his ailing mother in Delaware.)

"Hello, my dear Darleen!" he said. "Ready for our happy reunion? Only I'm afraid all the old biddies are going to be sobbing into their handkerchiefs because I won't recognize you at first, you know."

"They told me about that," said Darleen. She was very fond of good old Mr. Williams—they all were. "My Royal Papa has amnesia from being hit on the head."

"Indeed I do! Sorry, Charlie, just having a nice warm

bit of conversation with my darling princess daughter, Miss Dahlia Louise, known to all the world as Daring Darleen."

Uncle Charlie was beginning to look like a volcano again.

"Are you two ready to join the rest of us?" he said. "Some of us have a photoplay to film. Time's a-ticking. Come *on.*"

Mr. Williams stroked his kingly beard and gave Darleen a wink, and then he turned back to the prop document on his desk, which a Salamander, his face hidden behind a mask, was spreading out for him to read.

"And we'll GO!" said Uncle Charlie. The bad waltz started up again. Uncle Dan cranked the film through his camera.

Darleen slipped through the doorway and behind the curtain that was so conveniently draped right to one side of the door.

Uncle Charlie stopped the action and consulted with Uncle Dan.

"Dancers in the background are looking pretty good!" said Uncle Charlie. "We'll just pause to move the camera in a bit now."

That was done so that Mr. Williams (the poor exiled king of St. Benoix) and the wicked Salamander could be the focus of the next shots in that scene.

Mr. Williams was an old hand in the Legitimate Theater (which was what he called the kind of acting done on fancy stages in front of rich people in furs), and liked to speak his lines out loud, so once the camera started cranking again, he and the man playing the wicked Salamander (not the head of the Salamanders, fortunately, which meant not Jasper Lukes—*and thank goodness for that,* thought Darleen from her hiding place behind the curtain) got into a fairly entertaining discussion.

"This is the will and testament I'm supposed to bring to you, mister, so you can sign it all pretty and fast," said the Salamander, hamming it up. He had *not* come in from the Legitimate Theater. There was not a hint of Shakespeare to be heard in his twang. Of course, it didn't matter much that his phrasing was rough and tumble, because only the occasional lip-reader in the future audience would have any idea of the words he had actually spoken when the camera was filming. Most people would see the simple title card ("SIGN NOW, OR SUFFER THE WORST!") and fill in any gaps in the conversation themselves.

"Oh, can it be that I asked you to bring me this document, good man?" said the poor exiled King (oh, his gorgeous vowels! not to mention his consonants! But even the future lip-readers would never know how beautiful his diction was). “But I don’t remember any of this. A will? Why, I don’t even remember . . . my own name!”

“Never mind, never mind, mister,” said the Salamander. “See, we’ve written it all up for you nice and tidy. You don’t have to be able to remember anything. Not to worry. Just sign it here like a good fellow.”

“I’m so sorry to be causing such trouble,” said the poor exiled King, and Mr. Williams made a show of looking at the paper, rubbing his eyes, and putting his hands to his heart, to express his confusion and emotion.

“Not at all,” said the Salamander. “Here’s a lovely quill pen. If you’ll just add your John Hancock to this piece of paper, we’ll be all done.”

More emotion from the exiled, amnesiac King.

“Please, good sir,” said the King. “Give me a moment alone. I get nervous when you hover that way. And I must say that *horrible* waltz is going to *drive* me out of my *mind*! Wish you had a good fiddler out there instead.”

(Sometimes even Mr. Williams liked to ham things up a bit on set. He could even say one thing with his face while saying something entirely different with his voice. Mr. Williams also preferred to have a nice bit of violin playing along, to warm up the emotions of a scene. But there was no violin today.)

“Five minutes,” said the Salamander. “And there’d

better be a signature on this form by the time I get back — or else!"

"Excellent! Good!" called Uncle Charlie from the front of the scene. "Bad guy leaves, *closing the door behind him*. That's the way! HANK, YOU CAN QUIT THE OOM-PAH-PAH NOW!"

The horrible piano playing stopped with a bit of a bang on the keys, and Darleen could hear the extras being moved off the set behind the thin wall. No more dancing was needed now that the door was closed.

"Right, now Darleen!" said Uncle Charlie. "Creep out from behind those curtains and come up quietly, quietly, to Mr. Williams, your Royal Father! And you've been oh, so worried about him!"

Darleen's heart gave a twist in her chest; she couldn't help thinking of her own dear, bashed-up, real Papa, recovering as best he could in Aunt Shirley's armchair.

"Not *too* slowly, now, my girl!" said Uncle Charlie. "This is an adventure picture we're making, not a weepie."

But it was too late: Darleen was actually weeping. Actual tears were actually dripping down her cheeks. For the second time in less than twenty-four hours! And when Mr. Williams turned to look up at her, astonishment lit up his face.

"But, my heavens, what's wrong, dear girl?" he said, quite naturally.

"Papa," said Darleen. And in that moment, everything that mattered in the universe was held in that one little word. A hush fell over the set and began to spread, rippling out across the studio.

"Are you looking for your father, my dear?" said Mr. Williams, who at this moment was entirely the King in Exile of St. Benoix, and also the brave, often-imprisoned father of Crown Princess Dahlia Louise. "But tell me, pray, how do you think *I* can help you? What is your name, my girl?"

Darleen jumped a little and put her hands to her face for a moment (which was, fortunately, pretty much exactly what she was supposed to do), and then she was back on track again, enjoying this juiciest part of the scene, where she got to beg, beg, beg her Royal Papa to remember her, and to say things like, "I'm your own little Dahlia Louise! Don't you remember me? Oh, what will we do now?" and so on.

It was a great scene! At the end, the Salamander came back (Darleen hid behind those convenient curtains again), and when he saw that the poor, amnesiac King had not yet signed the new will (having been distracted by the girl he did not recognize as his daughter, the one now hiding again behind the curtains), that bad Salamander struck the poor fellow over the head with a conveniently placed statue (made actually of some very lightweight stuff, like an egg-white meringue, so Mr. Williams would not be damaged), and *that blow,* by the way and of course, made all of the King's memories return! (It always worked that way in an adventure film.) You could see Mr. Williams, the King, saying, "Dahlia! Dahlia Louise!" as he was dragged out the door.

"Well done, well done!" said Uncle Charlie, while Uncle Dan repositioned his camera. "One more bit now. Darleen: grab that will from the desk and climb out the window. Don't worry, it's stronger than the roof was this morning, or so say the carpenters."

There was some laughter here and there from those who had been around earlier in the day for Darleen's fall from the rope.

Darleen kept her scowl hidden inside. She went to the desk, picked up the will, and leaped right through that window as if it were an insignificant hurdle.

The extras cheered!

"And that's it for today," said Uncle Charlie. "Well, except for a few doorknob shots. Excellent work all around, and tomorrow we venture abroad: trains and balloons, out in the world. Get yourselves ready for that."

The technical crew huddled to figure out what needed to be transported for the next day's shooting. Uncle Charlie and Uncle Dan slapped each other and Mr. Williams on the back. Most of the extras wandered away.

Except for one *extra* extra, who was smiling from ear to ear at Darleen.

"Do you know, Miss Darling, this has been the most extraordinary day of my life!" said 'Bella Mae.'

"More extraordinary than the Alps?" said Darleen.

"I'm not sure whether Bella Mae would admit to having been to the Alps," said Victorine, looking around briefly to see if anyone was within earshot. Fortunately, nobody seemed to be. "Pardon me, but may I see that paper in your hand?"

It was the will. Darleen handed it over, and Victorine eyed it carefully, turning it over and over in her hands as if it were telling her some sort of secret.

"I have to go back to Aunt Shirley's now," said Darleen. "I'll be back later with some more food and things. Are you going to be all right?"

"Absolutely fine," said Victorine. "Perhaps better than fine. Oh, Darleen, I think I have the beginnings of what *may* prove to be a truly excellent idea — no, no, I won't say a single word more about it, not yet. I'm thinking it all through!"

Chapter 17

The Wishes of a Grandmama

Darleen checked in with her father (who was sitting up and looking much more like himself, though Aunt Shirley said she was keeping him out of circulation for one more day), and when she told him about the little trouble with the roof, it was like a balm for her spirit to be laughing about studio adventures again with her own dear Papa. Then she stayed for some supper and made off with some thick ham sandwiches for Victorine. She wasn't going to sleep in her own comfortable bed at home and leave poor Victorine camping out alone at Matchless Photoplay. And when she got back to her dressing room at the studio, she found that Victorine had been at work, making improvements. She had borrowed a rug from somewhere, and their nest in the corner was at least half again as soft and cozy as it had been.

And Victorine appreciated the sandwiches! In fact, she was quite radiant about them — but, as it turned out, not only about the sandwiches.

"Dearest Darleen," she said, very earnestly. "I don't think any kidnapping in the history of kidnappings ever led to as lovely an adventure as I've been having. I meant what I said earlier: this has been one of the grandest days I can ever remember! I realize now how small my world has become since the death of my poor Grandmama."

Dar squeezed Victorine's hand in sympathy and showed her the newspaper that had been waiting all day on the shelf here, along with the savory biscuits it had been used to wrap up. The biscuits were no longer as fresh as they had once been, but they tasted pretty fine all the same.

"See this, Victorine? Your cousins are already saying you've drowned. They showed the police a pair of soggy shoes!"

"So they wish!" said Victorine, looking like someone who would, in fact, be very hard to drown. "All those Brownstones care about is my Grandmama's fortune, and not the fate of my Grandmama's granddaughter, by whom I mean, you know, *me*. I wonder how long we have before everyone begins to believe their awful lies."

Darleen felt a great wave of indignant sympathy rise up in her heart.

"Honestly, Victorine, you were practically kidnapped already, the way your relatives were treating you."

Victorine clapped her hands together.

"Exactly," she said. "And that has made me think most seriously about what my Grandmama said to me when she grew so very sick and it became clear that she . . . that she . . . wouldn't be able to stay with me much longer, you know. It was the scene you were acting in today, Darleen, that made me think of it. Because, you know what? She was dictating to me the latest version of her last will and testament, and I was writing it down for her, all very neatly. She insisted *I* do it, not her. She wanted it in my handwriting, you see. She even had me sign her name for her. She was very firm about it."

"But isn't that strange?" asked Darleen. "I mean, that's not usual, is it, for wills?"

"What you must understand about my Grandmama," said Victorine, leaning forward as if she were sharing a great secret, "is that she was *exceedingly* intelligent and *brilliantly* eccentric, both at once. I don't think I'll ever know anyone quite like her. And she loved me to a wonderful degree."

"Of course she did!" said Darleen out of sheerest sympathy. "I mean, you're intelligent and eccentric, too, aren't you?"

And then Dar blushed, because it did *perhaps* seem a forward thing to say. But Victorine didn't look irritated at all. She seemed, in fact, pleased.

"She was hoping for the best — hoping that Mr. Ridge, her lawyer, would prove a forceful advocate on my behalf, and hoping that whatever persons he deemed most suitable to help raise me would turn out to be kind. But she couldn't help but realize that these hopes might be . . . unrealistic. And she worried about that quite a bit. Do you know what she said to me as I was writing out her will?"

"No," said Darleen, feeling almost as if she were watching a melodrama unfold on the stage or screen. "Tell me, please do. What did she say?"

"She said, 'Listen to me, Victorine. I do not trust any of them — I do not trust anyone in this great, wide world of ours — as much as I trust *you*.'"

"Oh!" said Darleen. "How sweet of her!"

"Not merely *sweet*," said Victorine. "She was trying to tell me something very important, I think now. I think it was a kind of hidden message, a sort of code."

"Really?" said Darleen. This story was sounding more and more like a photoplay.

"Really," said Victorine. "Because listen to what she said after that. She said that the problem with wills is that their writers are, naturally, absent from the scene when the wills go into action. 'And documents can be misused,' she said. She said she was doing her best to leave a will that would protect me from 'the greedy sharks already circling our little ship'—though, to be honest, she stopped at that moment and added, 'No, I'm misspeaking, of course. Our ship is not little. But it has felt small and cozy because you and I have shared it all these happy years. Our ship is large, and thus the sharks are many.'"

"Do you actually have a ship, Victorine?" asked Dar. She was beginning to get lost in the tangles of Victorine's story, or perhaps it was just the lateness of the hour that was making her eyelids flicker.

"No ship," said Victorine. "It's a figurative expression. And so are the sharks. The sharks are actually, for instance, my awful cousins, who care not a fig for me but are after the Berryman fortune."

Darleen made herself sit up a little so as to pay attention properly.

"They *are* sharks," she said. "Horrible, kidnapping sorts of sharks. But we won't let them have you."

"Thank you, Darleen," said Victorine. "Your courage has already saved my life several times over."

(That, thought Darleen, really was an exaggeration.)

"And I have grown more determined to be bold, as bold — as *daring* — as you are!"

(Goodness! More exaggeration!)

"I'm sure you're actually very daring already," said Darleen. "And anyway, I don't understand what being daring has to do with your grandmother's will."

"But that's the thing, exactly: Grandmama trusted me to be daring enough to take care of myself," said Victorine. "Grandmama said as much at one point, though I didn't understand her properly at the time. She said, 'I'm trying my best to make this a will that will protect you, but if it fails to do so — or if, heaven forbid, it becomes a cage — then I count on you, Victorine, to do *whatever is necessary* to make it better.' She said that, Darleen."

Darleen eyed the cracks and swirls in the boards of the dressing room wall. She was thinking about how complicated life was — how complicated even a single tree was when you turned it into planks and saw all of its secret inner patterns. But the thing was, you couldn't change the pattern on a board once it was part of a wall. You couldn't make it, for instance, *better.*

"But, Victorine," she said. "How can you do that? How can you make the will better? Oh!"

A big thought had suddenly come into Darleen's head.

"Like the photoplay, you said," she whispered. "They had rewritten the will in the photoplay. Are you saying —"

"Yes, Darleen. My Grandmama had me write out *her* will in *my* own hand," said Victorine. "And I think I finally understand why."

Darleen couldn't help herself; for a moment she sounded just like her own Papa.

"But that would be against the law. That would be forgery, and forgery is not just against the law, it's — it's —"

"It's a kind of *lie,* you mean to say," said Victorine. "I know."

Darleen blinked in surprise, but Victorine's truth-telling eyes looked as clear as they had always been.

"I have been thinking about this so very seriously, Darleen," said Victorine. "About why my Grandmama might want me to break my promise to tell only the plain truth — or worse, to do something against the law. And I think, you know, she loved me very much."

"Well, of course she did!" said Darleen.

"And the foremost thing in her mind when she was having me write out her will must have been my welfare — then and in the future," said Victorine. "So sheerly out of respect for my Grandmama, it does seem to me I have to take her wishes seriously. Despite everything! Because perhaps sometimes, Darleen, the wishes — the *will* — of a Grandmama must rise above any law."

Chapter 18
Time's Arrow Turned Around

The next day, Darleen went bumpity-bouncing off in the Matchless Photoplay motorcar to the next little town of Leonia, because there were no trains running through Fort Lee proper, and for Episode Nine, they needed a train.

"I'll be gone all day," she had said to Victorine very early that morning when they were sneaking across the dark street back to Darleen's empty house. They had decided that since Darleen's Papa would be at Aunt Shirley's for another day, there was no reason Victorine couldn't spend the day in an actual house, where she could work on improving her Grandmama's will without a hundred studio people looking over her shoulder or telling her to get out of the way.

She would have to keep her eyes peeled for human spiders, of course. But Victorine was not particularly frightened of any kind of spiders.

"I'll be so hard at work," she said, "I won't be worrying myself. My ears will keep watch while my brain and hands happily labor along. I will be the juvenile equivalent of a hermit in his alpine cave."

There was coal in the hob. And some not-too-perishable food items in the pantry. It wouldn't be luxury living, but it would be fine for a juvenile hermit. Victorine seemed well contented.

Worrying a little about Victorine's plans meant that Dar didn't notice the cat-that-swallowed-a-canary look on her Uncle Dan's face until they were unloading equipment at the train track cutoff in Leonia.

"Why is Uncle Dan grinning that way?" she asked Uncle Charlie, since, when a cameraman is thrilled about the challenges of a shoot coming up, it is often the case that the actors involved should be a bit worried. "There's no scary cliff here, is there?"

"Don't you worry about a thing, dear Niece," said Uncle Charlie, with almost as disturbing a grin as Uncle Dan's. "Just an air balloon landing on the tracks in front of a speeding express train. Nothing to trouble yourself about."

Not so comforting, really.

They strolled over the gravel to the track. Connections that Uncle Charlie and Aunt Shirley had carefully cultivated at the Leonia railroad depot sometimes let them use this old engine on a side track when Matchless needed a train. Any photoplay studio is going to need a train on occasion!

The train was sitting there on the tracks right now, looking huge and quiet and harmless, like a resting whale. Darleen tried to figure out what the plan was going to be.

There was a tall bridge over the track here, and to it the properties men had connected a big basket, the large sort of basket that might dangle from a fairground balloon.

"We borrowed it from the amusement park," said one fellow when he noticed a puzzled-looking Darleen staring at it. "We're going back there this afternoon to film the actual balloon, so they were all right with our borrowing this basket."

The basket was now resting right on the tracks, but you could see from the ropes and pulleys and so on that the men up on the bridge would be able to raise or lower the basket at will.

All of this was being set up right in front of the great iron nose of the train engine.

"Who's in the basket with me?" said Darleen.

"Nobody," said Uncle Charlie.

"What do you mean, 'nobody'? Who brought the balloon to rescue me from the Salamanders' attic, then?"

"Um, nobody," said Uncle Charlie. "Don't waste time with details now, Darleen. We couldn't agree about how to handle the balloon, so we decided it just picked you up, you know, by chance. Maybe the previous aeronaut fell out? Or it got unmoored and made a run for it or something? So anyway, you'll climb into the nice balloon basket, and there won't be anyone there, and you'll be a little surprised, but because you're Daring Darleen, you'll decide you need to stop the train and get on it. Because — oh, let's see if I can keep all this straight — the train's going to the mansion. Where the party is. Where they're trying to make your Royal Father sign a new will."

"You mean what we did yesterday."

"Right, right, right. Now, let's start with you climbing up onto the train and explaining to the nice engineers that you need a ride. Big gestures should do the trick."

It's not as easy to swing yourself up onto the engine of a train with grace, but after a few tries, Darleen got herself up to the car, where Mr. Jones, an actual train engineer they borrowed whenever they borrowed the engine, gave her a big grin.

"Nice to see you again, Miss Darleen. Your uncles have something strange in mind today, I see. Lowering you in a basket in front of my train, is that it?"

"You won't hit me, will you, Mr. Jones?" said Darleen, while hanging on to the side of the engine and making dramatic gestures.

"I'll try not to, my girl! Now I'm supposed to say, 'Come on in.'"

He was a very good sport, Mr. Jones. Darleen climbed into the engineer's cab with him, and they waited awhile, until Uncle Charlie shouted up that all had looked just fine.

"I'll be firing up my engines now," said Mr. Jones. "See you around, Miss Darleen!"

While Mr. Jones got the train ready to go, Darleen climbed into the basket that was going to dangle from its ropes as if there were an actual lighter-than-air balloon up above it and not three men on a bridge with ropes in their hands. Dar didn't yet see how this was going to work. She could see Uncle Dan readjusting the camera on its stand. In fact, it looked like he had just flipped the camera part of it right the way upside down.

What was he doing?

"Uncle Dan?" said Darleen.

"Pretty clever, huh?" said Uncle Dan, but Darleen wasn't sure yet what the clever part of the setup was supposed to be.

"All right, now, *listen,* Darleen!" said Uncle Charlie. "Some special requests for you. We're going to get you into a comfortable pose, and then your job is going to be not to move, because movement won't look good, says Dan. Why don't you grab the front of the basket with one hand and a rope with the other. Yes, like that."

"But why can't I move?" said Darleen.

"Because, see, we're doing this scene backward. When I give the signal, Mr. Jones is going to start backing up the train, nice and slow, and our guys up on the bridge will pull you up in your fake-balloon basket, and Dan will be cranking this a little slowly so there will be more drama in the scene in the future. Am I right, Dan?"

"Mmm-hmm," agreed Dan, checking over his upside-down camera.

"I thought I was supposed to be *landing* the balloon in front of an *approaching* train, not taking off in front of a train that's backing up," said Darleen.

"My darling, daring D.," said Uncle Charlie, "I said we're doing it *backward.* When the film is developed, we'll flip this bit of upside-down film over, and it will be as though we magically filmed it with time's arrow pointing the other way around. You *will* be landing in front of a huge oncoming train then. Just you wait and see!"

"Is this something Uncle Dan thought up?" said Darleen, feeling a bit suspicious. It sounded too complicated for words.

"Yup," said Uncle Dan. "Together with Bill, whose brain is clearly getting back into fighting form. Clever, right?"

Oh! Her own Papa! Well, then, Darleen was going to make this thing work, even if it seemed harebrained.

Uncle Charlie shouted and signaled, and the guys up high who were handling the ropes of Darleen's basket began pulling it up into the air. Meanwhile, Mr. Jones's huge engine roared and hissed and began reversing along the tracks. Darleen tried to look natural while not moving around — which is harder than you might think. Up, up, up, the basket went, while the engine chugged backward, away, away, away.

"That's it!" said Uncle Charlie. "Stop filming, Dan!"

And he and Dan danced a bit of a jig right there by the tracks, they were both so pleased with whatever they had just managed to do.

"All right, then, time to get some actual balloon footage," said Uncle Charlie, post-jig. "Great big ball of gas on a nice safe tether. Ready for the amusement park, Darleen?"

The amusement park! Sweet treats and Ferris wheels and doughnuts! Darleen was *ready*!

Chapter 19

Up and Away

Who, after all, needed Coney Island when you had Palisades Park?

Darleen had never been to Coney Island. It was far, far away, on the other side of New York City entirely, with at least two stretches of water between here and there. But when she counted up the many attractions at Palisades Amusement Park, her heart went pitter pat and (as it were) kicked up its heels: Shows! The almost-brand-new saltwater pool! The carousel! The roller coaster! And, apparently, a friendly purveyor of lighter-than-air balloon rides with whom the local movie studios had an ongoing friendly relationship (because every adventure picture worth its salt needed at least one scene in an air balloon. Who could argue with that?).

So Mr. Mancini, keeper of the balloon, met the crew on the lovely expanse of lawn in front of the dance pavilion and shook everybody's hands with the good cheer of a longtime business partner.

"What's on the docket today, Mr. Charlie?"

"We'll want a nice shot taken on the lawn so we can get the sky behind Darleen as she scrambles into the basket. And what else would you like, Dan?"

Uncle Dan looked up from his camera, which was back in its right-side-up position.

"Hot dog, please," he said. "Lots of mustard."

That made Mr. Mancini laugh as loudly and roundly as you would think a balloon keeper should laugh. (Then he sent his nearly-grown-up son running to get some hot dogs from the stand in the park.)

"And some shots of the balloon in the air, using the thin tether, all right? So it won't show."

"You got it," said Mr. Mancini. He knew all about these photoplay people: they wanted a balloon, but a tame balloon. So did amusement parks, for that matter! But the photoplay people didn't want the tameness to show, so they liked their anchor ropes thin and subtle, hard for the camera to see.

First, Darleen's uncles had her clamber into the basket, which was really unpleasant, to be honest, especially since the uncles remembered at the last second that Darleen's legs had been tied together in the attic shots the day before. Mr. Mancini had the balloon tethered solidly (the main rope disguised as the one Darleen was climbing up), but anyone who has ever climbed a rope and then over the rim of a swaying basket (all with bound feet) while the photoplay director is shouting, "A LITTLE MORE GRACEFUL, DARLEEN, PLEASE!" will understand that this particular scene was not Darleen's favorite of the day.

Uncle Dan was practically lying on the ground, his camera tilted up and at an angle so that it would look like all there was in the world was Darleen, a rope, a swinging basket, and the balloon above. All up in the air!

"All right!" said Uncle Charlie. "Look back down at — Where are you coming from again?"

"Attic," said Uncle Dan.

"Ha-ha, right," said Uncle Charlie. "The attic with the broken roof, eh, Darleen?"

Using every drop of her actorly self-control and skill, Darleen turned the scowl that was rising up in her into the furrowed brow of someone who has just clambered into a balloon basket and been surprised to find no one there. Then she made a show of looking at all the ropes and pieces, without actually doing anything that might cause trouble, of course.

"Now you sit tight, Darleen," said Uncle Charlie, "while we get the next scene set up."

Actually—and this was just a bit galling—Uncle Charlie and Uncle Dan, not to mention most of the film crew, were taking a cheerful pause to wolf down Palisades hot dogs while Mr. Mancini started working with the tether ropes. He would take off the big, too-visible ropes (or let them dangle if they were short enough), and they would be down to the one thin tether. Darleen took advantage of the pause to wriggle her feet free from the ropes, now that her feet were safely out of the picture.

"We won't let you go too far, not to worry, miss!" said Mr. Mancini. (Dar wasn't much worried about the balloon—she was mostly just wishing she had a hot dog too.) "Maybe twenty feet in the air, just enough to make the nice picture with the sky and all, and then we'll haul you right back down."

"Places, people!" said Uncle Charlie, licking his mustardy lips. "Dan, are you set?"

"Yep," said Uncle Dan.

"All right, then! Have a nice ride, Darleen! Up, up, and away! Let 'er go, Mr. Mancini, if you please!"

And the balloon bobbed up into the air, suddenly

enough that Darleen had to hang on to the sides of the basket quite tightly. It was a strange thing to be up twenty or thirty feet above the ground, looking out over the sparse crowds in Palisades Amusement Park. (It was still early in the afternoon on a Tuesday, after all.) Below her was Uncle Charlie with his megaphone, shouting, "DON'T LOOK BACK AT US!" to Darleen as if she were an absolute beginner.

And over there to the left — Wait! What was that?

Her attention had been caught by two men with their overcoat collars turned up and their hats pulled down. They wouldn't have attracted Dar's attention at all, except that they were moving rather . . . The only way to put it was *guiltily.* They moved like people not wanting to be noticed, and there's nothing more noticeable than someone slinking around trying not to be noticed.

Darleen made a show of looking out over the land, shading her eyes. That was all for the camera. And then she stole another glimpse. One of the skulkers was pointing up at her now, while the other one skulked yet more skulkily. And, oh, my goodness! The one pointing at her was that horrible man! The kidnapper who had driven that motorcar!

She almost shouted and pointed herself, but then she remembered that she mustn't do anything that might possibly alert the police to the whereabouts of Victorine, and she resisted the urge, although she felt a cold sweat break out on the backs of her arms.

And then there was a second very bad thing: the other man was Jasper Lukes. No wonder he was trying to be invisible! Anyone on the film crew would recognize him in a second if they got a good look. But all eyes were turned upward just at the moment. Darleen's eyes were the only ones glancing down at the ground — intermittently, of course, so as not to ruin the picture.

Second glimpse: the men seemed to be arguing about something but trying to do it quietly.

Third glimpse: the kidnapper had something shiny in his hands. Could it be . . . ? A knife! And he was slithering over toward Mr. Mancini. Darleen couldn't help it now.

She shouted, "Oh, be careful!"

"Looking good!" cried Uncle Charlie, who thought everyone was still acting.

Darleen looked over the edge of the basket, almost straight down now, where the kidnapper was only a couple of feet away from the thin tether, tied to a nice solid loop hammered into the ground.

"Oh, help, *no*!" she said. But too late! The balloon lurched upward, flinging her back against the other side of the basket.

"HEY!" they all shouted down below — Mr. Mancini,

Uncle Charlie, and Uncle Dan, who was still, Darleen saw, cranking away (because a true cameraman isn't stopped by mere disaster).

She saw the kidnapper running away with nobody going after him, but she couldn't see Jasper Lukes anywhere — rot his hide! Nobody on the ground would have caught the slightest glimpse of the kidnapper and his knife, because nobody had been looking anywhere but up.

Some of the younger crew started chasing after the cut tether, even jumping up into the air, trying to get it, but the balloon was so thrilled to be free that it was rising up, up, up, into the air.

"Oh, my," said Darleen. She was already so high that the whole of the park was spread against the horizon now, and there, to the right . . .

(Her heart, which was pounding hard, did a bit of a flip in her chest.)

There to the right — that is to say, to the east — was the Hudson River.

"Oh, no, oh, no!" cried Darleen. She was high enough now that it didn't matter what she did with her hands or her face or anything, because the camera couldn't catch it.

Way, way below her, and now somewhat to the north, she could see knots of ordinary people at the amusement park looking up and waving at her. *They must think I'm an aeronaut and this is all a show,* Darleen thought in alarm.

For a moment she looked in a panic at everything in that balloon's basket and wondered what could possibly be done with any of it. She had never been carried off by a balloon before, and it is hard to make a quick study of aeronautics when your heart is galloping so very hard, and a wild joy is waking up inside you. Her shocked eyes took stock of everything: the slats of the basket; the silk billowing in a huge cloud above her; a mechanical thing — a valve of some kind governing the pinch point of the silk, not far above her head. There were also a few sandbags hanging from the sides of the basket, but Darleen knew enough about gravity to understand that dumping a sandbag overboard would make the balloon rise higher, not descend.

The thing is, balloons aren't very biddable. They have independent spirits and more or less do what they want.

For now, thank goodness, the breeze that had picked up her balloon seemed to be headed gently inland, not out over the Hudson River, or — horrors! — past the Hudson toward the dangerously busy streets of Manhattan. But if the balloon kept sailing up and up, there was no telling where she might find herself!

If she twisted that mysterious valve, what would happen? Would the balloon be discouraged from rising? And how much of a twist would it take? She wasn't sure. The dancing balloon bobbled her about terribly, but somehow she managed to reach up and force the valve a bit to the left, hoping she had guessed the right amount of turning necessary and would now neither fly out to sea nor plummet to the ground like a stone.

And then she hung on to the sides of the basket and let herself gaze freely in all directions, willing her mind to remember these images forever. After all, she might never again see the world from such a colossal height! It was a thrill, a true thrill, and the feeling she kept bottled up inside her came out dancing. Everything was so tiny down there below her: toy motorcars rumbled slowly along thin threads of roads, and toy boats steamed back and forth across the Hudson. And over there, the buildings of Fort Lee and the various photoplay studios looked like dollhouses, some of them with those astonishing glass walls twinkling in the sun. It was all beautiful seen from this height.

That was when she noticed that the houses were growing somewhat larger.

The balloon was not meant for long voyages. And she herself had turned that valve. She reached for it again now, and — *Oh, no!* It refused to budge.

Everything began to happen too fast, which is the way accidents and disasters like to work. As the gas in the balloon escaped, the whole contraption began to sag, down, down toward the earth. For a moment, Darleen let herself feel that sharp (but wicked) pang of regret; it was so lovely being up in the sky! And then she focused on the more pressing issue, which seemed like it might be quite a challenge:

Getting back to the ground in — *oh, please, oh, please* — one unbroken piece.

Chapter 20

Snake-Charmer Falls from Sky

The balloon was swaying back and forth now as it drifted lower across Fort Lee. Darleen could see an open field ahead. Oh, but would she make it that far? Now that the balloon had decided it was coming down, it seemed very determined to get the job done fast.

She did not want to bang into any roofs! So she unhooked one of the smaller sandbags and threw it down, then another. The balloon gained a little height, so she was encouraged. One more sandbag over and away, and then she was safely past the roofs and drifting across the field, where, if the balloon didn't veer toward those houses on the right, there was nothing much to do her harm but the ground itself—and a surprised-looking horse being held back from bolting by the elegant woman on its back.

"Hold on!" shouted the woman to Darleen as the balloon angled itself toward the ground. Darleen was holding on to ropes, to the basket, to anything she could grasp. She braced herself, hoped for the best, and shut her eyes.

Bump! Bump! And then came a trailing series of little bounces as the balloon in its last gasp dragged its basket some way across the field.

Darleen stretched her limbs, opened her eyes, and fought to catch her breath. She was surprised to discover that, apart from an aching howl from her thigh, which had apparently made very rough contact with the top of the basket, her body seemed to be in one piece and only slightly battered.

The balloon, however, had lost any hint of its former rotund glory. It had become a flattened blob stretched out across the grass, like a jellyfish washed up on the Jersey shore.

The basket lay toppled onto its side. Darleen took another breath and crawled out into the solid, earthbound world that was where her feet (she told herself firmly) belonged. Oh, but her head was still spinning from its ride through that wide, wild, wonderful air!

The lady on horseback was already slipping off her

horse as gracefully as any circus rider (or, for that matter, as gracefully as any exiled princess).

"*Mais alors!*" the woman said, her face full of concern and surprise and even a hint of laughter.

Darleen's eyes snapped into focus, and now it was her turn to be surprised, because this person was indeed the very same elegant French-speaking woman she and Victorine had encountered on the ferry, the one who had been carrying a picnic basket full of Snake. "But it is one of my little snake charmers, fallen now from the sky! My dear girl, whatever has happened to you that you are crashing to earth in a balloon practically in my own front yard? Yes, I live over here, in this house here. Oh, do let me take your elbow, if you don't mind."

In fact, it was quite necessary, just for that moment. It turns out that it is completely normal for one's body to have a moment of feeling quite weak and helpless when one has just plummeted from the sky in a deflating balloon.

"There now, there now," said the elegant woman soothingly. "Do you think you can make it to my door? A few steps more and we'll be nearly there, Miss Darling. Look, the curious onlookers are beginning to arrive!"

It was true: some people were walking toward the field now. They must have spotted the balloon falling from the sky and were curious to see it up close.

"Please, won't you be a very kind fellow," the woman said to the first man who arrived on the run, "and trot off to alert the people from Matchless studios. They'll be at Palisades Amusement Park right now if I'm not mistaken. Is that Mr. Mancini's balloon, dear? I think they will be worried about their lost aeronaut. Tell them I am dosing her with a restorative tea."

She had quite a lovely way of giving orders: firmly and kindly, both at the same time.

The young man swept his hat off and nodded.

"Yes, of course. Pleased to be of service, Madame Blaché," he said, and then he turned around and ran back the other way. Someone else was already taking care of the horse.

Darleen gave a start. The lights had just turned on in her head, all at once. In fact, her head was so ablaze with sudden insight that it might as well have been Coney Island, lit up by thousands of electric light bulbs, all spelling out a name: ALICE GUY BLACHÉ!

"Oh, my," said Darleen. "Of course! That's why you seemed so familiar back on the ferry. You're Madame Blaché! Oh, my goodness."

Madame Alice Guy Blaché, the French-born founder of the Solax Company, whose film studio was located not two hundred feet from Matchless Photoplay.

That is to say, the most famous and most powerful

woman in all of Fort Lee. And for that matter, maybe the most famous and most powerful woman in all of New Jersey. Certainly one of the most artistically gifted women anywhere. Why, she had made hundreds and hundreds of pictures, first in France, and now here!

"That is who I am, indeed," said Madame Blaché. "How convenient that we recognize each other. Now can you climb the stairs up to the door?"

It was a lovely old house that Madame Blaché lived in, with a little porch that seemed practically octagonal, and windowed alcoves pushing forward and giving it an interestingly complicated air.

"You're so awfully kind," said Darleen as Madame Blaché guided her in through the doorway and beckoned to a maid. "I'm sorry to be causing so much trouble."

"Not a trouble, not at all!" said Madame Blaché. She settled Darleen into a lovely chair. "Poor girl, you are trembling. You will have a nice comforting cup of tea, and then you will tell me how this all happened. I am right to think it is the balloon from the Palisades that brought you here so unexpectedly? Mr. Mancini's balloon? But that is a great surprise to me. We have all worked with him before, and he has always seemed most helpful and dependable. But here his balloon seems to have galloped off with you! Have a sip of this tea, now, dear, won't you?"

The maid had brought in the pot of tea, and Madame Blaché poured a cup for Darleen and another for herself.

"There, now, is that a little better?" said Madame Blaché as Darleen took a sip of tea. "You are a brave girl! Though that was perhaps not your most elegant leap out there just now. Do you know" — her eyes were sharp and kind, both at once, as she leaned a little closer, over the teapot — "sometimes, in your pictures, when you jump so bravely from your railway bridges, and do a beautiful . . . how is it in English? In French we say *saut périlleux* — a perilous rolling in the air. Do you know what it is I mean?"

"A somersault?" said Darleen, feeling the warm tea spread through her veins already.

"That is it! *Exactement!*" said Madame Blaché with great satisfaction. "In any case, Miss Darling, when I see you in a glorious *somersault* or scaling the cliffs so beautifully, do you know what I think? I think, *This girl is a dancer at heart, like her mother* —"

Oh! It was not Darleen's fault that she dropped her teacup then, but of course she felt terrible about it, although Madame Blaché was so quick with the tea towel that almost no damage was done to the upholstery or carpet.

"There now, there now, I foolishly startled you," said Madame Blaché, handing her a second cup. "Let us try again with our tea, Miss Darling, and I will try to be less shocking."

"But you said . . . you said . . . *my mother*?" whispered Darleen.

"Yes, dear Miss Darling, I did say that," said Madame Blaché. "May I tell you a little story? I have been wanting to tell you this story ever since you girls charmed our naughty snake back into his basket on that ferry boat and I realized who you were. Have more sugar, brave girl. It is *most* helpful when one has suffered a shock."

She went ahead and popped another sugar cube into Darleen's slightly trembling cup of tea, and then she sat up quite straight and elegant again and said, "And so, my *histoire*! When I was very young and working as a secretary in a firm so as to support my poor, widowed mother—Oh, yes, I was a secretary! But already then, I worked very well with all the new machines. I was a typist-stenographer, you know, and I thought myself very *moderne*. And then one day, I went to an exhibition with my employer, and we saw some tall boxes with peepholes in them. 'These are the new kinetoscopes from America!' they said. 'In them is magic! Pictures that move!' And, Miss Darling, when I looked through the peephole into that great box, what do you think I saw?"

"Oh!" said Darleen, her heart too full with a sudden hope to say more than that.

"Yes, you have guessed it," said Madame Blaché. "I saw the tiniest, most beautiful dancer, so graceful with her wings and her flowing skirts. 'Loveliest Luna,' they called her, and I thought—"

"You saw my mother!" said Darleen, and Madame Blaché didn't seem to mind a smidge that she had been interrupted.

"Oh, brave girl, it is not just that I saw her!" she said. "It is that some creative ember, some spark, flared up in me when I saw her! I thought, *This new magic, these moving pictures—I want to use them to create beauty, to tell fairy tales, to make the world dance!* And so I did. More tea?"

Darleen blinked. Madame Blaché smiled very sweetly and lifted the teapot into the air.

"I cannot thank her, your mother, for showing me what a camera could do, but I can certainly serve you, her daughter, a grateful cup of tea!"

And then she looked out toward the field, where the blob that once was a balloon could still be seen, and laughed. "And shall I also pour a cup, perhaps, for your faithful young friend, the French-speaking girl who is incognita—and who is just now running so very quickly past my front window?"

Chapter 21

GIVE BACK THAT GIRL YUR HIDING

Oh, Vic—I mean, *Bella Mae*!" said Darleen, rising up from her chair. "Is she really here?"

"Does she have so many names, the anonymous one?" said Madame Blaché, and she added a few more words in French for the maid, who hurried to the front door.

In a moment, Victorine was in the parlor with them. In fact, she and Darleen had flung their arms around each other and for a while were very nearly sobbing with relief and surprise.

"When that balloon flew overhead," said Victorine, "and I looked up, and *there you were*! Of course, I understood they meant to film you today in a balloon, but an actual *crash*! An accident for real! How reckless these movie people are! Darleen, weren't you simply petrified? And to think that on the same day at your own home, there was — *Oh, madame, c'est vous!*"

Victorine had finally glanced in the direction of their elegant rescuer and hostess.

"How sorry I am! I didn't realize it was you, madame! Please, please, excuse my rudeness, do. I find I'm all in a dither."

Madame Blaché smiled with great benevolence.

"Of course you must be in a, as you say, 'dither,'" she said. "It is not every day one's friend falls out of the sky like the poor ancient Icarus."

And then, after the briefest pause, in which she poured yet another cup of tea and offered it to Victorine: "Tell me, Miss Bella Mae — as I believe Miss Darling called you — are you still hoping to remain incognita, dear girl? I, for one, would rather not be. I am Madame Blaché, as your friend has already learned."

"She founded Solax," said Darleen, a little worried that Victorine might not appreciate how illustrious a person Madame Alice Guy Blaché was. "That's another photoplay studio — not far from Matchless, you know. More or less around the corner. And her husband, Mr. Blaché — he runs a studio too. Two studios in one family!

But it's Madame Blaché who makes the *most* wonderful pictures!"

Madame Blaché made a dismissive gesture that said that even if her pictures were indeed made with considerable skill and dedication, they were not really the topic of conversation now.

"Since you mention Matchless, Miss Darling, I gather there was some trouble at Matchless the other day — an intruder, is that so? Oh, do not look so surprised, my girls. I keep always an ear, as you say here, to the ground, especially when there is talk of robbers and mayhem. Alas, Fort Lee! What is happening to our rustic little village?"

At that very moment, a child started crying in another room of that large house. Madame Blaché listened for a moment, gauging, as a parent will do, whether the crying would stop on its own or whether her presence was required. In the end, she stood up.

"Excuse me one moment, girls," she said. "Please make yourselves comfortable."

And as soon as she left the room, Victorine pulled her chair closer to Darleen.

"Oh, Darleen," she said. "I was about to tell you. The kidnapper, that bandit! He *came to your house*! Not with the Mr. Lukes who acts in your photoplays, not this time. All alone."

"What?" said Darleen. "What do you mean? The one

who drove the car? Do you mean he came in while you were there?"

"Yes, yes!" said Victorine. "That's the frightening part of it all. I was writing my Grandmama's will, you know, at the table in the kitchen, where the light comes in so naturally through the windows. All was peaceful. And then suddenly there was a crashing sound from the back-porch door! So I took my paper and pen and slipped right under the table — you know how low that cheerful tablecloth you have hangs down to the ground. I got under the table and tried to stay as still as any mouse, though, my goodness, I'm sure anyone listening with half an ear would have been able to hear my heart pounding away."

"You're all right, aren't you?" said Darleen. She was still feeling a little faint from the many shocks of that day. "You're here with me, Victorine, so you must be all right. You hid and stayed quiet? And there really was someone there?"

"Yes, indeed there was. His shoes walked across the kitchen floor. They were noisy, you know, and I saw them go by. Darleen, if he hadn't left the kitchen, I don't know — I'm afraid I might have simply screamed out loud and given myself away! That's how frightened I was. And then here's the horrible thing: he went upstairs, and he *shouted my name*. 'You, Victorine Berryman,' he shouted, with his ugly, ugly voice — and that's how I recognized him. 'Are you here? You'd better come out now if you don't want anyone else to get hurt!'"

"Oh, no!" said Dar. "Oh, how terrible! I guess they didn't believe me when I said I thought you had gone back to the city."

"And then he made an awful racket upstairs," said Victorine. "I think he was looking for something, opening drawers and closets and so on. I don't know whether he went away with anything. But he slapped something down on the table two inches above my head right before he left."

"You stayed hidden, though," said Darleen. "He didn't find you!"

She was so glad of that.

"He didn't find me at all, even though I was in fact directly under his nose. Those kidnappers are evil to the core, but I don't think they're very intelligent, to be honest. And so he banged out through the door again, and I waited under the table until I was sure, absolutely sure, that he had gone far away, and then I crept out — in relief, you can imagine! And I finished my work. But Darleen, here is the paper he left on your table."

She handed over the scrap of paper to Darleen.

On it was scrawled: YOU CANT MAKE FOOLS OF US GIVE BACK THAT GIRL YUR HIDING

SHES NOT YORES — WE WILL GO AFTER YORES NOW YOULL SEE

"His spelling isn't very good," said Victorine. "But of course we must overlook that. I have known many a person with poor spelling and poor grammar but who possessed a sharp brain and warm heart. Not that that is the case here. This man has no scruples and no sense. He is a brute."

"And then he came after me at the amusement park!" said Darleen. "He was with Jasper Lukes then. Why, I suppose it must have been Jasper Lukes who told him where our house was."

"That is possible, I'm afraid," said Victorine. "The more one learns about the depths of human nature, the more discouraging the whole enterprise becomes. Still, *most* people are good. *Most* don't kidnap children or hit people's fathers over the head."

"The gall of him!" said Darleen. "'SHES NOT YORES'! Talking about you as if you were a possession!"

"But of course that is exactly what I am to them," said Victorine. "A possible source of wealth, like the Black Sapphire in your photoplay. But anyway! Look what I have accomplished, bandit or no bandit!"

And she brought forward something that must have been in her hand when she came running, but that Darleen hadn't even noticed until now. It was a brownish-grayish rectangle that turned out to be ordinary kitchen wrap carefully folded around a thicker, whiter sheet, protected by sheets of blotting paper.

"My Grandmama's will," she said. "Improved and updated for the modern era."

And just as she pulled back the blotting paper to give Darleen a glimpse — it was a work of art in its own right, that will, with such beautiful old-fashioned handwriting that Darleen clasped her hands together in awe — just as the will appeared, Madame Blaché came smoothly sailing back into the room.

"But what have you there, my girls?" she asked.

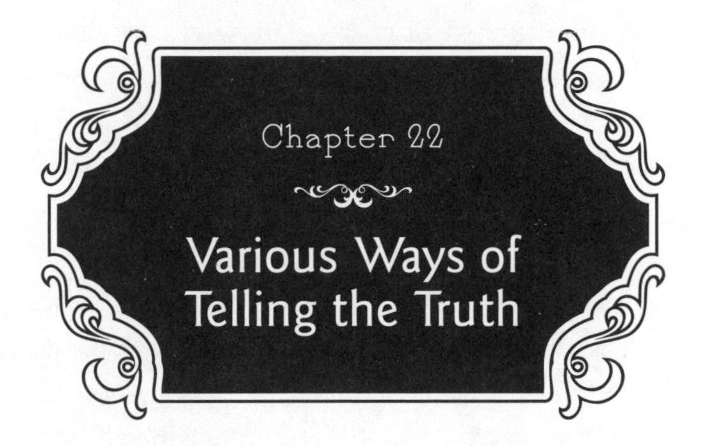

Chapter 22

Various Ways of Telling the Truth

Now, Darleen had had a trying day, with more than the ordinary number of bumps, shocks, and spills. And yet, in this moment of crisis, a brilliant idea came leaping into her mind. It seemed brilliant, at any rate, as it appeared, just as a pebble plucked from a stream looks opalescent and glorious before its coat of liquid evaporates into the air.

"Madame Blaché!" she said. "Please say you'll help us!"

"But what is the problem, dear child?" said Madame Blaché, and then she added, "Apart, of course, from the criminals who have undertaken such vicious attacks on

Matchless Photoplay — and there, I think, I am not the one who can help you."

"Well, you see," said Darleen (very conscious of having to make the words string themselves convincingly together as they spilled forth), "poor Bella Mae — Miss Goodwin here — is in awful danger. Because of *this*!"

And Darleen held up the paper that Victorine had just unwrapped.

"It's a very important document! It's a will, and not just any will, but the will of the late Mrs. Berryman. Have you heard of Mrs. Hugo Berryman? Of the Berryman fortune?"

"I do believe I have heard the name," said Madame Blaché.

"Well, she died, and some very wicked people have been trying to take advantage of her poor granddaughter, Victorine Berryman, which would have shocked her, I'm sure, because — in all the papers they always said it — Mrs. Berryman loved her granddaughter, Victorine, more than all the world. And would have wanted her protected from wicked people."

Darleen took a deep breath to fuel her last run of words, and Madame Blaché leaned forward.

"I'm sure you must be right in these things you say," said Madame Blaché. "But how do you know so much about Madame Berryman?"

Oh, dear! Darleen could only press gamely forward, hoping something would come to her in her moment of need, like a handhold on a rocky cliff.

"Because . . ." she said. (No handholds anywhere; no rescuing ropes.) "Umm . . . because . . ."

"Because, madame," said Victorine, and Darleen realized only too late that that tremor in Victorine's voice meant that *the truth* was bubbling up in her. Indeed, the truth was already spilling right out into the air. "Mrs. Berryman was my own dear Grandmama."

"Aha!" said Madame Blaché. "So are we to presume, Miss Bella Mae Goodwin, that you are some sort of *cousine* of that poor Miss Berryman, so sadly missing?"

"Oh, a cousin!" said Darleen. What a clever idea *that* was!

But Victorine shook her head. The truth-telling habit was clearly flaring up strong in her right now, and Victorine on fire with the truth was harder to navigate than an escaped balloon: no emergency valves anywhere.

"No, no, madame," Victorine said now. "I use Bella Mae Goodwin as my stage name, although all those names are actually my own—Bella Mae, you know, and Goodwin. But Victorine Berryman is what I am generally called. That's who I am: Victorine Berryman."

Darleen felt a very strong urge to hide her face in her

hands, but she did not. Victorine and the inconvenient truth! *Now* what would happen?

What happened was that Madame Blaché inclined her head politely.

"Mademoiselle Victorine Berryman," she said. "I'm so pleased to make your acquaintance finally."

"But you mustn't tell anyone who she is!" said Darleen. "She's in terrible danger."

"Really?" said Madame Blaché.

"Oh, yes," said Darleen. "There are kidnappers after her! Awful kidnappers, the kind that throw people into the river to drown when they don't get the money they want. And meanwhile, those Brownstones who are her very distant cousins seem to be wicked people, too, so greedy they won't even pay any ransom, and it's pretty likely all of these people would do anything — *anything!* — to prevent this will from falling into the proper hands!"

"Darleen! My goodness!" said Victorine under her breath. "You make it all sound so dramatic!"

"But it's all true as true," said Darleen. Victorine had to admit that it was.

"Ah! And which hands would those be?" asked Madame Blaché. "The proper hands, I mean, for this will that you have brought me."

"The hands of Mr. Ridge, the attorney. He was Mrs. Berryman's adviser, though she did think him . . . um . . ."

"Somewhat unreliable, unfortunately," said Victorine. "And rather weak."

"But if the will itself told him the right thing to do —" said Darleen.

"He would probably do it," said Victorine.

"But since we don't know whether he's *entirely* to be trusted, it seems reckless to march into his office and put the will — and dear Victorine — into his unreliable hands, doesn't it?" Darleen folded her own hands beseechingly. "It would be so much better, so much surer, if we marched in with someone he cannot bully or ignore. Someone like you, Madame Blaché!"

There was a long pause while Madame Blaché's face tried to make up its mind what sort of expression it wanted to adopt: horrified or skeptical, or perhaps something else entirely.

"My children," she said finally. "Explain to me: Where did you come across this will? And how do you know that it is truly the work of the late Mrs. Hugo Berryman? And that is but one problem with this fantastical scheme of yours."

"Don't people keep their wills in their houses sometimes?" said Darleen. "Don't they probably put them in drawers near their beds when they are very ill? And Victorine was living in her Grandmama's house right up until she was kidnapped, you know, so —"

"*Darleen!*" said Victorine. "Never mind all of that, Madame Blaché. What I *can* say is that this will is in precisely the same hand as the original. The handwriting will prove that the same person wrote them both."

"How remarkable," said Madame Blaché.

"Well, the main point is that that's *true*," said Darleen out of sheer loyalty to Victorine. "It *is* in the same hand as the original will. And the spirit of it is true as true. Mrs. Berryman would have been so upset to think that some distant relatives with wicked intentions would be trying to misuse her own poor Victorine."

"Aha," said Madame Blaché. "But there is one additional difficulty here, my dear girls. According to the morning's newspaper, you, Miss Victorine Berryman are, *hélas,* almost certainly no more. They fear the kidnappers may have drowned you in the Hudson River! How does that change your story, dear brave girls?"

"Not at all, since the truth is that here I am," said Victorine, standing very tall. "And I'm not drowned yet, thanks to our dear Darleen. She rescued me from those awful kidnappers. Why, she had us climb down the side of a building! I mean, technically speaking, over to a fire escape, and *then* down."

"*Brava!*" said Madame Blaché to Darleen. Then she took Victorine's hand. "You have been in danger, it seems. But do you truly think that getting this will you have found into the hands of your grandmother's lawyer will help?"

"I hope so," said Victorine.

"And you will be able to provide this lawyer, this Mr. Ridge, with some formal proof, dear girl, that you are in fact the Miss Berryman in question? I understand that the lawyers here in America are very enthusiastic about proofs and evidences."

"Oh, I have a great deal of proof, of course!" said Victorine, and then Darleen could see her face falling just a bit as she no doubt remembered that she had recently been kidnapped and actually had nothing but a pocket knife to tell the world who she was. "That is to say, I know where I can find it — proof that I am who I am."

"Excellent," said Madame Blaché. "Then let me take this will and think things over."

Darleen must have twitched a little, because Madame Blaché looked right at her with sparks of laughter in her eyes.

"Oh, you can trust me! But listen, I will take a photograph, and then we will have a lovely facsimile as a kind of insurance, and you can keep the original in your hands."

And so she did just that. She had a camera set up in the corner of the room, and she propped the will up on an easel and made a photographic image of it, just like that.

"I will develop it this evening, you see. I have my own little darkroom in the cellar, as one does. And then, later this week, let us see what I can do to be of help to you, Miss Berryman, dear friend of the brave daughter of Loveliest Luna, who taught me to dream so long ago."

Then a rumbly roar came up the road, and they all looked out the front window together.

"The Matchless people are arriving now, it seems," said Madame Blaché.

The motorcar had found the balloon.

"Did she really just say 'Loveliest Luna'?" said Victorine into Darleen's ear as Madame Blaché went to the door to greet the rescuers. "But what did she mean by that? Wasn't Loveliest Luna your—"

"Oh, Victorine, yes!" said Dar. "Oh, you can't even imagine everything that has happened. It's amazing. It's—"

She didn't have time to find the words to describe how her world had just blossomed, however, because Madame Blaché was already hurrying back from the door.

"Go on out to them if you are feeling adequately restored, Miss Darling—and if you are confident you can keep yourselves out of the reach of any kidnappers or murderers, because they do sound dangerous, and I would be very sad to have our new friendship cut tragically short."

"We're quite expert at hiding," said Victorine, and Darleen added, "We'll be careful. Don't worry!"

And then they thanked Madame Blaché most sincerely for all of her help and kindness and shook her hand.

As the girls left, Madame Blaché bent her head to them one last time and whispered, "If I may give you a word of advice, dear girls: next time you find an old will, you might wait until the ink is thoroughly *dry* before you take it out into the world to be shown to people."

Chapter 23

Hands and Doorknobs

Right in the middle of the hands-and-doorknobs shots the next day (the close-in images of little things that lend trustworthiness and visual variety to any photoplay), Aunt Shirley came stomping up to the set in a lather.

"Darleen Darling!" she said, just at the very moment Uncle Dan was about to start cranking his camera again, and Uncle Charlie turned to her and said pretty much what he always said when his sister came roaring onto the scene during filming.

"Dear Shirley!" he said. "We are smack dab in the middle of something, please! Can this wait?"

But he was (most unusually for Uncle Charlie) smiling

as he said it, and Uncle Dan turned away from the camera and said, "Good to have you back, Shirl!" which was a long-winded sentence indeed, coming from Uncle Dan. "And Bill, too."

It was true: Darleen's Papa had finally made his way (a bit creakily) back to the studio that morning. That brought general relief to Matchless. The laboratory part of the building felt wrong somehow without Bill Darling around. And without Aunt Shirley's strong and steady hand, the Matchless studios always felt like a motorcar taking a turn at too great a speed for safety.

"OUT FOR TWO DAYS, AND EVERYTHING FALLS TO PIECES?" Aunt Shirley was saying at top volume. "Darleen, I need a word with you!"

"Shirley! Been too quiet around here without you," said Uncle Charlie. "But our Darleen is — Oh, never mind. Go see what the trouble is, Darleen."

From Aunt Shirley's face, anyone could see that she was not about to wait patiently for her word with Darleen.

"Mmm-hmm, good luck," said Uncle Dan, as Darleen slipped past the camera and toward the human onslaught that was Aunt Shirley.

"Darleen Darling!" said Aunt Shirley as she drew near. "I have had *three* telephone calls in short order that make me wonder what on earth you've been getting up to! Please explain!"

Darleen tried hard to look like she was willing to explain if at all possible, while being reasonably certain she might *not* be able to explain a thing, since that was more or less the general theme of her life these days: inexplicability.

"Telephone calls?" she said.

Aunt Shirley governed the Matchless Photoplay telephone. It lived in her business office, which was shut up and locked whenever Aunt Shirley was not on the premises.

"Telephone calls *about you,*" said Aunt Shirley. "Indeed, yes. Let's take them in order, shall we, Darleen? *First* of all, I receive a telephone call from someone who declines to give a name, but who is, to judge from his voice alone, unsavory. This person says that I should tell Darleen Darling, 'that actress gal,' that she can't get away with 'hiding what ain't hers' and then says that if the stolen goods, as he puts it, are not returned entirely pronto, Darleen Darling's darling father and the whole studio will be beaten to a pulp and sent up in flames, too, mark his words. I tell him I'll be reporting his nonsense to the police and cut the connection. Thievery, Darleen? I must say that's a bit unexpected!"

"But I didn't—"

Aunt Shirley waved all words from Darleen away.

"That's not all!" she said. "One moment later, the

telephone clamors again. This time—oh, coincidence!—it's the police. The police, Darleen! And who do they ask about? YOU! 'So sorry to trouble you,' they say, 'but we've had a very serious accusation come in regarding people closely tied to your Matchless studios. Did the studio really arrange a kidnapping at the Strand Theatre?' they ask. 'Because these are serious crimes and no laughing matter, and if this anonymous letter proves correct, and that Darleen Darling of yours is found guilty of kidnapping—'"

"What!" said Darleen.

"To my credit," said Aunt Shirley, "I did not say what came first to my lips, which was 'Darleen, in trouble *again*?' I said there must surely be some mistake here, since Darleen Darling is a child of twelve, and the only kidnapping we arranged was a purely theatrical performance. Policeman was unmoved: 'Well, we work with the information we're given,' says he, 'and that's what I have, and it doesn't look good for Matchless studios, does it, to be the front for a criminal operation, leading to the disappearance and possible murder of a young member of High Society.' 'CRIMINAL OPERATION'! 'POSSIBLE MURDER'! Darleen!"

Oh, she was in full eruption mode now.

"How did you manage it, Darleen? Turning a simple publicity gag into a world-class disaster? No—quiet,

quiet, I'm not done yet. Because *then,* Darleen, there came a third telephone call, and this one was perhaps the most disturbing of the lot. Do you know who was on the line, asking to speak to Miss Darleen Darling?"

Darleen looked blankly at her aunt.

"Madame Alice Guy Blaché! The director of the Solax Company! Now, why would she be contacting her rival, Matchless studios, you might ask, and asking to speak to one of our star performers here?"

Darleen, no longer experiencing inner blankness, had to work hard to keep her reactions muted and, so to speak, offscreen.

She wanted to say, *But Madame Blaché once peeked into a kinetoscope and saw my mother dancing, and her life was never the same again!* But of course she knew she must not say any such thing.

"What did she say?" she asked, even though it was hard to get her voice to behave properly.

"Yes. What did she say? Well, you might ask that! She said, in that smooth Frenchified parlay-voo of hers, that she was calling to see if she could borrow Miss Darling tomorrow, since she and Miss Darling have come to some sort of 'business arrangement' that requires, apparently, a joint trip to see a lawyer-type person in New York City! Explain me *this,* Darleen Darling! Because *this,* if you ask me, is going several steps too far."

Darleen gulped.

"It's not what you think, Aunt Shirley," she said.

"Oh, excellent," said Aunt Shirley in a voice that implied that this was the very exact opposite of excellent in every way. "That's good to hear. Because, frankly, I don't even know what I think at this point. Our Darleen, a thief and a kidnapper, that's bad enough, but *willing to skip out on Matchless entirely*? That is simply too much. We have raised you up from babyhood—we are not just your studio, Darleen, we are your *family*. Does family mean nothing to you anymore? What could Darleen Darling possibly have to do with Solax? Oh, those French businesspeople! Too clever by half! I hear Mr. Blaché doesn't quite trust that clever, clever wife of his. Maybe that's why he went and started that Blaché Features business. Maybe that's why he went to the Poconos last year for two weeks on his own."

(Aunt Shirley was an enthusiastic reader of the gossip columns in *Moving Picture World*.)

"And now his wife comes trying to poach one of us Darlings! But Darleen, why? Are you so discontented with your treatment here, with starring in an adventure serial under your own name, with all the care and attention we've given you over all these years? Well! That Madame Blaché put me right in a state, I'll tell you! I told her I would consult with your father, Mr. Bill Darling, and I hope my voice froze her heart into an icicle when it reached her over the wires, I do."

At least here was something Darleen could deny outright.

"Aunt Shirley!" she said. "I would never run away from Matchless! How could you think that? It's not photoplay business that Madame Blaché wants to help me out with. It's something else."

"Something else *what*?" said Aunt Shirley. Aunt Shirley was relentless; that was how she got so many things done. But sometimes that blunt relentlessness could make a person feel rather pummeled. "'Something else' of a criminal operation sort of ilk?"

"Something else — that isn't my secret to tell."

"You are a child," said Aunt Shirley plainly. "You aren't allowed to *have* secrets."

That was ridiculous, but Darleen gulped down any protest. All of tradition and all of the law, of course, would be on Aunt Shirley's side in this matter, even though Aunt Shirley had no idea how many secrets Darleen was carrying around at this point, did she?

Darleen had to think fast. And — oh, miracle! — she did. The first hint of an idea came into her brain, and she grabbed its front paws and pulled.

"I told you, it's not *my* secret," she said. "I can't explain it to you, but Aunt Shirley, I'll talk to Papa about it tonight, and if he says I may go, then I'll go. Did Madame Blaché say what time she wanted to leave tomorrow?"

Aunt Shirley huffed and puffed, but eventually she reverted to honesty and directness and answered the question.

"She said she'd come around in a motorcar for you at your father's house at eight thirty in the morning. I told her it would be a waste of good petrol because it was hardly thinkable that Mr. Bill Darling would agree to let you go, and she said, cool as a cucumber, that she would trust Miss Darling's powers of convincement. Now maybe that word's in the dictionary, maybe it's not. I asked Miss McNulty, who writes scenarios and knows a million words if she knows a dozen, and she said she thought so, but, Darleen, I am skeptical."

There was an abrupt pause in the progress of Aunt Shirley's train of thought; indeed, it had switched tracks and was beginning to roll in an unplanned direction. Aunt Shirley applied the brakes with force:

"Don't you go derailing our conversation!" she said (which was, thought Darleen, unjust). "Because I have *one more thing* to say to you, Darleen: Couldn't you have managed that scene yesterday without destroying Mr. Mancini's very expensive balloon? You seem *determined*, dear girl, to be the ruin of Matchless, and in every possible way."

Chapter 24

Who Is This Man?

Mr. Mancini's balloon! Aunt Shirley's rant seemed so unfair that Darleen, even though used to her aunt's ways of arguing a point, had to blink back tears. And then she remembered that although the ruined balloon had not been her doing, she had indeed kept secrets and might indeed be somewhere on the far side of the law and could even possibly be said to have put the people of Matchless at some kind of risk (without meaning to, of course! By accident!), and she blinked again.

To save Victorine's life! she reminded herself. *To save Victorine!*

But at what price?

And as if to rub the hurt right into the soft parts of her

heart, she turned and saw her own wounded father coming across the studio floor to where the uncles were standing. He looked flustered and worried, and a moment later, the three Darling brothers seemed to be arguing about what to do about something — about something that was lost?

Oh, now Darleen caught the essential phrase: "missing footage from the Strand."

The stolen reel, she thought, and her curious ears angled themselves toward the uncles like flowers turning toward the sun.

Aunt Shirley made an exasperated noise.

"Fine," she said. "Pay no account to anything I say. Fine, Darleen. If you bring reckless ruin to all of us, you'll see how you feel then. But I warn you: if I get one more telephone call about you today, I may lose my patience."

(Which was already long gone, as far as Darleen could see.)

And then Aunt Shirley spun around and stormed back to her office at the other end of the studio.

The Darling brothers were still having a heated discussion about what to do. Uncle Dan was proposing finding a storefront in Fort Lee that they could dress up to look "at least a little bit" like a theater entrance and refilming the bit with the motorcar and the kidnappers. Uncle Charlie groaned. "But we had actual pictures of the *Strand*!"

"Darleen," said a quiet voice very nearby. "Are you all right? I'm afraid your aunt seemed very angry with you."

It was Victorine — well, *Bella Mae* — and as soon as Darleen heard her voice, an idea came into her head.

"Listen to that! They want pictures of the Strand. Could you run upstairs and fetch that little strip of celluloid that we saved and hid?"

"Yes!" said Victorine, and a moment later she was gone. She had impressive skills in coming and going without clomping noisily around.

After a minute or so of mental preparation, Darleen walked right up to that discussion and tugged on her Papa's sleeve.

"Papa, wasn't there a strip of film from the Strand hanging on the wall, that awful day when the burglars came?" she said.

"Gone now," said Papa. "Fellow was thorough."

"But Papa," said Darleen. "I was just talking to one of the extras, and she told me she'd found something, just by chance, you know. Oh, here she is now! I asked her to run and fetch the thing she'd found."

Victorine was hurrying toward them across the floor, a bit of folded paper in her hand.

"Here you are, Miss Darling," she said. "I do hope it's useful in some way."

Darleen unfolded the paper, and there it was: a small but very clear image of the kidnapper turning around to stare at the camera while Darleen tumbled into the seat of the motorcar.

"Oh, look at this, Uncle Charlie!" she said. "And Uncle Dan! And Papa! This is Bella Mae Goodwin, one of the extras. Look what she has found!"

"Found" was only very approximately the truth, so Darleen hurried to push forward the little piece of film, framed in her hand, before her uncles could think of follow-up questions they might want to be asking.

"Well, I'll be," said Bill Darling. He held it up to the light. "Look, Dan! That's the outside of the Strand Theatre it's showing, isn't it? Thief must have dropped it."

"Too bad the thief didn't drop the whole reel," said grumpy Uncle Charlie. "This doesn't do us much good. All right, let's get back to —"

"But we *could* use this, couldn't we?" said Darleen. All the men (and Victorine) turned to look at Darleen in some amazement. Everyone knew better than to *interrupt* Uncle Charlie. Darleen had probably never intentionally interrupted Uncle Charlie since she'd precociously reached the age of reason at about four.

The advantage to breaking a rule like that the first time is that everyone is stunned for a moment, leaving, as it were, the door of opportunity swinging: Darleen pushed on through.

"I've thought about it. Uncle Dan, couldn't we turn this into one of those intertitles that looks like, you know, a newspaper? Call it *The Observer* or *The Post* or something and then have a headline—no, *two* headlines! 'EXILED PRINCESS KIDNAPPED OUTSIDE STRAND!' with this picture, right? And then 'WHO IS THIS MAN?' Something like that?"

"Ah!" said Victorine (standing a little behind Darleen). That word was enough to let Darleen know Victorine had understood instantly the cleverness of this plan. Here was a way to get the kidnappers into trouble *without going directly to the police.*

People were so starry-eyed about the photoplays. They wanted to believe they were as true as true. If you ran the picture of someone like this in *The Dangers of Darleen,* Episode Nine, then you could be quite certain that people would be contacting the police with tips every time they saw a similar face. Most of the time, that would be a bit of unfair awfulness for the poor, innocent actor involved. But for once, this was no "poor, innocent actor." Let him see his own face, labeled in a photoplay as *what he really was,* a kidnapper, *and let him sweat*!

Darleen's heart swelled a little with pride, and that was even before her Papa's face and her Uncle Dan's face and even her Uncle Charlie's face lit up with what you might call creative hope. They weren't thinking about exposing kidnappers, of course, but they seemed to like what they'd heard.

"Could do that, Charlie," said Uncle Dan. "What do you think?"

"Hmm," said Uncle Charlie. "I figure we could open Episode Nine with a title like that. Then go to the attic scenes. Hmm. All right, let's try it. Bill, you up for putting the title card together?"

"Sure," said Darleen's Papa, and he beamed at Darleen—and then looked more closely at Victorine (who was standing right behind Darleen) and blinked a couple of times.

Uncle Charlie went back to shouting orders: "ALL RIGHT! EVERYONE BACK TO WORK! Darleen, five minutes!"

Everyone in this part of the studio began to find their places again. Darleen's Papa now had the piece of film in his hands. He was cradling it, but he was looking at Victorine.

"Excuse me," said Darleen's Papa to Victorine. "My head's a little fuddled ever since the thief conked me. What's your name again, miss?"

"Goodwin," said Victorine. "Bella Mae Goodwin. At least, that's what my Matchless Photoplay form says. I'm an extra here, you know. Your daughter has been showing me how things are done. Oh, and I'm awfully glad you are mending, Mr. Darling!"

"Miss Goodwin," said Darleen's Papa. "But, dear child, have we met before? I feel somehow that we have. It seems to me — in a dream — you were kind, when I was ill, or perhaps I am mixing things up terribly . . ."

"Oh, Papa!" said Darleen, because she could see the puzzlement fogging up her father's eyes. She could see also that Victorine was tongue-tied from the pressure of staying as close to the truth as possible despite leading a life now that was almost entirely based on deception — or at least "acting," which may not be deception exactly but can feel like it's coming pretty close. "Papa, you are right to think well of Miss Goodwin! She *is* kind! Oh, Papa, may she stay with us at our house tonight? She has had some misfortunes, and she has been a good friend to me these past few days while I was all alone and worried about you!"

"But of course, of course!" said Darleen's father. He blinked a last time and came back, as it were, into focus.

"And now," he said, "I'd better get to work on this clever idea of yours, Darleen. I'll have one of the scenery people draw up a bit of fake newspaper for me if they aren't too busy."

"You know who also does a lovely job with writing and drawing?" said Darleen in a second fit of inspiration. "Miss Goodwin!"

Darleen's Papa looked again at Victorine, this time with businesslike seriousness.

"Could you imitate a spot of newsprint, dear girl? I can show you some other title cards we've done in the past, along these lines."

"Yes, Mr. Darling," said Victorine. "I'm sure I can manage what you describe, with the help of pen and ink and paper."

"We can rustle together all of that! Come with me, then. I'll show you some of the ropes, since you're a friend of my Darleen's."

And off they went, each being so very kind to the other, like a child and a grandpa in a photoplay, and Darleen's heart felt a little more settled than it had in a long while. Now at least Victorine would have to hide a little less of herself.

And then Uncle Charlie's voice rolled over their heads like a tidal wave and ended that peaceful moment:

"DARLEEN!" he was shouting. "TIME FOR YOUR DAYDREAM ABOUT THE LOST KING!"

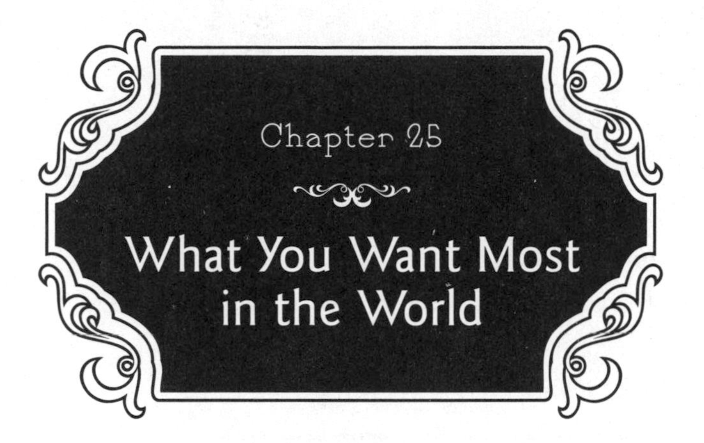

Chapter 25
What You Want Most in the World

One more little scene, that's all I ask," said Uncle Charlie. "We'll get this done, and then I think Episode Nine will be ready to be chopped, dried, and served out on fine china!"

That was his odd way of saying *developed and edited.*

"All right, back into your ropes. This is a tender moment from your lonely captivity in the Salamanders' attic."

"Before the balloon rescues me, all on its own, with no person in it," said Darleen.

"Correct," said Uncle Charlie. "Now, is that exactly how the ropes went when you were tied up yesterday?"

"Day before," said Uncle Dan.

"Day before yesterday, then," said Uncle Charlie. "I'm just asking for us to be careful so that the foolish ropes don't jump all over the place when we cut from one shot to the next. That's reasonable, isn't it? To want things to be smooth?"

The crew fussed with the ropes, and Darleen thought little hungry thoughts about luncheon while tamping down other, more fretful thoughts about how she would explain to her father that evening that she and Victorine would be heading into New York City the next day with Madame Alice Guy Blaché.

Meanwhile, Uncle Dan was fiddling with his camera. He had added a kind of bracket right in front of the lens, and into that bracket he was fixing a small dark card.

"What are you doing?" Darleen called over from her attic set to Uncle Dan, perched on his little ledge with the camera.

"Well, you'll see!" said Uncle Dan. "It's for the daydream!"

"But what do daydreams have to do with cards in front of the lens?"

Uncle Dan smiled from ear to ear.

"Saving a place for it," he said. "Saving a place for the dream."

That seemed more like poetry than an explanation,

as far as Darleen was concerned. But Uncle Charlie was ready to get things underway. The set was almost the same as it had been two days ago, but the props and scenery people had tacked a black-velvet cloth over the whole of the attic back wall, and Uncle Dan's camera was positioned a little differently, so that Darleen (tied up in those annoying ropes and slumped in that foolish chair) would now be in the left-hand part of the frame, against the black-velvet wall.

"All right, Darleen, dear," said Uncle Charlie. "For this scene, all I need you to do is think about what you want most in the world."

What? Darleen stared at him, and for a moment her head felt like all the ideas in it had been emptied out and replaced by black velvet.

"No, no, no! What kind of expression is *that*?" said Uncle Charlie (but with a smile, because Uncle Dan hadn't been cranking the camera yet). "I mean, what I need you to do is to *look* like you're thinking about what you want most in the world. Can you do that? We'll do this scene three times, just to make sure we get a good one for Dan to work with. Ready, Dan?"

"Yep," said Dan.

"All right, let's go! Darleen, you're trapped in that attic, you're thinking about what you want, what you long for most in your life."

And somehow those words sent Darleen's brain spinning. Because, really, when she thought about it: What *did* she want most in life?

She knew her father's answer, the dream he had had, and lost, and longed to have again: a quiet cottage; a little farm; roses; feet on the ground.

At the very thought of it all, the feeling gave a rebellious wriggle from somewhere deep inside. She pushed it back down.

Of course she wanted to be a good daughter.

Or at least not to be a bad one.

She knew, she knew: her Papa's happiness depended on her.

"Feet on the ground," she said to herself, and she made her inner self very stern. In fact, she scolded herself.

And the feeling kicked against all the secret ropes she had wound around it inside her soul, and it said a terribly wicked word: *no.*

Because it wanted her to be *free*; it wanted her to be *real*; it wanted her to want things that were not just everybody else's dreams. It told her all of this without even bothering to use words; it just opened its wings the slightest bit, and she saw.

Try as she might, Darleen could never be an onion. No. She couldn't be one clear thing, all the way through. She had been trying so hard to be good, but she couldn't help it. It looked like she would always have secrets rustling inside her, wanting to come out and change her world.

The feeling danced a little in her heart — yes! yes! — but then it sagged again, like a balloon weighed down by sandbags, and the sandbags were all the reasons that that feeling of hers could never be allowed to soar off and take her wherever it wanted to go. *She had promised her Papa she would not fly away.*

"And maybe shed a tear or something, thinking of your Royal Father," Uncle Charlie was saying.

That brought Darleen back to Matchless studios with a jolt. Oh, yes! For example, a better actress, a better daughter, a better *person,* would have been thinking of her Royal Father. Or at least of her unroyal Papa.

"Good!" said Uncle Charlie.

He had them do the scene three times over, and then finally Darleen could wriggle out of those ropes and be slightly freer once again, someone who could at least stand up and sit down and walk about whenever she wanted, even if sandbags still weighed down her wobbly heart.

They moved the camera very carefully over to the desk and wall of the mansion set, where the King was supposed to be suffering from amnesia and imprisoned by the wicked Salamanders.

Uncle Dan set up the camera just so, looking at Mr. Williams from a somewhat greater distance than he had used in the attic set. He switched out the card stuck in front of the lens too. Now it was three-quarters of a card, covering up all the bits of the frame that the previous card had left clear. Then he checked the camera's position one last time while Mr. Williams strolled about, getting into his kingly persona.

"What's the plan, Dan?" said Mr. Williams.

"You'll sort of float," said Uncle Dan. "Like a thought balloon in the comics, you know."

Mr. Williams raised a kingly eyebrow and settled into his chair, his body positioned at an angle to the desk so that his kingly face could be seen to its best advantage by the camera lens.

"Here we go," said Uncle Charlie. "Who's running my stopwatch?"

That was a young man from the sets department.

"Thirty seconds," said Uncle Charlie. "Shout out every ten, boy, you hear me? And . . . START!"

Uncle Dan cranked his film. Mr. Williams tried to look as much like a tender father as he could manage (considering he had no children of his own).

"Ten seconds!" said the young man with the watch.

"Good! And now, Mr. Williams, why don't you

stretch your arms longingly out to the right of you and down a bit?"

"Twenty!"

"That's the way! It will look like you're reaching for dear Darleen."

"Twenty-eight, twenty-nine, thirty!"

Uncle Dan stopped cranking.

"That's one done," he said. "Two more chances."

They started in again. Darleen was beginning to understand how it all worked, more or less, but it still seemed almost miraculous to her. Light came pouring in through the glass panes of the studio building, bounced off Mr. Williams's body, and ricocheted into the camera through the unblocked parts of the camera lens. And then the light hit the chemicals coating the filmstrip and changed them, leaving a ghostly trace of Mr. Williams on the celluloid. But most of each frame had been covered up with that card to protect the image that was already there: Darleen in those dreadful ropes. Darleen thinking about what she wanted most in life. And after the film was processed, those two images would be there together, just as if they had been filmed at exactly the same time.

"It'll be dandy," said Uncle Dan. "Like magic."

And then, also a bit like magic, Darleen's Papa came striding back across the studio floor, and he was carrying a newly created title card very carefully in his hands.

"One last title card ready for your camera, Dan," said Darleen's Papa, and he held up the card, which showed something very like the front page of a newspaper, only somewhat more beautiful in its lettering, and there they were! The very titles she had suggested: "EXILED PRINCESS KIDNAPPED" and "WHO IS THIS MAN?" What's more, in the middle column of the pretend newspaper was the picture of Darleen tumbling into the motorcar, with that kidnapper's face right in the center of the frame, clear as could be. And, oh, a brilliant extra little touch: in the newspaper columns to the right of the image and the main headlines, Victorine had made sure to have the name *Brownstone* visible, as if by chance. Really, thought Darleen, the newspaper idea couldn't have turned out more beautifully. It would put all of those wicked people on notice.

"It was *Darleen's* idea," said Darleen's loyal parent (and there's little that's sweeter than hearing your Papa speak of you with such glowing pride). "And then that new girl, Miss Goodwin, made it look like gold. She's got real talent, that new girl."

At the end of the day, a happy trio emerged into the twilight outside the Matchless studios: Darleen, Darleen's Papa, and Bella Mae, who was coming over to have supper and spend the night with the Darlings.

There were many rather daunting adventures to be faced across the Hudson River in New York City the next day, but now was now, a peaceful moment and one not to be missed. In life, even in the midst of storms and wars and film production, there are shutter-brief periods of peace and quiet — what people sometimes call *grace* — and those should be savored, since they are rare and since the storm will return soon enough.

Darleen's father was glad to be headed home after his days spent as a coddled invalid at Aunt Shirley's place. He was also pleased to have had a good day back on the job, and to have been able to rescue Episode Nine, thanks to the quick thinking of his own dear daughter, Darleen, and the pen-and-ink talents of that nice new friend of hers, the gifted extra, Miss Goodwin.

"Sausage-'n'-apples for supper, girls!" he said with an extra little lilt to his step. "Shirley sent me home with a string of sausages, bless her heart. I have them right here in my satchel."

Darleen was happy to have her Papa back, and in what seemed very much like one piece. She was glad (but nervous) about the plan she had worked out for tomorrow and hopeful (but nervous) about all those different pieces coming together properly. And it felt very, very good to have Victorine here beside her and not having to hide like a rat in the dressing room.

"Your Papa is such a good and kind man," said Victorine now as the girls fell a little behind Mr. Bill Darling and leaned their heads together. "I really think, Darleen, that we should tell him the truth—"

"Most of the truth," Darleen interrupted. "Oh, that's what I was thinking too. He needs to know that we should bar the doors of the house, and I think he can be trusted not to hand you over to the Brownstones or the police, now that he knows you. It can be our new motto, Victorine: As Truthful as Possible."

"That's a fine, fine motto," said Victorine. "Not as perfect as 'Completely Truthful All the Time' would be, but I'm pretty sure that Grandmama, under the circumstances, would approve."

This is a short chapter because happy scenes don't last very long in adventure serials. But be assured that the Darlings (and Victorine) had a lovely evening together, and Mr. Darling learned a great deal about the previous few days that made the hairs on the back of his neck stand straight up, but those feelings of horror faded quickly because there was Darleen, right across the cheerfully patterned oilcloth tablecloth from him, and there to his right was Miss Goodwin, for whom he had developed over the course of that one day a great deal of respect and affection. Whatever name she might choose to call herself seemed fine with Darleen's Papa. And the sausages were very good, too.

Chapter 27

The Room of a World-Wandering Librarian

The next morning at 8:30 on the dot, a fine new motorcar pulled up in front of the Darlings' small and ramshackle house, where two eager (but nervous) young people stood waiting in freshly pressed clothes: Miss Darleen Darling and Miss (Victorine) Bella Mae Goodwin (Berryman).

Madame Blaché was not at the wheel today (although one felt certain that she would be as competent behind the wheel as she was on a horse or directing a film). She explained as she hopped out of the rear seat in greeting: "Good morning, my dear snake charmers! In my experience, those in the lawyerly professions are very sensitive to those little clues pointing to class and position. So as you see, I have brought my driver along with me today, and we will be careful to do everything very properly. How are your hats and gloves, girls?"

They were fine (after some emergency laundering the evening before). Not quite as elegant as Madame Blaché's — but of course that degree of elegance was rarely achieved by mortals.

"Excellent," said Madame Blaché, and she told the driver to take them down to the ferry, "without taking any truly inordinate risks on the turns today, since there are guests in the motorcar."

"And now for a brief review of the day's program," Madame Blaché continued. (A person who makes films understands the art that has to go into constructing a schedule.) "There is the newly discovered version of Madame Berryman's will, yes, to present to this Mr. Ridge. That I understand. But first we will procure the evidence of your identity, Miss Berryman."

"From my dear old home," said Victorine with a sigh. "Yes."

That was the riskiest and most daring part of their plan.

By the time they were on the ferry, everyone had an assigned role in the operation. Madame Blaché even volunteered her driver, whose name was Henri, as an honorary coconspirator, and he graciously accepted.

"So perhaps Mr. Henri can knock at Mr. Brownstone's door," suggested Darleen, "and ask some made-up questions that will lure him away from the house for a moment, and while he talks Mr. Brownstone's ear off, Victorine and I will slip into her house through the servants' door in the back and run up to her room and down again in the fewest possible minutes."

"And will it be so easy, going right in through the servants' door?" Madame Blaché asked, but her voice stayed calm.

"I have carried the key around my neck all this time," said Victorine, and she showed them her necklace, which was really two keys on a pretty chain.

"Then that's settled," said Madame Blaché. "And you are not in the least bit worried about running into other people in your house, people who might not be so . . . friendly?"

"Mr. Brownstone fired our old servants already weeks ago," said Victorine. "To save money, you know. There's his sister, Miss Brownstone, but she tends to keep to the fancier rooms downstairs. I think we have a reasonably good chance of avoiding unfortunate encounters."

"An adventure, then!" said Madame Blaché as the buildings of Manhattan grew nearer and the ferry blew its whistle. She seemed quite pleased to be part of this complicated plan thought out by her young snake-charming friends. "Off we go!"

It took a while to drive from the 125th Street ferry building to Victorine's neighborhood on the East Side (on Fifth Avenue, if you please). It was a genuine mansion, among many other grand buildings, and as they drove by, they had to swerve a little to avoid a taxicab parked right out in front, into which a small woman in fashionable black clothes was just then stepping, assisted by a young man whose face was hard to see because the motorcar was in the way.

"Oh!" said Victorine, shrinking back a bit. "It's Miss Brownstone!"

"Going somewhere," said Darleen. "That's good for us, isn't it?"

Madame Blaché had the driver park discreetly around the corner, and then she sent him to the mansion's door to inquire at great length about an incorrectly delivered package.

"Henri was an actor in France before he became a driver in Fort Lee, New Jersey," said Madame Blaché as her driver rounded the corner. "I think he is relishing this unusual opportunity to use his talents."

"How will we know when he has gotten Mr. Brownstone out of the building?" asked Victorine.

"I myself will stroll to the corner, I think, to observe the clearness of the coast," said Madame Blaché.

Darleen had to remind herself to breathe. *Oh, please let this work!*

Victorine and Darleen watched Madame Blaché, and then watched Madame Blaché some more, and then all at once she turned very slightly and nodded to them: *Time to go!*

Victorine led Darleen quickly down the street, not running exactly, since they didn't want to draw attention to themselves. They passed the front steps and then ducked down a little service alley, where there was a side door meant for receiving deliveries.

Victorine lifted her chain over her head and used one of the keys to open the door.

"Oh, good!" she said in relief as the door swung wide. "I did have worried moments when I wondered whether that Mr. Brownstone might have gone and changed the locks. Up these stairs, now — very quietly, just in case."

They slipped up those stairs as silently as two breaths of wind, except for a squeaking stair that caught Darleen's left foot by surprise.

"Oh, dear," said Victorine. "I should have warned you about that step. Now here's the door to the upstairs hall."

It was such a grand hall! There were mirrors on the walls, and art from all around the world, and, with a few dead or dying plants in the most elaborate porcelain planters in certain corners, it looked like a place that was beginning to lose hope that its true people would ever return.

"Oh, Darleen," said Victorine, suddenly stopping short. "Suddenly I feel . . . I feel . . ."

"Of course you do," said Darleen. "But you mustn't, not now. Don't think about anything. We are here to grab whatever documents you most need and leave. We can't let ourselves get stuck!"

So Victorine shook her head to clear it of old thoughts and opened the door to her bedroom, where it was Darleen's turn to gasp and get stuck. It was the loveliest room Darleen had ever seen, with a large window seat (with Victorine's books strewn upon it), a comfortable-looking canopy bed with fancy curtains looped around it, rugs upon the floor in which little woven birds hopped cheerfully through winding woolen branches, bright pictures on the wall, and a venerable old rocking horse in the corner. The colors were all soft greens and blues, comforting and lovely. It was, in short, the perfect nest for a child who would grow up knowing she was loved and wanting for nothing, as long as her doting millionaire grandmother could manage to provide it.

"You really live here?" Darleen whispered in awe.

"Yes, oh, yes," said Victorine. "Between travels, I

do. Or *did,* I suppose. Oh, Darleen—all my books! Oh, look at them! There they all are. The fairy tales! And *A Christmas Carol*!"

You could well believe that this room belonged to a girl whose heart's dream was to become a world-wandering librarian!

Darleen had never seen such beautiful bookcases. They were built along the walls on either side of the windows, with more books beneath the three angles of the window seat itself. And along the tops of the bookcases was an assortment of wonders: little porcelain statues of a milkmaid and a cow, a snow globe with a tiny Eiffel Tower in it, and the sweetest, smallest brown teddy bear Darleen had ever seen, tipped ever so slightly to one side. Someone had balanced a gold locket in his fuzzy arms. He was so tiny that it looked almost like he was carrying a shield.

Hanging on the wall was a sketch of a baby smiling in her parents' arms, along with a pretty painting of a goatherd tending animals near a cottage in what Darleen suspected was the Alps.

For a moment, Darleen turned slowly around and around, soaking in all the particulars of this magical room, and then she straightened the little bear so that he wouldn't look so sad. But that didn't help; the bear pleaded with her not to leave him behind.

Victorine, meanwhile, was pulling books off a shelf, paging quickly through them and sadly blowing dust off the tops.

"So many happy hours," she was saying, when suddenly there was one of the most horrible sounds Dar or Victorine had ever heard in all their lives: the slam of the majestic oak front door, two floors below.

Chapter 28

The Rescuing of Theo

The girls froze.

"Victorine," said Dar as quietly as she could. "Is that—?"

"Oh, no!" said Victorine. "Oh, no! I think it may be Mr. Brownstone! Oh, quick!"

She started pulling books off the shelf, fast as fast.

"Victorine!" said Darleen. "Shouldn't we—"

"There it is!" said Victorine.

A thin leather box was now in her hands. She tucked it into her sash and jumped to her feet.

"And now the back staircase!" she said. "Quick!"

But before taking another step, Victorine stopped and

took one last look around the room. Dar felt herself trembling, half from wanting to skedaddle and half from sheer sympathy on Victorine's behalf.

How hard it must be to leave so many memories behind.

"Thank you, dear everything, and for now, at least, goodbye!" Victorine said to the books and the pictures and the rocking horse, and then she took Darleen's hand.

"Now we must be *very* fast and *very* quiet," said Victorine. "Here we go."

She opened the door into the hall an inch's worth, and they listened. Footsteps were coming up the main staircase quite fast.

So they fled! They made their way down the hall to the back staircase. Victorine went ahead, and Darleen followed fast.

But as she took her first step onto that wooden staircase, a voice came bellowing from the other end of the hall:

"What's this!" it said. "What's going on? Is it you, Victorine? THIEVES!"

There was one second when Darleen was stopped in her tracks by the sheer *anger* in that voice, and then Victorine said, "Hurry!" and Dar's feet started moving again while the angry man — Mr. Brownstone, she assumed — came pounding heavily down the hall.

The girls scurried down those stairs faster than either

one of them had ever descended a staircase before. There is nothing like being chased by an angry, dangerous, *shouting* man to make your feet move like the wind!

At the bottom of the stairs, they lost about half a second as Victorine fiddled with the door latch with trembling hands, and then they were back outside in the little alley. And there — oh, wonder of wonders! — was Madame Blaché's motorcar, blocking the Fifth Avenue end of the alley so that it could be as close to the girls as it could possibly be. Its rear door swung open, and a voice with the loveliest of French accents was saying, "Quickly, quickly, girls!"

And twenty seconds later, Dar and Victorine had tumbled into the motorcar. It left the curb with a jolt, before Mr. Brownstone had gotten even halfway down that alley. Madame Blaché settled back in her seat with a smile on her face. She seemed to have enjoyed this adventure.

"Tell me, Miss Berryman, did you manage to find that document you wanted?"

"Oh, Madame Blaché, I did!" said Victorine, and she pulled the thin leather box from under her sash, where she had so carefully tucked it.

She opened the lid of that box. Inside were a couple of what looked like letters, folded, and an old official-looking document of some kind.

"What's that?" asked Darleen.

"That's my birth certificate," said Victorine. "My Grandmama impressed on me that it is always important to have some means of proving who you are."

She thought a minute.

"Or, you know, who you used to be," she said more quietly. "If you are now becoming a different person entirely."

"That all sounds perfectly sensible to me," said Madame Blaché. "And now, off we go to discuss things with Mrs. Berryman's lawyer."

That was when Darleen realized her hand was still clenched around something small and fuzzy.

"Oh, look at this, Victorine!" said Darleen, unfolding her fingers. "I forgot: as we were leaving, I grabbed it for you. I thought . . ."

In her hand was that tiniest of teddy bears.

"I thought . . . He didn't seem to want to be left behind," said Darleen.

Victorine took the little bear from Darleen slowly, like somebody to whom a small wonder has come when utterly unexpected.

"My Theo!" she said. And then she gently plucked the locket from his small arms. "And look what else he has. My Grandmama gave this to me."

Inside the locket were two tiny photographs.

Victorine's breath seemed to catch in her throat a bit as she looked at them.

"See, these are my parents," she said, pointing to the man and woman on one side. "I remember my father some but not, of course, my poor mother, though I hear she was very accomplished. And on this side here is my dear, dear Grandmama."

Even in that miniature portrait, Darleen could see that the old woman had eyes that practically crackled with intelligence and good humor. She did look like a person who would greatly enjoy guiding someone through the wild places of the world.

"Who is that man sitting next to her?" asked Darleen.

"Why, that's my tragical Uncle Thomas, who went out on a solitary stroll, long before I was born, and never returned."

They admired those pictures together while the motorcar made its way through the busy New York streets, skillfully avoiding streetcars, other motorcars, men dashing across the streets, and the poor beleaguered horses, who must be wondering why their city in recent years had gotten so much louder and faster and filled with dangerous roaring beasts made of metal.

"She must have been a tremendous woman, your *grand-mère*," said Madame Blaché.

"Oh, yes," said Victorine softly, and then she went

very quiet. Darleen could see a little tremor in her fingers as she put the locket back around the bear's small neck.

"Oh, dear," Victorine said finally. "Do you know, I'm having a funny sort of thought."

"What sort of thought?" asked Darleen.

"About — about Theo," said Victorine. "It's very silly of me, I know, but look at his little face. He was all alone in that great big house, and he must have thought I had gone for good! If you hadn't rescued him, he would have waited on and on in that room, with no one there to give him a kind word or to pat him on his fuzzy head occasionally. I told you it was a silly sort of thought."

She wiped her eyes, and Darleen was so full of sympathy that she felt as wobbly as gelatin.

"It is not easy to leave one's home," said Madame Blaché. "This I know well, Miss Berryman. This I know very well."

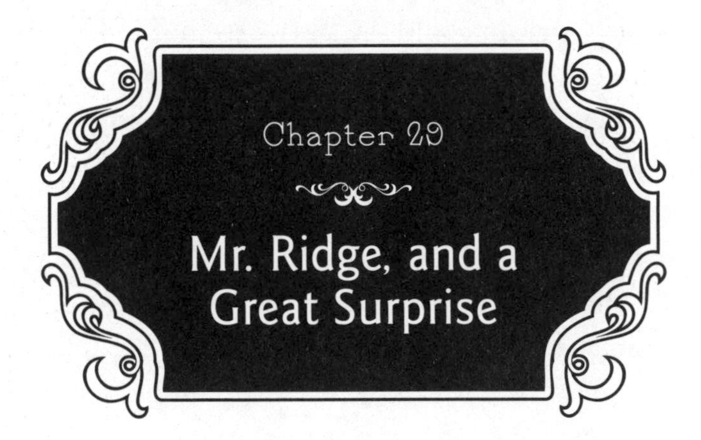

Chapter 29

Mr. Ridge, and a Great Surprise

The offices of Mr. Ridge were in an impressive building, all dark paneling with brass accents. They were on the seventh floor, and, most thrillingly, there was a mechanical elevator that carried you up into the heights. Darleen had never been in an elevator before, and the jolt as the box started up reminded her a little of her adventure in the lighter-than-air balloon. It was a most interesting and peculiar sensation. Her stomach was slightly unsettled anyway because of the upcoming conversation with the lawyer. Like elevators, lawyers were not something that Darleen had encountered before in her everyday life.

"You will follow me into this meeting room of his, I think, girls," said Madame Blaché. "And then, after I have explained the situation to your Mr. Ridge in an introductory way, you, Miss Berryman, will take over the conversation."

That was the plan.

Madame Blaché sailed in through Mr. Ridge's door, and the girls followed in her wake. Mr. Ridge looked rather nervous, as well he might, since he could not know what this visit was about.

"Good afternoon, Mrs. . . . er, Blatchy?" he said.

As she handed over her card, she said, "So delighted to make your acquaintance, Mr. Ridge. I am Madame Blaché, director of the Solax Company, which produces photoplays. You have heard of us, perhaps?"

Mr. Ridge mumbled polite phrases while his puzzled eyes made little questioning zigzags as he tried to figure out what any of this meant.

But as he studied Madame Blaché's card, the puzzlement shifted to a kind of awe. Perhaps he was remembering something he had heard or read about Madame Alice Guy Blaché, about the work she did, the company she ran, or perhaps even her photoplays.

"What, er, brings you here today?" he asked, wringing his hands. "We have not spoken previously, I believe?"

"These brave girls here have discovered a document

that I think you will find most interesting and valuable: an *amendement* — I believe in English you would call it a 'codicil' — to the will of the late Mrs. Hugo Berryman."

Mr. Ridge looked quite shocked, which was only to be expected.

Then Madame Blaché took the will out of its protective brown-paper envelope and popped it right into his surprised hands.

"You should know, Mr. Ridge," she said in a mild-mannered way, "that I have made a number of photographic copies of this document, since I am convinced as to its importance. Those photographs are safely in my possession. I say this merely as an aside."

"Yes, yes," said Mr. Ridge. "But there must be some mistake. Mrs. Berryman, bless her soul, is no longer among the living and therefore cannot be providing new versions of her last will and testament."

"I think you should tell Mr. Ridge the story of this codicil now, Miss Berryman," said Madame Blaché, and at the sound of Victorine's name, Mr. Ridge actually gave a start, quite as if he had run by accident into a fence.

"What?" he said, blinking at Victorine. "Who? But this cannot be. Miss Berryman's personal effects washed up on the shore of the Hudson. The police tell me that she has almost certainly drowned, poor girl."

"Mr. Ridge, it is, however, I. I am Victorine

Berryman," said Victorine. "You will recognize me eventually, I am sure, if you look closely. My grandmother did introduce us at several points. Although perhaps you took no notice of me since I was merely a child. Oh, and here, in case you mistrust your eyes, which I suppose would be understandable, is my certificate of birth. And this little locket, in which you see my dear Grandmama's picture. You must certainly recognize my *grandmother.*"

He stared at her face and then long and hard at the birth certificate and the little locket, with its pictures of a happy family long ago, and then, after taking several rather furtive glances at Victorine, he set the locket down on his desk and passed a trembling hand over his eyes.

"But this is extraordinary," he said, quite overcome. "The young heiress rising up from her watery grave! And to think that at this very moment, in the office next door, we were just — But never mind."

Darleen saw Madame Blaché raise two skeptical eyebrows (very few people, in real life, can raise only one eyebrow at a time, despite what novels tell us), but Mr. Ridge was already continuing:

"Really, now, Miss Berryman, if you were not drowned, why did you not swiftly return to your loving guardians and relatives, the Brownstones? Mr. Brownstone has been very concerned about your safety and whereabouts. I know he has written a number of times over the past few days — until the sad discovery of your shoes in the river — to ask whether I had heard anything from or about you."

That's a lot of nerve on the part of the Brownstones! thought Darleen, quite indignant about it. But she kept quiet so as not to make anything more difficult for Victorine. She just reached out and squeezed Victorine's hand to convey her support and her affection.

Victorine sat up even straighter than usual and said, "Oh, Mr. Ridge, I know my grandmother most explicitly asked you to be sure that I would be kept safe from harm, that the guardians you appointed would be honorable and kind people. But in the case of the Brownstones, you have made an awful mistake. Perhaps we would not now be in such difficulties if you had consulted with me in person before securing my guardians, but you did not. As I explained when I spoke to you on the telephone, the Brownstones seem to care only about selling off all of my grandmother's most prized possessions. I thought you would surely come to my rescue when you heard how dreadfully the Brownstones were behaving — because you had had so much respect for my grandmother, you know. But that's not what happened. Those awful Brownstones fooled you, and you went away without helping me at all. And do you know what happened then? Mr. Ridge, it was terrible!"

"I must say — this is . . . this is . . . er . . . really —" said Mr. Ridge, stammering a little. "I hardly recall —"

"What happened next," said Victorine, not relenting one bit, "is that after you left that day, Mr. Ridge, Mr. Brownstone came to my room in a terrible temper. He kept shouting at me, 'You went crying to strangers; now we'll see how you like crying alone!' And from that day on, they kept me for the most part locked in my room."

After a moment of dramatic hush, Mr. Ridge wiped his brow and said a bit weakly, "Oh, dear. How awkward this all is."

"Yes, I suppose it is," said Victorine. "Awkward and awful both. For a moment, when I realized no help was likely to come from my grandmother's trusted attorney, I despaired a bit, I admit. My fate seemed very hard."

Mr. Ridge squirmed in his chair.

"But then imagine my happy surprise," said Victorine, "when one day Miss Brownstone came to my door and told me I would be going with her to the grand opening of the Strand!"

"Where you were kidnapped," said Darleen. Hearing Victorine tell her sad story made the little gears in her head begin turning.

"Where I was kidnapped," echoed Victorine. "Yes."

"And taking you to the theater was the first kindness the Brownstones had shown you in ever so long," said

Darleen. "And we know they aren't very kind people, not really. So why?" The gears were turning faster and faster. There is a particular speed — about sixteen frames a second, or thereabouts — at which individual images suddenly become a *moving picture,* and the ideas churning in Darleen's head were now running at something approaching that magical threshold: they were coming together and beginning to move.

"Yes," said Victorine. "Why?"

"Victorine!" said Darleen, putting her hand to her mouth. "Don't you see? Perhaps it wasn't by chance, all of it. Your cousins, the Brownstones — What if they found out about my *fake* kidnapping from that wicked Jasper and decided to arrange your *real* kidnapping at the same time? Because the police would think the *real* kidnapping was just the *fake* one. Oh, Victorine, your own cousins! What if it was *them,* all along?"

"Oh!" said Victorine, and Madame Blaché said, "How dreadful," and Mr. Ridge stared at Darleen in horror.

"What? What?" he said. "Who *is* this loud young person here?"

"This is Miss Darling," said Victorine. "And I'll have you know, Mr. Ridge, that I owe my life to her. Several times over!"

Darleen wasn't sure what etiquette demanded on such occasions, so she nodded slightly and tried her best to look modest. Mr. Ridge stared at her and shook his head, evidently still not understanding.

"Mrs. Blash-ay," he said (coming just a bit closer to the correct pronunciation). "I'm grateful to you, madam, for bringing back our lost lamb, Miss Berryman. I will be sure to return her safely to her guardians, the Brownstones."

"*No!*" said Madame Blaché, Victorine, and Darleen all at once.

Mr. Ridge gave quite a start. He had perhaps never been so thoroughly contradicted—and interrupted—by females in his whole life.

"Have you not been listening, Mr. Ridge?" said Madame Blaché. Suddenly she was all business, so that you could well imagine her spending her days telling dozens of people exactly what to do. "Perhaps we have not been sufficiently clear. As Miss Berryman has explained to you, Mr. Ridge, these people you refer to as 'guardians' have behaved very badly, and possibly criminally. Henceforward, therefore, she will no longer be living with these Brownstones."

"But according to the terms of the late Mrs. Berryman's will—" said Mr. Ridge.

"Aha!" said Madame Blaché. "But you see, Mr. Ridge, this is exactly the point we have come to discuss. Please be so kind as to take a moment to read the recently discovered codicil. I think you may find it illuminating."

Everyone else in that room already knew quite well the contents of the document Mr. Ridge now put his glasses on to read:

"'Last Will and Testament of Mrs. Berryman: Addendum.

'Since it has always been the writer's intention that Victorine Berryman, granddaughter and principal beneficiary of Mrs. Hugo Berryman, be protected from those who might seek to profit from her fortune or otherwise bar her from the free exercise of her own good judgment, the following remarks are to be added to the original will:

'1. Any guardians appointed for Miss Victorine Berryman must not only be exceptionally trustworthy and kind individuals but also meet with the approval of Miss Berryman herself.'"

(When he reached this point, Mr. Ridge looked up in alarm: "Approve her own guardians! But that would be highly irregular!" he said. Madame Blaché had to gesture rather firmly at the will, to remind him to keep reading.)

"'2. Should Victorine Berryman (heaven forbid!) vanish, disappear, or die, the entirety of the Berryman estate must be held intact; no money or material goods may be transferred to any person, company, or entity until the date that would have been Victorine Berryman's twenty-first birthday. At that time, IF she has not appeared to claim the estate, or IF definitive

proof has at some point been received of her death, the entire estate will go to the NEW YORK PUBLIC LIBRARY, *for the construction of a dedicated reading room for the children of New York so that they may enjoy books as Victorine has always loved them. This change in the will should guarantee that no so-called guardians or other parties will have any reason to try to exert control over Miss Berryman or to cause her harm.*

'3. A sum of money, not less than five hundred dollars, shall be deposited every half year in the safety deposit box of Mrs. Hugo Berryman at the American Bank of New York, a box for which Mr. Ridge, attorney-at-law, and Miss Victorine Berryman both possess keys.'"

When Mr. Ridge finished reading, he set the will down on his desk with a trembling hand and dabbed at his forehead with a handkerchief.

"Goodness, goodness," he murmured.

"I am sure you agree with me that this new will seems both practical and wise," said Madame Blaché, as if they were in the middle of an ordinary conversation. Mr. Ridge opened and closed his mouth a few times without making a sound.

"Mr. Ridge, are you all right?" said Madame Blaché after a moment.

"Yes, yes, of course," said Mr. Ridge, pulling himself together. "But this is *not* how these things are done! And anyway, how can we have any assurance this codicil represents the genuine wishes of Mrs. Berryman?"

"If you look at my grandmother's original will," said Victorine, "you'll see the handwriting is exactly the same. *Exactly* the same."

Mr. Ridge sat quite frozen for a moment, his hand still slightly quivering. And then he pulled himself together and said, "In any case, this is a muddle. I'm afraid that your fanciful story here — and this peculiar addendum to Mrs. Hugo Berryman's will and testament — are not only irregular. They may also be irrelevant, ill-timed, perhaps even illegal."

"I don't understand," said Madame Blaché.

The lawyer stood up from his desk.

"There are complications. Dramatic complications," said Mr. Ridge. "It has been a most surprising day. *Most* surprising. And trying. The girl who was drowned by her kidnappers is no longer drowned. Mrs. Berryman's will is no longer what we thought it was. And that is not all."

He stuck his head out his door and said to his secretary, "Please do send them in now, Miss Green."

Darleen, Victorine, and Madame Blaché all jumped very slightly in their skins. What was this about?

The door opened, and in came a man with remarkable eyes (one dark brown, and the other quite light and glittery), followed by the very woman in black whom they had seen getting into a taxicab on Fifth Avenue that morning.

At this point, everyone in that room except for Madame Blaché and Mr. Ridge made sudden sounds of astonishment or distress. And Victorine slipped her hand into Darleen's so that they were standing together again as they had stood when facing the kidnappers a few eventful days earlier.

"Miss Berryman," said Mr. Ridge. "Here are your cousins, Mr. Brownstone and Miss Brownstone, his sister. Before your rather unexpected arrival, we were discussing the future of the Berryman estate."

"The future of the Berryman estate?" echoed Victorine. Darleen could tell from her voice that she was truly, deeply shocked.

Mr. Brownstone closed his especially glittery light brown eye for a moment, letting the other, dark brown eye pierce Victorine on its own. Then his face changed its shape entirely and became all sadness and perplexity. The sadder version of Mr. Brownstone gestured in Victorine's direction and said, "But I don't understand. Just who is this young woman claiming to be?"

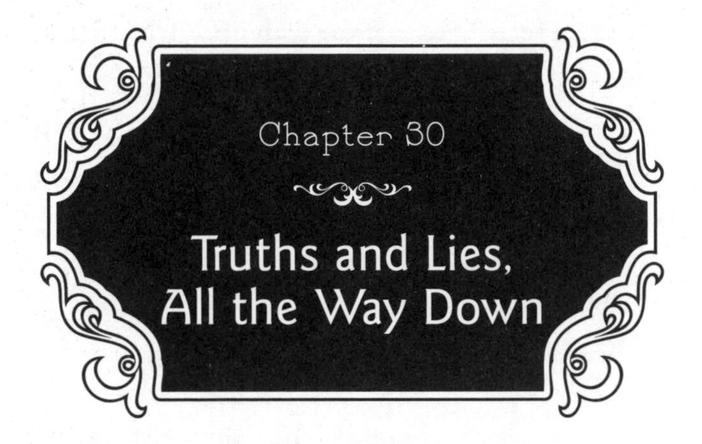

Chapter 30

Truths and Lies, All the Way Down

For a moment even Darleen fell under Mr. Brownstone's spell; he seemed so very puzzled, so honestly concerned. But then his expression flickered for a moment, and Darleen saw the meanness hiding there, and a surge of indignation raced right through her, quite like the shock those new electric wires might give you when handled carelessly.

"This, of course, is Miss Victorine Berryman," she said. "As you very well know!"

"And you? Who are you?" said Mr. Brownstone, but really he hardly bothered to glance at Darleen. "Our poor Miss Berryman is in the process of being declared legally deceased. Drowned in the Hudson River, alas. It's a very sad day for us, I'm sure. Not a good time, Mr. Ridge, for foolish conversations."

Victorine gasped. Darleen gasped, too, but inwardly. She felt that this was a scene in which every line and gesture might matter, and she drew every bit of herself into one powerful concentrated force, as focused as a lens.

"How can you say Victorine isn't alive!" said Darleen. "She's standing before you right this minute!"

"And I'm not in the least bit drowned," said Victorine. "Thanks largely to Miss Darling here."

Mr. Brownstone ignored everything the girls were saying and instead settled an arm on Mr. Ridge's shoulder, as if to steady him somehow.

"Now, Mr. Ridge. Let's be logical. Have they shown you any evidence of who they claim to be?" he said. He sounded very reasonable. "Because really, Mr. Ridge, this is *most* inconvenient and cruel, just when we are mourning the loss of our dear young cousin."

Mr. Ridge looked very uncomfortable.

"She does look *rather* like the Miss Berryman I knew," he said. There was a wavering in his voice that Darleen didn't like. "But children are all so similar, aren't they? Although she has presented a birth certificate as proof, you know —"

"And a picture of her own grandmother!" said Darleen.

"Well, well, well," said Mr. Ridge. "What a puzzle. It

does seem more likely than not, doesn't it, that she probably really is—"

"But this is ridiculous!" said Victorine. "Of course Mr. Brownstone knows perfectly well who I am! He practically held me a prisoner in my room for ages!"

"And he was running after us just an hour or so ago, shouting 'Victorine!'" added Darleen. "Why would he be shouting 'Victorine' if he thought she was actually dead?"

"Excellent question," said Madame Blaché. "We seem to be hearing some dreadful and irrelevant nonsense."

"What are you calling 'irrelevant nonsense,' madam?" said Mr. Brownstone, as if deeply offended. The dark brown eye darted back and forth, examining his audience (but the light brown eye stayed very still). "The question of Miss Berryman's identity can hardly be 'irrelevant nonsense' if we are Miss Berryman's legal guardians! Indeed, we are more than that—we are her closest kin."

"Not so very close," said Victorine through slightly tense lips.

"Ha, ha!" said Mr. Brownstone, as if she had just dealt him the winning card in a game with rules too complicated for any mortal to understand. "*Very close.* Tell her, Ridge."

"Well, now," said Mr. Ridge, who had been oddly silent for the past few moments. "It seems that on this interesting topic, we have been presented, you know, very recently — I mean, this morning — with some new information."

New information? Darleen and Victorine exchanged glances, and then Mr. Brownstone drew the woman in black forward from where she had been standing behind him. Darleen looked at her pinched, querulous face, and a little shock of recognition went through her. Was it just that she had seen her getting into that taxicab this morning? No, the shock seemed to want to say something more, but the language of shocks can sometimes be hard to decipher.

"My poor, bereaved sister," said Mr. Brownstone, and his tones were rather theatrical, "will finally be able to tell her full story."

"Is this 'full story' necessary?" said Madame Blaché. "I have business to attend to at Solax. And I'm quite sure Miss Darling here is wanted at home."

Was it Darleen's imagination, or did the woman in black flinch slightly at Madame Blaché's words? That electrical sensation became stronger, buzzing about in her, leaping from nerve to nerve, as if knocking on all of Darleen's inner doors in alarm.

"You will remember, Mr. Ridge, that when we first came to take charge of poor Miss Victorine Berryman, alone in the world after her grandmother passed away, we explained that we were — well, I believe we said we were *distant cousins*," said Mr. Brownstone, smooth as silk. "But at that time, we were simply worried about shocking poor Miss Berryman with too many surprises, just when she had had the shock of losing her grandmother. But now that Miss Berryman is possibly drowned—"

"Not drowned!" said Victorine fiercely.

Mr. Brownstone blinked. "You do resemble her somewhat, I'll give you that. But it hardly matters anymore."

"What?" said Darleen. How could Victorine's identity not matter?

"Because, you see, Mrs. Hugo Berryman had *two* children."

"Now that's quite right," said Mr. Ridge. "She had two boys."

"One was the father of Miss Victorine Berryman. He was the younger son. But he had an elder brother, and that brother, Thomas Berryman, was something of a troubled soul."

"Who died very young," said Victorine. "He was a wanderer by nature, said Grandmama. He wandered through the gorges and ravines of southern France, until one day he broke his leg and died in some lonely canyon of thirst. It was a most tragic accident."

"How well informed you are!" said Mr. Brownstone. "You have prepared carefully for this role if you are an impostor."

"She is *Victorine,*" said Darleen. "And you know that's true!"

"As I said, it hardly even matters. Because the accident was more tragic than you know," said Mr. Brownstone. "During his wanderings, something happened that would change many lives forever."

Every nerve in Darleen's body was alert by this point and looking out for danger. She stepped a little to the left, where the window was, and glanced down at the street far below. Of course she got no new information there, other than that seven stories above the pavement is very high indeed. (Her nerves jangled, and the feeling woke itself right up and fluttered a bit.)

"During his wanderings, young Thomas Berryman met a beautiful woman with whom he fell deeply, deeply in love, and they were secretly married in a small church in the village of Venasque just before his unfortunate death in a local gorge—and before he learned of the happy event that would transpire in the following year."

The woman in black put a handkerchief to her eyes, although Darleen would have been willing to swear that those eyes contained no tears.

"What are you saying?" said Victorine. "Mr. Ridge, what can he be saying?"

"Mmm," said Mr. Ridge. "He is saying, Miss—well,

whoever you actually are — he and Miss Brownstone are not actually *distant* Berryman relations . . ."

"Aha!" said Darleen, but Mr. Ridge continued on.

"But instead, the person we have known as Miss Brownstone —"

The woman in black dipped in a tiny curtsy, but the tension never left her face.

"— is actually *Mrs. Thomas Berryman*," said Mr. Brownstone in triumph, taking over Mr. Ridge's speech.

"Miss Brownstone is my aunt?" said Victorine. "Surely not!"

"Good heavens!" said Madame Blaché. "How complicated this is all becoming."

"Most relevantly in terms of the law," said Mr. Ridge, "Miss Brownstone — Mrs. Thomas Berryman, I mean — is the mother of Mr. Hubert Berryman, cousin to the recently lamented Victorine Berryman and presumptive heir to the Berryman estate."

A stunned silence filled that room and hovered there for quite some time.

Then Victorine said, "Do you mean that I have a cousin? But then where is he?"

"Mr. Hubert Berryman is waiting outside in the hall," said Mr. Ridge. "And so, even if you were Victorine Berryman —"

"But I am, as you know. I even showed you my birth

certificate. And there must be witnesses who knew my Grandmama and me. You can't keep saying I'm not who I am, Mr. Ridge! It's impossible!"

Mr. Ridge looked very torn.

"Oh, dear," he said. "You look so very like her, I suppose it must be true. Well, then, let's say you *are* Victorine Berryman."

"Yes!" said Darleen. "She certainly is!"

And then something very peculiar happened.

Miss Brownstone (the widow of Thomas Berryman — could it really be?) flung her arms around Victorine and began to cry.

"*My darling niece!* We were so *afraid* we had *lost* you! Come, let's go along home."

Mr. Ridge looked rather moved, but Darleen was shocked, as was Madame Blaché, who clapped her hands in irritation.

"Oh, now," she said. "This seems quite a sudden change in attitude."

"We will take her in again, won't we, dear brother?" said the former Miss Brownstone. "She must be very sorry for having worried us so."

"By being kidnapped!" said Darleen.

"And even though her claim on the Berryman fortune has now been superseded by that of my own darling Hubert, surely we can open our arms and —"

"All right, dear sister," said Mr. Brownstone, checking his large pocket watch by bringing it up close to his dark brown eye. "She comes back home with us. Time to go, Victorine. Come along quickly now."

"Yes, quickly," said the woman in black, and suddenly Darleen knew where she had seen that face before. This woman in black! The two-eyed man! And then her brain went *clickety-clack, clickety-clack* (approximately the sound of long lines of dominoes tumbling against each other), and in a mere instant, Darleen figured out all sorts of other very interesting things too. Why, it was like a photoplay after all! In the photoplays, villains were always needing to be confronted and unmasked!

So Darleen pulled herself up to her tallest height and became as close a copy as possible of the Crown Princess Dahlia Louise (known in her exile as Daring Darleen):

"No!" she said. "Miss Berryman won't go anywhere with you! I absolutely forbid it."

"Who are you?" said Mr. Brownstone. "*You* can't forbid anything."

"I can," said Darleen. "I can, and I will, and I do! You may not know who I am, but I'm beginning to think I know who *you* are! Let's see if I'm right!"

She darted forward and grabbed the locket from where it lay on Mr. Ridge's desk.

"Here's something that can help us: *my locket*!" she

said. It was the most bold-faced lie she had told all day. She could hear Victorine's sudden, horrified intake of breath — so Darleen simply made her words louder and more dramatic, to drown out any qualms of conscience from Victorine.

"In my locket are pictures, you see," said Darleen, and she swooped the open locket right up close to the woman in black's face with a gesture bold enough to impress any camera back at Matchless studios. "The people here in these photographs are *my family*!"

(Another slightly strangled noise from Victorine — but never mind that!)

"*My family!* Do you recognize them? Look closely, please do!"

The woman in black glanced at the miniatures, but her face stayed puzzled and blank. (Oh, Darleen was quite certain now. She was positively, absolutely sure.) "What nonsense this is," said the woman. "I've never seen any of these people before in my life. Step aside, little girl. These pictures have nothing to do with me!"

Darleen imagined the camera closer to her now. In her mind's ear she could almost hear Uncle Charlie shouting, "Emotion, Dar! Emotion!"

Emotion! She let her face crumple, like that poor old fairground balloon when it had sagged to the ground, all deflated with no air left inside. "Oh, dear. Have I gotten confused? I could have sworn you were — Are you quite, quite certain?" said Darleen, and she made her voice match her face, all sheepish and hopeless.

Mr. Brownstone stepped forward and frowned at the pictures in the locket. "You are quite mistaken, girl," he rumbled. "The people in these photos of yours are nobody we know and entirely irrelevant. Enough of this nonsense. Stand back and hush!"

But Darleen had no intention of standing back — nor of hushing, for that matter. Not a bit of it.

"Oh, dear," she said — and she couldn't resist adding a slight tone of *regret* to her speech. "Then it is as I feared. Here is *your* locket back, Miss Berryman — yes, *yours*, not mine —"

("Oh, Darleen," said Victorine, shaking her head as she took the locket.)

"Your locket, dear Miss Berryman!" Darleen repeated grandly. (She was still being formal; the scene was not quite over. Not yet!) "Filled with photographs of *your* family. Not only of your dear parents and your departed Grandmama, but also of your tragically deceased Uncle Thomas —"

She paused then, of course, because drama is absolutely built on suspenseful pauses, and she was pleased to notice, during that pause, that every single adult in that room looked thunderstruck. Except for Madame Blaché, on whose face a wise and delighted smile was beginning to take shape.

So Darleen continued: "The very same Thomas Berryman whom this woman claims to have married! But now they say they have *never seen him before*! Now tell me, how can a person be married to a man and, goodness, *have that man's child* and yet never have set eyes on him in her life? How?"

A moment of electric silence. Then—

"Enough of this charade!" roared Mr. Brownstone, and he grabbed one of Victorine's arms and pulled.

And that was when chaos broke out. Darleen leaped up onto the windowsill and swung the window open, and it was as if she had just let the feeling out of its cage. It spread its wings and crowed in triumph.

Five pairs of eyes were fixed on her in horror. Some of those eyes looked angry enough that Darleen could imagine their owners trying to give her a helpful shove.

"*You listen to me, all of you!*" she said, as the breeze from the street canyon tickled the back of her neck. "If you do not do exactly as I say, I will proceed to climb right up the outside of this building, and that will be a spectacle no one in New York City will soon forget. And who knows? Perhaps it will even bring the police running."

She held on to the window frame and leaned back a bit, just to confirm that this was one of those buildings with fussy little decorations everywhere. Yes, it was. The feeling wanted to dance its way up, from ledge to curlicue to ledge.

"Darleen!" said Victorine, her hand to her mouth. "Oh, dear! Darleen!"

"Madame Blaché," said Darleen. She was trying to be extraordinarily dignified, to the degree possible when you are standing on a windowsill. "Will you be so kind as to place a telephone call through to my Aunt Shirley at Matchless? You won't object to our using your telephone, Mr. Ridge?"

Mr. Ridge shook his head rapidly back and forth. His face had gone green.

"Stop this right now!" said Mr. Brownstone, but Madame Blaché was already talking to an operator.

"And what shall I tell your aunt once we are connected, Miss Darling?" said Madame Blaché, who proved able to keep a very cool head under trying circumstances.

"Tell her that she should urgently send here — to this address — my uncles, and they should bring with them the largest photograph pinned to the wall of my dressing room. They'll know what I mean. The group photograph. The old one. Tell her it is a matter of life and death. Oh, and tell her please not to tell my Papa, because he'll worry so. But my uncles, yes, they must come right away."

Madame Blaché was making energetic explanations

on Mr. Ridge's telephone, but she had turned to face the wall so that she wouldn't distract Darleen in any way. Meanwhile, Victorine's eyes had not left Darleen's face for a moment, but Darleen didn't dare look right at her in case seeing Victorine's face did something to the feeling that was carrying her so bravely along at the moment.

People were beginning to shout in the street below. *Good,* she thought. *Let them shout! Let the police come up to the seventh floor to see why a girl is balancing with such joy on the windowsill.*

"What? What?" said Mr. Ridge, looking ill. "Whatever are you *doing,* you reckless girl?"

"Your uncles are on their way with the photograph you requested," said Madame Blaché calmly as she set the telephone back down on Mr. Ridge's desk. "So, brave Miss Darling, what can we do to be helpful now?"

"Would you mind popping your head out the door and asking the secretary to send that mysterious young Mr. Hubert Berryman person in here? Bring him in. Bring him in! Because I'm pretty sure I know who he is. I know who he is, because I know who *she* is."

And she pointed one of her feet at the woman in black.

"And that means I am also certain I know who this person calling himself Mr. Brownstone is too! It's that eye that gives him away! Oh, I think I know who *all* of them are! And they aren't sister and brother at all, at all!"

The feeling was kicking up its heels inside her now!

"Stop this, right now!" said Mr. Brownstone. "Mr. Ridge, this abominable young person in the window now is nobody. Worse than nobody. I've heard about her. She is the kidnapper of Miss Berryman, and a shameless thief. And a liar. Victorine, come away from this madness. It's time for us to go."

His own lies were piling up into quite an odd and inconsistent tower, thought Darleen as she shifted her hands a little on the window frame and carefully steadied herself once more.

Tears were slipping down Victorine's cheeks, but she was smiling through them as she shook her head and moved herself in between Mr. Brownstone and Darleen's window, just in case Mr. Brownstone got any ideas about sudden moves.

"She is *not* nobody. She is the opposite of nobody," said Victorine. "She is my dear friend, and she is wonderful, and she is *Daring Darleen.*" And she added, for Darleen's own sake, "Oh, Darleen, you really, truly are."

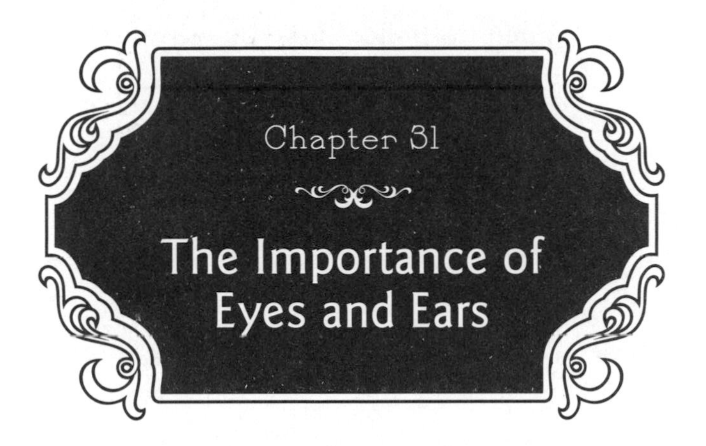

Chapter 31

The Importance of Eyes and Ears

Madame Blaché slipped back through the doorway after her consultation with the secretary in the hall outside.

"The young man on the bench out there refused my invitation to come into this office," she said, still cool as a French cucumber. "Are you still doing all right, Miss Darling, in that window? It may be a very long time indeed before your uncles arrive."

"I'm fine," said Darleen. She didn't think she would have to wait as long as all that. Some part of her had been paying close attention to the sounds from outside, and so she was pretty sure some help might arrive well before her uncles. "When the police come in, we will have to ask them to check his ears."

"Police?" said Mr. Ridge. "Surely not."

"Darleen?" said Victorine with some concern. "His ears? Are you all right?"

There was a commotion outside the room — doors opening and someone shouting.

"They're here," said Darleen. "The police. Tell them — Tell them this woman here who says she's your aunt used to be Somebody-or-Other Lukes. Claudette? Was it Claudette? My uncles will remember the name. And this man with the two-colored eyes is also no Brownstone at all, I'm quite, quite sure. Oh, Victorine, catch me! I'm coming down."

And she tumbled forward, hard enough that both she and Victorine rolled to the floor.

"You're not hurt? Darleen, you're all right?" said Victorine, as they scrambled to sit up again. "My heavens, what a wonderful actress you are! But wait! Where are those awful Brownstones going?"

The pair of them had slipped right out through the door into the commotion of the hall.

"Quick! Before he talks his way out!" said Darleen, and Victorine helped her scramble to her feet. For some reason Darleen's legs were suddenly wobbly, although she had felt so strong and steady in the window. Uncle

Charlie had told her once that sailors sometimes feel queasy when they come back on shore after a long time at sea, so perhaps this was something like that.

The girls staggered together through the office door and into a very confusing scene indeed, a tangle of heated arguments.

"There she is now!" said Mr. Brownstone to a policeman, and he pointed an enraged finger in Darleen's direction. "A wicked girl! No morals! Kidnapper! Lawbreaker! Practically holding my ward prisoner and slandering us all!"

"That little girlie there?" said the policeman, and he scratched his head. "Which one of you was threatening to jump out of that window?"

"Nobody," said Victorine. "I'm Victorine Berryman, and Miss Darling here was merely preparing to climb up the side of the building. Out of necessity. Because this woman and that man and that . . . that strange younger person over there —"

There was definitely something strange about the man who was supposed to be Victorine's cousin. He was practically huddling under his hat on the office bench, trying to get as far from Darleen as possible.

"They are all pretending to be my relatives," said Victorine. "But they aren't."

"They're Lukeses!" said Darleen. "I'm sure they

are all Lukeses, not Brownstones or Berrymans at all. Impostors!"

"Oh, now, we can't have that," said the policeman. "Nor we can't have children climbing up buildings, neither. Public disturbance."

"But Miss Darling is a professional," said Victorine. "She is Daring Darleen. Haven't you seen her in the photoplays?"

"Daring Darleen?" said the policeman, and his whole demeanor softened for a moment. "Well, now! We think the world of Daring Darleen at my house! Is that a fact!"

"Then, please just hold these people here until my uncles come," said Darleen, and she swept her hand around to include all of the Brownstones. "They're bringing the photograph — the *proof* — that'll show who these people really are."

"You're not going to believe anything she says, are you?" said Mr. Brownstone (actually, Lukes). "She's an actress, not fit to mix with quality. She earns her living telling lies."

"Acting is not the same thing as lying, Mr. *Lukes,*" said Victorine. "And you yourself have told an astonishing number of lies right here and now. Distinctly more than the rest of us."

"Speaking of lies, won't you please ask that young man over there to take off his hat?" said Darleen to the nearest policeman. "He claims to be Hubert Berryman, but he's not. I'm pretty sure he has dyed his hair black, and if we could just take a look at his ears —"

"Ears?" said the policeman, but Madame Blaché was already walking over to the young man, and she plucked the hat right from his head. And there, just as Darleen had suspected, was a pair of extraordinarily pointy little ears.

"See? That's right. I knew it! *That's* Jasper Lukes," said Darleen.

Madame Blaché leaned in to get a closer look. Jasper Lukes glowered, but couldn't come up with a word to say in his own defense.

Suddenly Darleen felt so tired that she had to sit right down on that bench (but at the end farthest from Jasper Lukes). "Just don't you let these pretend Brownstones go. You'll see in the photograph when it comes. That's Mr. Lukes, and one of his eyes is a fake, I'm pretty sure, and that's his wife, and that's Jasper Lukes, whom they left behind all those years ago when they wandered off. I guess they must have wandered back again and caught him up in their nasty plans! He's an actor, too, by the way. Maybe you've watched him in *The Dangers of Darleen.*"

"Miss Darling is quite right about this young man here," said Madame Blaché, eyeing Jasper Lukes. "I have faithfully followed the adventures of Daring Darleen, and this man is without a doubt the villain in those pictures, the one they call the *Grand Salamandre*. Well, I suppose there's nothing left for us to do but to wait for these Darling uncles."

And she joined Darleen on the bench. Fortunately that bench was quite long.

The uncles came quite some time later, and as soon as they entered the room and saw Mr. Brownstone, they said, "Oh, if it isn't *Lukes*! Where'd you get that extra eye?" That was already very convincing for the policemen and office people watching, especially when Mr. Brownstone snarled back at them like a caged lion and began struggling to get himself out of the policeman's grasp.

And then the uncles passed around that old photograph so that everyone could see, plain as plain, that the woman in black had indeed been Claudette Lukes back in the 1890s, and the uncles put their fingers on the blurry man next to her in the photograph and solemnly swore that there was "no mistaking Lukes, even if he did switch his patch for a fancy glass eyeball," and the baby with the pointy ears (infant Jasper) was no baby Berryman, but a little Lukes. The three were Lukes, Lukes, and Lukes the whole way through.

But the best thing of all was not the arrival of the uncles; the best thing was the man who pushed through all the police to gather Darleen into his arms: her own dear Papa, beaming with pride.

"Is it true you've been helping our Miss Goodwin in her hour of need?" said Papa. "Good for you!"

The police were bundling the protesting Brownstones — who were not Brownstones at all — out of the office.

"My feet weren't on the ground, Papa," said Darleen into her father's dear old ear. "They weren't at all on the ground."

"I suppose sometimes we have to be willing to break a rule here and there," said her father, "when it's to rescue a friend."

They quite filled Madame Blaché's motorcar to bursting, but nobody minded the lack of room. By the time they got off the ferry on the New Jersey side of the Hudson, the sky was dark. Henri drove them up the winding roads with skill, however, and they were all so cheerful that the drive went very speedily indeed.

"Back to the Darlings' home, please, Henri — past the studios, you know," said Madame Blaché.

The Solax Company and the Matchless studios were quite close to each other, and the Darlings' little house was just on the other side of that street.

It was such a lovely evening. The moon made the photoplay studios glitter like palaces in fairyland.

"Go slowly, here, please," said Madame Blaché, and she turned to Victorine. "Miss Berryman," she said. "There is something I have been considering— Wait, now! What's that? Henri, to the right, by the studio wall!"

Henri showed his dexterity behind the wheel by turning the car suddenly to the right so that the headlights would illuminate the side of the Matchless building.

And for a second, a surprised face was caught in that bright light. A face and a most suspicious-looking metal can.

Several voices exclaimed at once in that motorcar.

"*Mon dieu!*" cried Madame Blaché. "Can it be? An arsonist! Henri, we must help!"

"But that's that kidnapper, back again!" said Victorine in horror. "The one who came looking for me at the Darlings' house!"

The uncles both shouted at once.

Everyone spilled out of the car and sprinted into action as if they had rehearsed this scene a hundred times before. Anyone who had anything to do with the photoplay business knew to fear fire more than anything else in the world.

The kidnapper went darting off to the left, and Henri

raced after him and soon brought him down with a satisfying *oomph.* (Henri was evidently a motorcar driver with many useful skills, sort of like a human version of Victorine's folding knife.)

Madame Blaché ran to the emergency fire bell that hung by the laboratory door and pulled the rope there with vigor, and the bell rang out with all its might. The Darling uncles and Darleen's Papa ran for water.

And as the fire bell sang out its urgent alarm, Henri shouted and pointed. The kidnapper had gotten up again and was scrambling away, right past the girls, which was, of course, a bad choice on his part.

Darleen went for the kidnapper's right arm at the same moment that Victorine caught his left leg, and they brought him down like a rotten tree.

"Hold on!" the girls told each other.

The kidnapper looked satisfyingly terrified in the dim, confused lights cast by the moon, the motorcar's lights, and the many lanterns coming toward him at a run—and by the flicker of fire at the far end of the studio.

Voices attached to those approaching lanterns were shouting, "What's happening? What's wrong?"

Madame Blaché said urgently, "Keep those lanterns away! We have arsonists here, I fear! Oh, look! Over there—Fire!"

"I'm going for the sheriff!" shouted someone.

And others were calling out, "Water! Water!" and passing along buckets from hand to hand.

Darleen and Victorine kept holding on to their kidnapper while the flames crept closer along the studio wall.

"You kidnapper! You villain!" said Darleen. She found she was completely furious with the kidnappers, with Jasper Lukes, with the Brownstones, who were not Brownstones at all — with *all* the people who had caused them such trouble.

"It wasn't my idea!" whined the kidnapper. "It was the boss's idea! That's who it was. Mr. Smith! He wanted the girl kidnapped — and dumped in the river too. He wasn't going to pay no ransom. He wanted the film destroyed. He wanted that big old house burned, and the studio too — it was all Mr. Smith!"

The flames came nearer, and there was great confusion as more and more help arrived. Fire trumps everything, so before anyone could do anything to help the two girls who had leveled the kidnapper (and arsonist) and were still holding him now, all the arriving crowd attacked the flames. Somebody emptied a bucket of water right over Darleen and Victorine, and *still* they held on, despite the shock of the cold water in that awfully cold spring air.

"K-k-k-keep holding on!" said Dar to Victorine, her teeth chattering.

They kept holding on.

And then finally, several men materialized all at once to grab the kidnapper, and Darleen and Victorine could roll away from his angry limbs and gasp for breath and shiver, a few feet away from the main action.

"Fire's out!" someone down the line finally shouted. "Checking for sparks and cinders!"

"The studio," said Darleen in disbelief. "They were really trying to burn down the studio!"

"Warn't my idea!" said the kidnapper. "It was Mr. Smith's!"

"Oh, right, 'Mr. Smith,'" said the local sheriff, who already had the kidnapper firmly by the arm. "Tell me another one, why don't you. Why there's probably a hundred thousand Smiths in New York City alone. And it's been quite the day for fires, seems like. Over in the city they say that the Berryman mansion went up in flames this afternoon. Quite the show."

"What?" said Dar, and Victorine said, "Oh, no!"

The sheriff was too busy having the kidnapper tied up to notice that the girls who had captured him were clinging together now like they had suffered a great shock.

"Come on, boys, help me get this rotter into the wagon now."

"Mr. Smith," insisted the kidnapper. "He lives in New York! 'Burn everything'—that's what he said. For the insurance, I guess. He's a wealthy sort of man. The wealthy ones like burning things. He has a glass eye, he does! 'Dump the girl in the river,' that's what he said, first off. And then, 'Burn it all down!'"

"But that's got to be Mr. Brownstone he's talking about," said Darleen. "Which is to say, not Mr. Brownstone at all, but Mr. Lukes. Your 'Mr. Smith' is in jail, you awful man."

Victorine was standing very still there in the dark. Darleen could feel her trembling, though, as the sheriff and the kidnapper moved farther away.

"I will be brave," she was saying. "I will be brave. It was just a house. Without Grandmama there, it was just an empty house."

"And you aren't alone," said Darleen in a whisper.

"No," said Victorine, although her voice wobbled for a moment as she took Darleen's hand. "Not alone. And to think, Darleen—you didn't only rescue me. You even rescued Theo!"

An hour later, everyone was gathered around the table in the Darlings' cozy kitchen: Darleen, Victorine, Darleen's Papa, Madame Blaché, and Henri (who had certainly earned his cocoa that night!).

"We're grateful to you, Madame Blaché, and no

mistake," said Darleen's father. "You helped save Matchless tonight."

"Well, now," said Madame Blaché modestly. "Let us be glad we were there at the moment of need! And it was Henri and my brave, brave, snake-charming girls who brought down the wicked assassin!"

Darleen's Papa looked a little puzzled by the reference to snakes, but he was soon busy pouring out second mugs of coffee and cocoa.

"So, dear Victorine Berryman," said Madame Blaché. "I am sorry for all the troubles you have had. I will be hoping that this new chapter of your life will be a happier one. Will you be continuing your new acting career, do you think?"

"Oh, madame, I think I will, for a while," said Victorine. She was pale, as you might expect someone to be who had just wrestled a kidnapper to the ground and learned of the destruction of her family home. "And I'll stick to my stage name, too. *Miss Bella Mae Goodwin* seems a name much less likely to attract kidnappers or greedy cousins. To be honest, I'm curious to see what kind of life I may be able to build for myself. You know, the way that Crown Princess Dahlia Louise became Daring Darleen, once here she was, in America, and in disguise."

Then Victorine actually almost smiled.

"Oh, dear," she said. "In the spirit of Daring Darleen, I guess I had better be Bookish Bella Mae!"

"Brave, Beloved, Bookish Bella Mae!" said Darleen loyally, and then the others around the table added some other likely adjectives beginning with *B*, and eventually Madame Blaché rose gracefully from her chair and gestured at the clock.

"It is well past my usual hour for retiring," she said, "and my poor, dear children must be feeling quite abandoned, with me gone all this long day and with Monsieur Blaché away again on business. So, Henri, I think we should motor on home, as long as you girls are quite settled in here. But first I have two things to say."

Everyone had stood up out of politeness when Madame Blaché rose from her chair, and now they hushed like a very interested audience (which, of course, they were). Madame Blaché took Victorine's hand in both of hers and smiled over in Darleen's direction too.

"First of all, my dear, highly valued, sometimes incognita Miss Goodwin! If you ever decide you need someone to serve as a guardian, please do consider me. It would be an honor, truly. And should you find yourself in need of employment in times to come, I would be glad to hire you myself, as a secretary or — well, I suspect you may be capable of a great many things! And finally, if at some point you decide to move on from Fort Lee, I know people in the photoplay business out West, for instance, in Hollywood, in the state of California, who might also be glad to employ you."

Victorine said something in French that showed how grateful and overwhelmed she felt, but Darleen's Papa interrupted with, "No need, no need — she's always most welcome in the laboratory here."

And then Madame Blaché turned her warm eyes in Darleen's direction.

"And you, my other snake-charming child. To you I will say, you have definitively proven yourself to be — off the screen as well as on — worthy of your name: our own Daring Darleen!"

And there was some cheering around that table then. Yes, there was!

That night, as the girls lay waiting for sleep to catch up with them finally, in Darleen's cozy little room in the Darlings' cozy little ramshackle house, the glow of Madame Blaché's words lingered about them, giving hope to a girl who had just in a single day lost and gained a home.

"You know, Darleen," said Victorine, wiping her eyes, "I have been thinking about my old dream, to become a World-Wandering Librarian, and it occurs to me now — now that I know that I really *must* wander . . ."

She rolled over to face Darleen.

"It occurs to me that perhaps working in the photoplay business might be at least a little like that. Do you see what I mean?"

"Perhaps you'd better explain," said Darleen, who did *not* see, not yet.

"It is sharing stories about the world, as a librarian would do — that's one thing. And then there is the possibility for travel. Not merely in balloons, Darleen! Madame Blaché mentioned California."

"Well, that's true," said Darleen. "A few of the studios have already moved out there. So far away! But they say there's no winter to speak of in Hollywood, and of course that makes the filming easier. And you can have an orange tree in your own backyard!"

They were silent for a while, considering the wonder of oranges growing right there on an ordinary sort of tree.

"I wonder whether orange trees are good for climbing, though," said Darleen, and then they both smiled in the dark, because Darleen would always be looking for cliffs and tall trees and other places where that feeling inside her could let loose and fly, and they both knew it.

"I'll tell you what," said Victorine a while later. "I think we should work very hard to learn as much as we can about the photoplay business — about every part of it, you know. And then someday, I think — I think perhaps we should go out to California together and see what Hollywood is like."

"And have more adventures," said Darleen, just as a yawn caught her.

"More adventures!" said Victorine. "Yes, I suppose. For your sake, I'll hum my way through. I guess we can have as many adventures as we can think of, but this time they won't be forced on us by wicked kidnappers."

"No," said Darleen. "We'll make them up ourselves."

There was a quiet moment in which the house creaked a little and settled again, like an old dog dreaming of rabbits.

"Well!" said Victorine. "How interesting and complicated everything turns out to be. I really did think I preferred things to be simple and clear. But then I got kidnapped and met you and lost everything from my old life except Theo, and now I'm Bella Mae during the day and pretending all sorts of things in front of cameras. I'm not sure I can even call myself an onion anymore. But I do still think it matters, the truthfulness of things. You will tell me, won't you, when I get *too* far from being an onion."

"I'll try," said Darleen, and she felt herself smiling again. "You're really very onionish still."

"Well, that's reassuring," said Victorine. "Maybe that's what friends are for: to help us keep one eye at least on what's true. And also to stand in windowsills on our behalf when necessary. Wouldn't want to forget that!"

Truth is, friends make many things in life easier: even knowing when *not* to keep our feet on the ground.

Out on the ridge of the roof, the moonlight danced and was not sad. It was here for now, and for now not afraid of flying away.

The Dangers of Darleen, Episode Nine:
THE MYSTERIOUS BALLOON

Darleen and Victorine stood together for a while, admiring the advertisement in the window of the Fort Lee movie theater.

"Well, shall we go in?" asked Darleen's Papa.

They were all three of them, one way or another, in disguise: incognito.

Nobody would recognize a man from the Matchless laboratories, so Darleen's father was safely anonymous, whatever he might wear.

Darleen had plaited her hair and was wearing a simple sailor dress that was as far as possible from anything Daring Darleen would ever wear.

And Victorine was in the sort of practical but comfortable outfit that a Miss Bella Mae Goodwin might be able to afford (with her father's knife still secretly tucked up against her leg). No one would look at Victorine and think she was the heiress to one of the greatest fortunes in New York City (a fortune now being held in trust). No, she had crossed the Hudson River and left luxury behind. And to tell the truth, she was as happy as she had ever been — at any rate as happy as she had ever been since her Grandmama's death had thrust her into sorrow, adventure, and (eventually) an entirely new life.

In short, nobody turned a head or raised an eyebrow as the three of them entered the movie theater. It was a lovely feeling to be so successfully anonymous.

And then the picture started!

The girls were soon in agreement: Episode Nine of *The Dangers of Darleen* was quite possibly the most wonderful photoplay that Matchless studios had ever made. The brilliant title card at the beginning, with the kidnapper's scowling face so cleverly framed in a newspaper! The drama in the attic! The heartrending look on Daring Darleen's face as she imagined her Royal Papa reaching out to her. And the way the exiled king's image was right there in the attic with her, letting us see what Daring Darleen must be imagining. That was brilliantly done. And then there was that amazing moment when the enormous air balloon seemed to land right in front of an express train!

Dar and Victorine let themselves shriek a little, they were so caught up in the excitement of the picture.

A child turned around in a seat ahead of theirs.

"Don't you worry," he said. "Our Daring Darleen's very clever. She'll be all right."

And then came the visit to the old mansion, where the Salamanders and their entourage were having a masked ball.

More muffled shrieking ensued from Victorine and Dar.

"There you are!" said Darleen. She whispered so that they could hang on to their anonymity. "Look at you! You're so good!"

Victorine had been the smallest of the extras, but her footwork in the dance was by far the most elegant. It was a pleasure to watch Victorine dance.

On screen, Daring Darleen pushed her way through the dancers, looking for her lost Royal Father.

"Through that door!" suggested Victorine aloud, quite as caught up in the action as the boy in the seat in front of them clearly was.

The movie Darleen did exactly that: went in through the door. And then she was in the very room where they had been keeping her Royal Papa prisoner, and there he was — her long-lost Papa, with the forged will spread out like a menu in front of him. But he had taken an awful blow to the head in Episode Eight, and he didn't recognize his own daughter, not at all.

And of course Daring Darleen didn't know why her Papa wouldn't acknowledge her, and then, just as he was dragged out of the room, after having been banged on the head again — by chance — you could see the light come on in his eyes.

And Daring Darleen grabbed that fake will from the desk and leaped beautifully right out the window —

"TO BE CONTINUED" said the title (and the girls read aloud the words together, with such satisfaction and joy), "IN EPISODE TEN of *THE DANGERS OF DARLEEN: THE DEADLY GIFT.*"

"I can't wait! Can you?" said the boy in the seat ahead of them, turning around.

"Can't wait!" agreed Dar and Victorine.

"That was *very* good, girls," said Darleen's Papa, as he ushered them out of the theater. "And now we'd better get some rest, because you know what tomorrow brings."

The beginning of work on Episode Ten!

And eventually, one day, perhaps some tomorrow would even bring . . . California.

The girls had a pact now. They would learn how to be the heroes of their own lives. And while they learned, they would savor the miracle and sweetness and promise of those three most wonderful words, which are as much about the adventure of life as about any story or photoplay:

To Be Continued!

Although *Daring Darleen, Queen of the Screen* is a work of fiction, it is based on the thrilling true story of the rise of the film industry. In the mid-1890s a number of inventors in several countries had figured out how to make photographs seem to move by recording many pictures per second and then running those images quickly and precisely through a peephole system or, eventually, a projector that would allow films to be screened for larger and larger audiences.

By the time our story begins in the early spring of 1914, cinema was becoming a big business. Between late 1912 and about 1917 a new type of movie was all the rage:

the serial adventure film, where "cliffhanger" endings brought audiences back in week after week to see their favorite heroines (most of these films starred courageous and athletic young women) triumph over villains by performing great feats of physical danger. Jumping off bridges, climbing up the sides of buildings, clinging to the outsides of moving trains — nothing seemed impossible for the intrepid stars of these serials.

I teach film history, and the idea for *Daring Darleen* came to me quite out of the blue one morning as I was walking to class to talk to students about the young women who starred in silent adventure serials, and who not only often performed all their own tricks but were also often asked to take part in publicity stunts out in the real world. I thought, *And what if the publicity stunt happened to be a fake kidnapping? And what if it went quite terribly wrong? And what if the whole adventure had something of the flavor of a silent film?* And then I was happy, because I could feel a story beginning to take shape — a story into which I could pour my silent-film-loving heart.

Darleen Darling and her adventure serial, *The Dangers of Darleen,* may be fictional, but Darleen's role in this story and the title of her film series are based on the work of real silent film stars: Kathlyn Williams in *The Adventures of Kathlyn* (1913–1914), Pearl White in *The Perils of Pauline* (1914) and *The Exploits of Elaine* (1914–1915), and

Helen Holmes (later replaced by "Helen" Gibson) in *The Hazards of Helen* (1914–1917).

And where were these serials filmed? In many cases, in Fort Lee, New Jersey! In those early days Hollywood was not yet the undisputed epicenter of American film. As early as 1907 and 1908, New York City filmmakers started crossing the Hudson River to the little town of Fort Lee, where the woods, rustic streets, and rocky cliffs of the Palisades provided the perfect scenery for every possible photoplay. Soon elaborate studios started being built in Fort Lee, and although none of those studios bore the name Matchless Photoplay, my fictional studio is based on a number of real Fort Lee companies: Peerless, Champion, Eclair . . . and Solax.

Yes, Solax is entirely real, and so is that incredible pioneer of early film history Madame Alice Guy Blaché. She was not only the first woman to run a film studio, she was one of the first filmmakers *ever.* Born in France in 1873 to parents who tried — and eventually failed — to run a bookselling business in Chile, Alice Guy had to find a way to support herself and her mother after her father's early death.

Alice was an enterprising and modern young person, to say the least. She learned the then-high-tech skills of typing and stenography, and found herself a position as a secretary in a photographic company. This was a stroke of luck and good timing, because in March 1895, Léon Gaumont (one of the people running the company) invited Alice along to see a demonstration of the Lumière Brothers' exciting new invention, the *cinématographe*, or moving photography. Alice immediately saw cinema's potential for storytelling. She asked for permission to try her hand making short films. These were so successful that between 1897 and 1906, Alice Guy was the head of film production for what was by then called the Gaumont Company. She made every kind of film: funny films, trick films using double exposure or reverse motion, fairy-tale films, dance films, even films synchronized to sounds recorded on wax cylinders (decades before "sound film" became the norm).

In 1907 she married another Gaumont studio employee, Herbert Blaché, and they were sent to Cleveland, in the United States, to try (without much success) to whip up American enthusiasm for early sound films. By 1910, now with a toddler in tow, the Blaché family had moved to New York, and Alice Guy Blaché decided to leap back into filmmaking by founding the Solax Company. Her films for Solax were so successful that in 1912 she built an elaborate, state-of-the-art, glass-walled studio in Fort Lee, New Jersey, where she produced many much-praised photoplays.

With World War I — and ensuing shortages of coal

for heating and power — warm, sunny Hollywood finally replaced Fort Lee as the center of American cinema. Alice Guy Blaché made her last film in 1920 and lived the rest of her long life quietly. She was one of the great artists of early film history, however, and deserves to be remembered.

If you would like to learn more about Fort Lee, early cinema, or Madame Alice Guy Blaché, here are some sources I can recommend to you:

- Richard Koszarski's wonderful *Fort Lee: The Film Town* (Rome: John Libbey Publishing, 2004), filled with primary sources that bring early-twentieth-century Fort Lee back to vivid life.
- *The Memoirs of Alice Guy Blaché*, translated by Roberta and Simone Blaché and edited by Anthony Slide (Lanham, MD, and London: Scarecrow Press, 1986).
- Alison McMahan's *Alice Guy Blaché: Lost Visionary of the Cinema* (New York and London: Continuum, 2002).
- There is even a lovely picture book now about Madame Blaché: *Lights! Camera! Alice! The Thrilling True Adventures of the First Woman Filmmaker*, written by Mara Rockliff and illustrated by Simona Ciraolo (San Francisco: Chronicle, 2018).

As I worked on *Daring Darleen,* I read many issues of the *New York Times* and *Moving Picture World* (a publication dedicated to film news, ads, and gossip) from 1912 to 1914. Old newspapers and magazines are a wonderful way to get to know a different era, and both of these publications are available online. The Strand Theatre really did hold its grand opening on April 11, 1914, and there really was an article about "mercurial poisoning" on the front page of the *New York Times* for April 12, 1914. Check it out!

Sample episodes of *The Hazards of Helen* can be found online, as can some of Alice Guy Blaché's films. You might enjoy her *Falling Leaves* (1912), for instance, in which child star Magda Foy tries to stop time and save her ailing older sister by tying leaves back onto tree branches.

Oh, and take a look at the film William K. Dickson made in 1894 for Edison's Kinetoscope: *Annabelle, Butterfly Dance.* That was my model for "Loveliest Luna Lightfoot," and I think you can see why that little film might make Darleen's heart ache and Madame Blaché's artistic imagination take fire.

Working with Kaylan Adair on *Daring Darleen*'s thrilling adventures was one of the most satisfying creative experiences I've ever had. Those winter weeks where we were powering through the line edits together! Pure joy! What a gift it is to work with someone who is determined to make every page as perfect as possible.

Ammi-Joan Paquette makes being daring seem like a reasonable life choice. My life is wider, deeper, and more sparkly because of her. Thank you a thousand times over, Joan!

Erin Murphy has turned one special corner of the literary world into an oasis. How is that even done? I remember with particular gratitude one June evening when I was feeling completely stumped by revisions, and a bunch of brilliant friends took me into the next room and had me talk about Darleen until water had refilled the well. Thank you, thank you, to Janet Fox, Janet Carey, Elizabeth Bunce, Jillian Coats, Nancy Day, and Vicki Lorencen, and to all the other minds and hearts who helped bring this story into the world.

Everyone associated with Candlewick is both kind and phenomenally talented. *Daring Darleen* owes so much to everybody who helped turn this manuscript into a lovely object: Mary Lee Donovan, Pam Marshall, and Maggie Deslaurier, who kept the creative ship from crashing into icebergs or hidden reefs. And of course the designer and the artist who created the cover (which for a writer always seems simply miraculous), Matt Roeser and Brett Helquist. Thank you also to the interior designer, Lisa Rudden! I feel particular gratitude to Anne Irza-Leggat and Phoebe Kosman for taking such good care of authors and their books.

My friends and family make life worthwhile. Thank you to Eric, Thera, Eleanor, and Ada for being such a source of love and support. I am so lucky. Jayne Williams, Roo Hooke, Will Waters, and Sharon Inkelas have a way of keeping the world bright with creative potential. Darleen Young is my real-life hero. My students (especially those in Film 25A: The History of Film, Part One) remind me every year how exciting it can be to discover the past, over and over again.

I would like to acknowledge that the location where most of this novel is set — now called Fort Lee, New Jersey — is part of the traditional territory of the Lenni-Lenape people. This place contains many stories beyond the one I am telling here.

This book is dedicated to my dear friends and colleagues in the U.C. Berkeley Department of Film and Media, with whom I have watched thousands of silent films over the years at the great annual festival in Pordenone, Italy (the *Giornate del Cinema Muto*), at the Pacific Film Archive, in many classrooms in Dwinelle Hall, and at our various homes. You have been such a central and inspiring part of my life, with your bright minds and warm hearts. Thank you!